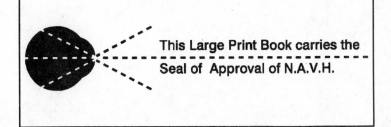

This Large Print Book carries the
Seal of Approval of N.A.V.H.

DEAD SEA RISING

DEAD SEA RISING

JERRY B. JENKINS

Dr. Craig Evans, Biblical Consultant

THORNDIKE PRESS
A part of Gale, a Cengage Company

Farmington Hills, Mich • San Francisco • New York • Waterville, Maine
Meriden, Conn • Mason, Ohio • Chicago

LIBRARY OF CONGRESS CIP DATA ON FILE.
CATALOGUING IN PUBLICATION FOR THIS BOOK
IS AVAILABLE FROM THE LIBRARY OF CONGRESS

ISBN-13: 978-1-4328-5851-3 (hardcover)

Published in 2018 by arrangement with Worthy Publishing, a division of Worthy Media, Inc.

Printed in Mexico
1 2 3 4 5 6 7 22 21 20 19 18

To Buster —
Redeemed and whole.

■ ■ ■ ■

THE DEAD SEA CHRONICLES
DEAD SEA RISING —
BOOK 1

■ ■ ■ ■

"I was drowning in a sea,
lost as I could be,
When you found me with your
boundless love."
Lyrics from "Boundless Love"
by John Prine, Dan Auerbach,
and Pat Mclaughlin

CHAPTER 1

Manhattan, New York City

"It's your mother," Nicole Berman's father said over the phone.

She rose from her desk at the sound of his voice. "What happened?"

"Broken hip. She's at Sinai on Madison."

"Hip? How, Dad?"

"You know what I know. How soon can you get there?"

"On my way," she said, juggling her phone to pull on her trench coat.

"Use a foundation car, Nic."

"Quicker to walk. It's rush hour here. What time is it there?"

"Coming up on eleven," he said, "and there's nothing leaving here tonight. I'm on standby out of de Gaulle in the morning, but I'm way down the list. I'll charter if I have to."

"Oh, Dad! You sure?"

"Are you moving, hon?"

"At the elevator. Should be there in twenty minutes. Want me to call, tell her I'm on my way?"

"No, they tell me she's already sedated for surgery. Text me as soon as you know anyth—"

" 'Course, but don't charter till I find out how serious this is. You're probably looking at —"

"Six figures," he said. "I know. But even picking up six hours, if I get out of here by eight in the morning, it's gonna be noon before I get into the city."

"Mom wouldn't want you to spend —"

"Don't bother her with that! We're flush as we've ever been and —"

But the call dropped when the elevator closed.

Nicole's lengthy strides made up for having to wait to cross Lexington and then Park Avenue. The fall sun had already dipped behind the buildings on the west side of Park, leaving a nip in the air that only quickened her pace.

At Mount Sinai Hospital, Reception summoned from upstairs a petite, black woman of about twenty-five. She introduced herself as Kayla and gave Nicole a visitor badge. "I'll take you directly to ICU, Dr. Berman."

"It's that bad?"

"With top-tier patients we take every precaution," Kayla said as they walked. "Let me express on behalf of our entire administrative team how grateful we are for The Berman Foundation. We —"

"I appreciate that, but what happened? Did she —"

"Housekeeper says she tripped on a rug. That's common among —"

"Not for her. She's still active, works out . . ."

"The surgeon will bring you up to speed. And a heads-up: he only *looks* twelve. He's thirty-five and one of our best ortho guys."

In ICU, Kayla began to introduce personnel, but Nicole brushed past them and cupped her mother's face in her palms. "I'm here." She leaned close and studied a bright red scrape on her mother's forehead that appeared to have been treated with ointment. Nicole turned to the surgeon. Script sewn above the breast pocket of his lab coat read "L. Thorn, M.D." It was good Kayla had warned her. If this guy was only a few years younger than she . . .

"We assume the contusion is a rug burn," he said.

"Oh, Mama, what happened?" Seeing her like this made everything else in Nicole's

13

life pale — and her plate was loaded.

Her mother appeared to try to raise a hand but closed her eyes, brow furrowed as if in pain. "Doctor, thish ish my . . ."

A nurse said, "She's been talking about you nonstop. You're up for some sort of a license or permit or — ?"

"She shouldn't have to suffer, should she?" Nicole said.

"She won't remember any of this," the anesthesiologist said. "There, she's out now."

"Doctor, my father should be here tomorrow. Could you delay op — ?"

Dr. Thorn shook his head. "Unwise. Waiting increases the risk of mortality, especially for someone your mother's age. Fortunately, she has no history of heart disease. But the sooner I get in there, the better chance I'll have to restore mobility. We're next in line for surgery."

Nicole sat alone in the waiting room, trading texts with her father. She left out the doctor's mention of mortality and asked if he had been informed by the new housekeeper. He wrote no, that he had heard from his assistant, Abigail.

No surprise, Nicole had had to get the word from her father from across the Atlan-

14

tic, despite that Abigail sat in the adjacent office at The Berman Foundation. But now was not the time to revisit that years-long cold war.

Her father texted that he wouldn't have been able to understand the housekeeper anyway, "but praise God she was there." He added that he had finagled a seat on the eight a.m. flight. "Thats 2 a.m. ur time so c u by noon tomorrow"

Nicole prided herself in writing properly even when texting. "And what did that finagling cost?"

"2× what the guy paid"

"Meaning?"

"€15,000. way less than charter"

She definitely would keep that from her mother, the former accountant for the foundation. "Get some sleep and have a safe trip, Dad."

"Any word on the permit, Nic?"

"Nothing. Can't think about that now anyway."

For months it had been all she thought about.

Nicole had never been good at waiting. She wouldn't be able to concentrate on any of the more than two hundred ebooks on her phone. And she could think of nothing to

15

pray beyond, "Be with Mom and spare her." She and her mother had never been closer than now. Tripped in her own home? Nicole couldn't make it compute. Her mother was still youthful, active at sixty-six.

Plaques on the wall honored her parents. This very waiting room had been "generously provided by Benzion and Virginia Berman." In the reflection off the glass of one framed certificate, Nicole noticed Kayla approaching the door behind her. She steeled herself, silently rehearsing dismissive language she hoped wouldn't offend.

But Kayla handed her a large coffee. "Two creams, no sugar, right?" she said.

"Exactly," Nicole said, thanking her. "Have we met before? Sorry if I —"

"No, no, we just do our homework. What I don't know is whether you prefer to be alone or would like me to —"

"Kind of you, but I confess I —"

"Not at all," Kayla said. "Here's my card if you need anything." She glanced at her watch. "I'm off at six, but call any time. I do just want to say that I almost majored in archaeology myself. You're such an inspiration. Not many women —"

"I've been fortunate. Without my father's foundation . . ."

"Still," Kayla said, heading toward the

16

door, "you've earned it. I — well, sorry, I'll leave you, but maybe I'll join one of your dig teams some day."

Two hours later, Nicole had tossed what was left of her coffee and sat with her coat draped over her knees, one foot bouncing.

The news and celebrity magazines didn't appeal, nor did the TV. She stared at the glacial clock, willing Dr. Thorn to appear. Why hadn't she asked how long this should take? Nicole almost wished she'd taken Kayla up on her offer of company, but why spoil a young woman's time off?

Most frustrating was not knowing when or if she should start worrying. Nicole began to Google it, but before she could finish, her mother's surgeon entered and she leapt to her feet.

"Sorry, Dr. Berman," Thorn said, "no news yet. Previous surgery went long, and housekeeping just got in there to disinfect. We can get started as soon as everything's dry."

"Surely not every operating room is in use," Nicole said.

"The ortho ones are, and they have the equipment I need. Plus, this is providential. I didn't expect to have the sales rep in the room, but we had time to track him down."

17

"Sorry? Sales rep?"

"Sold us one of the pieces of equipment, and he knows more about it than I do. It'll be handy to have him there."

"Actually during surgery?"

The doctor nodded. "He's just there to advise. This has become common. I assumed you knew."

Nicole shook her head.

"We had to sell the idea to your father months ago to get the grant. Naturally the equipment costs a lot more when it comes with a live consultant."

"Does my father know this will be the case tonight?"

"I haven't spoken with him."

"It might not sound like such a good idea to a man whose wife is on the table."

"Oh, believe me, you'd rather have the rep in there than not. He's only going to be of help."

"One more thing. My mother was anesthetized more than two hours ago. What happens now?"

"My anesthesiologist can handle it. Of course, she won't be charged for the delay or the extra meds —"

"That's hardly the issue."

Dr. Thorn shrugged. "I don't suppose your family will be charged at all." He seemed to study Nicole. "You must get your height from your father. Your mother's not that —"

"Is she comfortable?"

The doctor grinned. "We should all be as comfortable."

"How long do you expect this to take?"

"Assuming no surprises, figure an hour of prep and two hours of surgery, max."

"You still have to prep her?"

He nodded. "Most of that we can do only once we're in the operating room."

"And what kind of surprises are you talking about?"

"Well, the x-ray and scan show a straightforward fracture and no muscle tear, though I suspect soft-tissue trauma. And you never know how complex things are until you get in there." Dr. Thorn's phone chirped and he peeked at it. "Room's ready. Try not to worry. I do a lot of these."

CHAPTER 2

Shinar, Mesopotamia
2000 BC

"Terah!"

At the shout from the throne, King Nimrod's chief officer came running — not easy for a man of seventy. He panted and bowed low. "King Amraphel," he managed, using the name the ruler had bestowed upon himself.

"How wonderful to see that at long last Belessunu is great with child! Send word to me with haste when she brings forth your firstborn so that I may rejoice with you."

"I will, oh King," Terah said. "But may I speak forthrightly?"

"Of course!"

"Why did you forbid me concubines when for decades Belessunu was unable to bear me children? Even she fretted over her failure and was willing . . ."

The king looked away. "It was convenient.

20

For me and for you. It freed you to do so much more for me. You must share my pride in how the realm has grown."

"I do! But my legacy, my name —"

"Will forever be linked with mine and the glory of Mesopotamia, the Land of Nimrod. Even if Belessunu does not bear a son."

"I pray the gods *will* grant me a lad."

"Naturally," the king said. "I will also pray that Utu will favor you with a manchild. And may he live a thousand years."

"I am deeply grateful," Terah said.

That royal blessing was not beyond reason, for Terah's first child would be the tenth generation since Noah, still alive and nearly 900 years old. And Noah's grandfather had been Methuselah, who had perished in the great flood at 969.

The king was himself a grandson of Noah's son Ham. Noah had cursed Ham's offspring in the wake of Ham having mocked his father for passing out drunk and naked. So Nimrod bore no royal blood. In fact, because of Noah's curse of Ham, by rights Terah was the more likely king and Nimrod the servant.

But Nimrod had made himself kingly by growing up mighty and strong, a cunning hunter and leader of men. He built legions of admirers — including Terah, who early

21

on had turned his back on his and his wife's God-fearing heritage and became Nimrod's chief assistant. As his kingdom grew, Nimrod soon declared himself a deity, called himself Amraphel, and worshipped and prayed to a plethora of divinities — primarily the sun god Utu.

When Terah left the throne room, Ikuppi, whom he had hired years before as a member of the king's guard, beckoned him from the shadows. "Tread carefully with the king," the guard said.

"Did you not hear him, Ikuppi?" Terah said. "He's praying we'll have a son and wants me —"

"To bring him word, yes. I long to be mistaken, Terah, but he has been consulting with his stargazers."

"What are they saying? Will we have a son?"

"The king's meetings with them leave him sour."

"You heard them talking about me, about our child?"

Ikuppi looked down.

"Tell me, my friend!" Terah said. "Else I must take him at his word. I have served him faithfully for many years, so he has no reason to —"

"Bring him only news, then, Terah," Ikuppi said. "Do not bring him the child."

"If he asks, I must!"

"Terah, please . . ."

"Ikuppi, your countenance gives you away. If you know more, tell me."

"I owe you my role in the realm, Terah, and I know whereof I speak only because of access you have given me. But if I speak ill of the king, you hold my life in your hands."

"Rest assured I will not betray your confidence. But I fear you are suspicious without cause."

"I am not."

"Then visit me tonight and pray tell me of any danger to my child."

CHAPTER 3

Manhattan

Nicole hadn't thought she could eat, but knowing her mother wouldn't even be moved to the recovery room for three hours — let alone a regular room until midnight or later — made her suddenly ravenous. She left her cell number at Reception, said she'd be back within two hours, called for delivery from the Chinese place near her building for an hour later, and grabbed a cab.

Thirty minutes later her doorman said, "Was worried about ya, Doc. Didn't think you were out of town."

She told him why she'd be spending the night at the hospital.

"Sorry to hear that, ma'am. Let me know when you're coming back down and I'll have a ride waiting for ya. And give Ginny my best, hear?"

"Didn't know you knew her that well, Freddie."

He cocked his head. "Always nice to me when she visits. Classy."

Nicole grabbed her mail from her slot in the lobby and riffled through it on the elevator.

And there it was.

A regular business-sized envelope from Saudi Arabia. Could this be it — what she'd dreamed of for so long? No. It couldn't. Had it been, they would have informed her via email it was coming. And it would be bigger, thicker.

Nicole was not even tempted to open it. Not now. Business letters carried bad news, not good — rejections, not licenses to dig. She shook her head. A less-than-an-ounce response to her two-hundred-page application! Had she tried too hard to counter all the reasons they wouldn't find her qualified to finally become lead archaeologist on a dig?

This was the worst possible time for news — good or bad. She didn't need one more thing on her mind. Good news would be spoiled by her mother's ordeal, and bad news . . . well, she had expected that. But Nicole couldn't endure another blow, not right now. She tossed the mail and her keys onto the table just inside her door.

She rushed to shower and change and

pack a bag before the Chinese food arrived. She loved that the restaurant owners were as precise as she was. They delivered when she asked, not a minute before or after. That's the way things ought to work. If only the hospital were run by the Chinese. Nicole was setting her bag near the door when the bell rang.

She sat to ladle the steaming, pungent selections onto her plate, and fatigue washed over her. Shoulders sagging, emotion welled in her throat. She bowed her head. "Blessed are You, El Shaddai, Lord God Almighty, King of the universe, Who gave us the way of salvation through the Messiah Yeshua. Blessed be He Who provides vegetation for the service of man, that he may bring forth food from the earth. In the name of the Anointed One, amen."

How comforting the prayers her parents taught her as a child. She hadn't learned until she was old enough to understand that her Gentile mother had led her father to faith in the Messiah. And as she ate, Nicole still glowed from what Freddie had said about Mom. It was just like her to insist that strangers call her Ginny. It spoke volumes that others obviously felt connected enough to be so familiar.

She had long known her mother had

wanted more children — at least one. And at times Nicole had wished for a sibling. But she also enjoyed her parents' attention. Now she couldn't shake the surgeon's reference to senior mortality rates connected to hip fractures. If anything happened to her mother . . . She envied those who had a brother or a sister to summon — to share the worry, the affection.

Her mother had seen her through everything, including sixteen grueling years of post-high school education. Mom always said just enough and not too much when Nicole suffered from an ice queen image and roller-coaster loves and losses. Sometimes her support proved as concise as "Good riddance, he didn't deserve you anyway." And only last week she had told Nicole, "You just have yet to meet the man who deserves to be as happy as you could make him."

Bone weary from the stress alone, Nicole seemed to chew in slow motion. Still, she relished the savory combinations on her tongue. But she couldn't quit watching the clock and soon stored the boxes of leftovers in the fridge and called downstairs. "On my way, Freddie," she said.

On her way out, Nicole considered taking the Saudi envelope and the rest of her mail.

She would likely face hours of tedium and could easily work through it. But no. If landing another Saudi Arabian archaeological ID — this time to become the first woman under forty to lead a dig — meant so much to her mother that she bragged about it before it happened, it was sure to be the first thing she'd ask about as soon as she was conscious. Better for Nicole to be able to say she didn't know yet than to have to tell the truth — especially if the news was as she feared.

Her father had warned her that, despite her résumé and her two doctorates, she was unlikely to be approved by the Saudis.

"But I was co-director on a site there at thirty-six."

"A technicality, hon," he said, "and you know it."

She couldn't argue that. After having been a volunteer at the Dead Sea and surrounding sites with her dad from her early teens, during grad school Nicole was appointed as a square (or trench) supervisor on her next several digs. Though supervised in each instance by a licensed archaeologist, she was still too young to become a site co-director. But every lead archaeologist sixty or older is required to have a younger co-director, in case the lead dies before the excavation is finished or the reports are published. It happened that the archaeologist she served under at Mada'in Saleh in Saudi Arabia had been killed in a plane crash on his way home, and the co-director moved into the lead role to compose the site reports. He frequently consulted Nicole as he wrote and cited her in the documents as co-director, adding an impressive credit to her curriculum vitae.

More importantly, while working in Mada'in, Nicole had become obsessed with that site and was determined to dig there again. She had uncovered a find so rare that she believed it could change Middle Eastern history. If she could only find a fragment corresponding to the one she'd listed among those catalogued from the dig — and Nicole believed with her whole being that it was there somewhere — it actually had ramifications for the centuries-long Mideast conflict. Her dream was to uncover that the very divide between the three major religions of the world was based on myth, not history.

What she was determined to find made it mandatory that she be the lead archaeologist. It had led her to leave her associate professorship at Harvard to accept a fellowship with her father's foundation so she

29

could undertake the exhaustive application process. Nicole's colleagues at Harvard would have howled at her hubris and her conviction that she could uncover what she believed she would.

Even her father was skeptical, and he was the only one in whom she had confided besides the dig leader and co-leader. "More power to you, Nic," he had said. "You deserve this and could do it, but I can't imagine the Saudis licensing a young woman who's never led, or really even co-led, a dig."

"Then you apply for it, Dad, and make me co-leader for real."

He waved her off. "My lead days are long gone, along with these knees."

She pleaded with him, reminding him that his exposing her to the caves at Qumran where the Dead Sea Scrolls had been found was the reason a little girl had made archaeology her life. "You show me the greatest find in history and you won't dig with me to find the next?"

He smiled. "How about I promise to come visit if you do get your ID?"

Nicole had spent her first six months as a fellow at The Berman Foundation formulating the application. Her father coached her through it, reminding her — too often — that she should not get her hopes up. Nicole documented for Saudi authorities her experience properly recording data, that she had developed contacts where she could safely store the finds, and that she would produce detailed and timely annual reports, longer major reports every three years (which she hoped would form the basis for renewal of the permit as needed), and eventually a final report.

"They'll want to know you have the funding," her dad said.

"And do I?"

"We need to talk about that."

"So let's talk," she said.

It was the same cat-and-mouse game with him every time, and it had started years before when Nicole's elementary school friends started referring to her as the rich kid. She had asked her mother if it was true. "Are we rich?"

For some reason that made her mother laugh. "That's a question for your dad, honey."

He did not laugh. First he wanted to know why she asked. Nicole started to tell him what her girlfriends were saying, but she grew impatient. "Just are we or not?"

"Well," he said, pressing his lips together,

"I am. You're not." She realized that was why he expected her to contribute at least half the cost when she wanted anything he considered a luxury. "Having skin in the game is what's going to make you a success — not getting whatever you want just because I can afford it."

As she grew older, Nicole became aware of the truth. Rich wasn't the half of it. Her father had inherited the generations-old Berman Foundation from his parents, but as a rebellious teen he had tried to refuse it. The Berman ancestors had amassed the family fortune through shrewd European real estate investments between the world wars before immigrating to the US. Benzion, the first Berman born in America, had been raised in understated privilege. His parents eschewed shows of extravagance, though Benz, as his mother called him, had a nanny, attended private schools, and spent summers at exclusive camps.

When Nicole went through her own minor rebellious phase as a teenager, her father finally revealed his own story. "I had a reason for rebelling," he told her. "You don't."

"I just want to be treated like an adult," she said.

"I wanted to be treated like I existed," he said.

"I thought Grandma and Grandpa gave you everything."

Her father shrugged. "Everything but themselves." Desperate for their attention, he said his excelling in school made them even more complacent about him. "So I resorted to bad behavior — anything to get them to focus on me."

"What kind of bad behavior?"

He hesitated. "Not sure I want to tell you."

"I'm not looking for permission, Dad. I just want to know."

"Why?"

She snorted. "You tell me you wanted your parents' attention and wonder why I want to know you?"

Her father sat back and interlaced his fingers behind his head. "You'd sure be easier if you weren't so smart." He had a way of slipping in compliments.

"Genetics," she said, parrying with her own.

"Ever wonder why you're in public school when we could afford prep school?"

Nicole shrugged. "Sometimes, I guess. But I'm glad. I'm no preppy."

"It's a risk," he said. "We want you to go to any university you want, and you just about have to be valedictorian in public school to have a prayer of getting into the Ivy League. I don't want you letting things slide now."

"Nice move, Dad."

"Hmm?"

"Changing the subject."

"The subject is rebellion, Nic. Like I said, I had a reason."

"I'm not rebelling, and I'm not letting anything slide. I'm just growing up."

The love in his eyes pierced her. "It's so easy to make mistakes you'll regret," he said. "I almost did."

"Like what?"

He sighed and told her of bouncing around northeastern prep schools, booted from one and then another for drinking, smoking dope, skipping class. "The only reason new schools kept accepting me was because my dad would write a big check and wind up on their boards — much as they had to hate having a Jew involved, let alone enrolled. Dad and Mom both said I'd meet a higher class of people there, but I never got called *kike* or *Jewboy* more than there."

"That's awful. But somehow you graduated."

"No *somehow* about it. I had no interest

34

in college and didn't mind embarrassing Dad and Mom, but I wasn't about to be a dropout."

"I always wondered why it took you so long to start college," Nicole said.

"Figured I'd run into the same so-called higher class there. I did, but I'd grown up a lot by then. I owe that to your mother. And the Lord, of course."

"And Vietnam?"

He got that faraway look and shook his head.

"This time a night ya gotta go in through Emergency," the cabbie told Nicole.

She was stunned to find Kayla sitting just inside the sliding doors — no longer in her dress suit. "No worries, Dr. Berman," the young woman said, rising.

"Don't lie to me, Kayla. What's wrong?"

"Nothing, really. Your mother's case manager just asked me to come in and keep you informed. Let me take you to where you can spend the night. It's called Eleven West, and it's where your mother will —"

Kayla had started toward the elevators, but Nicole wasn't moving. She set her bag down. "Not till you tell me what this is about."

"Your mother's not in danger, but she *is*

35

still in surgery and could be for another hour."

"Why?"

"That I don't know. You're aware they got started late . . ."

"I am."

"Room prep may have been part of it. Your mother had to be anesthetized a second time . . . And the surgeon may have found more than he expected."

"Surely you know."

Kayla shook her head. "I'd tell you. I would."

"Kayla, have you ever been assigned to do grief counseling?"

"Believe me, that's not what this is."

"But have you?"

Kayla nodded. "We're taught not to delay or soften the news. I wouldn't do that to you."

"But my mother's caseworker learned something that prompted her to call you in after-hours to babysit me?"

Kayla's gaze fell.

Nicole said, "I didn't mean it that way —"

"It's all right, ma'am. I under —"

"And can we stop with the *ma'am* and the *doctor* if we're going to spend this much time together? Friends call me Nic."

36

"Well, I wouldn't be comfortable with that, but I can call you Nicole if you prefer."

"Let me tell you what I prefer, Kayla. I want you to find out exactly what's going on with my mother, and then I want you to go home."

"Actually, I'm honored to stay —"

"Kayla. Find out. There must be a phone in the operating room if someone talked to the case manager."

"Oh, I couldn't call, Nicole! Can you imagine?"

"Then scrub up and slip in there."

"I'm a civilian," Kayla said. "I'm not allowed —"

"I know better than that," Nicole said. "There's a sales rep in there!"

"You're not gonna let this go, are you?" Nicole stared at her. Kayla pressed a finger to her lips. "Give me a second." She turned her back and pulled out her phone. "I owe it to Dr. Berman to tell her what they told you," she whispered. "What's going on in there? . . . Thank you."

Kayla turned back and suggested they talk at Eleven West.

"You don't get it, do you, Kayla? No more jerking me around."

"I wouldn't have come back in if I was gonna do that!" Kayla said, clearly on the

37

verge of tears.

Nicole crossed her arms.

"Okay," Kayla said. "I don't understand all the terminology, but the doctor's concerned about the advanced deterioration of your mother's bone density. The fracture was severe enough that he wanted to consider a hip replacement, but now he's not sure."

"So can't he stabilize her and decide tomorrow?"

Kayla looked down. "There's another thing — something he doesn't like about the break. He considers it suspicious."

"Suspicious how?"

"He had the case manager notify the police."

CHAPTER 4

Ur of the Chaldees

Terah welcomed Ikuppi to his home after nightfall. The guard removed his long, bronze sword and leaned it against the doorframe outside. He greeted Belessunu but refused her offer of food or drink. "I apologize for troubling you at this time of your discomfort."

"Discomfort," she said, smiling and resting her hands on her massive belly. "Is that what this is?"

"It has been for my wife," he said. "Thrice."

"And I'll say it if you won't — she is half my age."

"You're right!" he said, chuckling. "I won't say it."

Terah showed Ikuppi the large table that dominated the great room. It bore his entire inventory of several dozen eight- to ten-inch idols fashioned from ivory, stone, clay, and wood — in neat rows a few inches apart each.

"Beautiful!" Ikuppi said. "You make these?"

"I do," Terah said, beaming.

"They look like the silver and gold ones in the palace."

"I make those too. The king provides the materials. My handiwork is my gift to him."

"And all these are for your own use?"

"Oh, no, Ikuppi. We get lots of visitors. Citizens often bring sacrifices and kneel right here, leaving the meat and other foodstuffs for us. That's why I have to fight not to look great with child myself!"

"Amraphel does not insist on the sacrifices coming to him?"

Belessunu emitted a scoff. "The king does not deign to eat food provided by commoners."

Ikuppi smiled. "So you eat well! And your husband is the highest paid and most trusted member of the king's staff. Good for you!"

Terah leaned forward. "In reality, that is not the extent of my recompense. I also sell these to locals and travelers. It's a thriving business."

"Which I must conduct for him," Belessunu said with a sigh. "These pilgrims come during the day when he is busy running the palace and making life easier for the king. That thriving business means I must entertain visitors every day."

"That has to be difficult," Ikuppi said. "Especially now as your time draws near."

"I thought you were going to say 'at my age,' " Belessunu said.

Ikuppi held up both hands. "Not me!" He pointed to an ivory icon. "Beautiful!" he said. "This is Marduk, is it not?"

"Patron deity of all of Babylonia. You could tell from the robe?"

Ikuppi nodded. "May I?"

"Of course," Terah said.

Ikuppi picked up the idol, slowly turning it over and over. "You must let me buy this one."

"Consider it a memento of your visit," Terah said.

"Oh, I couldn't!"

"You must! You honor me by being here."

"I'll cherish it."

"I hope you'll do more than that," Terah said. "May Marduk answer all your prayers."

"Thank you both!"

"Don't thank me," Belessunu said. "He's the one who believes a carving can hear prayers."

Terah shot her a look. "We have much to

discuss, Ikuppi — on the terrace."

"You'll forgive me for not attempting the climb," Belessunu said.

"Of course," her husband said, having chosen the roof so he and Ikuppi could speak privately anyway. His visitor followed him outside and up the steps, bearing his gift.

Despite the setting of the sun, the windless night proved not much cooler than the blistering heat of the day. Still, Terah lighted a torch, believing he could better judge the veracity of Ikuppi's report if he could see his face. The man seemed weighed down by the burden of his concern — or was it fear?

"Tell me everything, friend," Terah said softly to keep his voice from carrying into the night.

Ikuppi sat and leaned toward Terah. "You must know the king worries about usurpers to the throne."

"I know better than anyone. I am constantly alert for interlopers. All kings face such worries, and they must."

"But Amraphel more than most."

"Perhaps."

"I believe he has put so much faith in you because you have proven your loyalty, Terah. He is less sure about your progeny."

"Without reason," Terah said.

42

"That's not what his stargazers are telling him."

CHAPTER 5

Manhattan

Nicole narrowed her eyes at Kayla. "Police? Why?"

"You know what I know, Dr. Berman."

"Then point me to the case worker's office."

"Oh, she's not here this late, ma'am."

"Kayla! The surgeon has her call the police and she's planning to manage this from home?"

"That's why I'm here."

"But you don't even know what's going on! Get her back on the phone."

"I really can't do that."

"Then my mother's out of here as soon as she's out of surgery."

"Oh, no, Dr. Berman! You don't want to do that."

"Somebody's gonna tell me what's going on or —"

"How about you talk to the police as soon

as they get here."

"Not a second later."

"Let me get you set up in your mother's room. When they arrive —"

"I hope they know more than you do."

On the way to Eleven West, Nicole began texting her father, but what was the point of troubling him when all it would do was rob him of sleep? And there was little he could do from halfway around the world, despite that he and the hospital brass were on a first-name basis. She would tell him only if she ran into any more roadblocks.

Eleven West proved as elegant as any five-star hotel, the most luxurious patient rooms Nicole had ever seen. "Concierge service and everything," Kayla said. "I've already checked you in as an overnight visitor in your mother's room."

Nicole had just set her bag on the bed when Kayla took a call and informed her NYPD was in the lobby. "Get settled here and I'll arrange where you can talk —"

"No, let's just go."

Kayla looked as if she'd resigned herself to the idea that Nicole always got her way.

In the lobby they were approached by a plainclothes detective who left two uniformed officers waiting. The detective, Nicole guessed midfifties, had a trench coat over his arm and wore a lived-in suit with one shirttail hanging out. He flipped open his notebook. "You Kayla Jefferson?"

"I am, and I've arranged for a conference room where —"

"And this is?"

"I'm Nicole Berman, daughter —"

"Of the victim?" he said.

"Victim?!" Nicole said.

"So you've been told nothing." He reached to shake both women's hands and introduced himself as Detective George Wojciechowski of the New York Police Department's Senior Services and Domestic Violence Unit.

Nicole blanched. The young detective turned his smartphone toward her, showing Wojciechowski's name. "If that's too much of a mouthful for ya, call me George or G-Dub."

"My mother tripped on a rug, Detective. How is that domestic violence?"

"That's what I'm here to find out, ma'am."

"But —"

"Hold on," Wojciechowski said. "You got questions, but so do I, and this is my investigation, not yours."

Kayla said, "Why don't we take this to the conference r—"

Wojciechowski held up a hand. "First I gotta know where the victim is now and where she's gonna be for the rest of the night."

"Would you stop referring to her as a victim?" Nicole said.

"You're about to find out why we're here, Ms. Berman, but my first priority is your mother's safety, so let me do my job. Ms. Jefferson?"

Kayla said, "Virginia Berman is in surgery and she'll be in a recovery room within the hour. Then she'll be moved to her private room in Eleven West until she's released." Kayla wrote the number on a card.

"And when do they expect she'll be released?"

"Normally within a week, but with this development . . ."

"Got it. Let whoever needs to know that our uniforms'll set up outside the operating room and accompany her to Recovery and then to her room. And we'll need anyone entering that room to have hospital credentials."

"I'll be with her too," Nicole said.

"Maybe," Wojciechowski said.

"What does that mean?"

"Let's not get ahead of ourselves. You and I need to talk."

47

Nicole began to respond, but the detective turned away and told the uniformed officers to get to the surgical ward.

"Why does my mother need protection?" Wojciechowski turned back to Kayla. "Okay, that conference room?"

CHAPTER 6

Ur

"His wise men have warned the king that a threat to his throne lurks on the horizon," Ikuppi said. "He even proposed having all pregnant women in the realm brought to the palace to give birth. Those delivering female babies would be rewarded."

"And conversely . . . ?" Terah said.

"Mothers of males will be honored for their sacrifice and urged to return home and try again."

Terah found himself unable to speak. Finally he whispered, "Sacrifice? But he blessed me with the wish that we would have a son who lived a thousand years!"

Ikuppi shook his head. "He has vowed to kill male babies with his own hands."

CHAPTER 7

Manhattan

Nicole followed Detective Wojciechowski into the conference room. "Actually, I'm going to start with Ms. Jefferson," he said. "So I'll ask you to wait outside. I won't be long."

"Can you just tell me —"

"Listen, there's things I gotta know before I tell you anything, let alone question you."

"You're going to question me?"

"As soon as you stop questionin' me. Now, please."

Nicole dropped onto a bench in the hallway, frustrated she couldn't make out Wojciechowski's conversation with Kayla. And it took longer than she expected. But then it was her turn, and she and Kayla traded places. Wojciechowski pointed to a chair directly across from him, and as Nicole sat, she said, "Listen, I —"

"No, you listen, ma'am. I don't jump to

conclusions or pass judgment. I'm just the researcher here. I gather information. So —"

"You're not paid to determine —"

"I'm not sayin' I won't have my opinions, and I been doing this long enough to know when someone's lying, so —"

"I'm not a liar, Detective."

"Yeah, well, we'll see," he said, flipping through his notepad. "You and your parents have separate addresses . . ."

She nodded. "We live about forty minutes apart."

"Their address, if you don't mind my saying, is in a swankier part a town."

"Naturally."

"But you've got two doctorates, just like your dad."

"He owns a foundation. There's not much money in academia or archaeology."

"I wouldn't know. You visit your parents often?"

"Often enough. I work with my father, so maybe not as much as I might otherwise."

"You and he get along?"

"Of course."

"But you don't wanna see him outside the office?"

"I didn't say that."

"Well, say what you said again then. I

thought that's what you were implyin'."

"All I meant was that I might see my parents a little more often if I didn't work in the same office as my dad — and my mother worked there for years too."

"Got it," Wojciechowski said, scribbling. "Any problems with her?"

"No! Why? She trips on a rug and breaks her hip and —"

"I think you know it was more than that . . ."

"What're you saying?"

Wojciechowski narrowed his eyes at her. "I think you were there when it happened."

So much for not jumping to conclusions. "There when it happened? I got a call from my dad in Paris at about four this afternoon. That's the first I knew about it."

Wojciechowski thumbed through his pages again. "So he's got an alibi."

"An alibi? For what? She —"

"She went down hard, Dr. Berman. Hard enough to break her hip and bang her forehead, and there's no evidence she even had time to break her fall. No pain or damage to her hands."

"Meaning?"

"Meaning she may have been knocked to the floor."

"That seems a leap in logic."

"When's the last time you had a fight with your mother?"

"Never."

"An argument?"

"We don't agree on everything, if that's what you mean. I thought she was wrong to retire from the foundation a few years ago, but that was just a difference of opinion — a discussion, not a fight."

"And you don't resent your lifestyles being so different? You don't live now the way you did growing up."

"Resent it? No. I'm proud of my parents."

"But didn't they just inherit their wealth?"

"My father did, yes, but he's built on that."

"And handsomely."

"Yes."

"You don't have a housekeeper."

"I don't have enough house to need a keeper. Now, please, what's this about? I want to know what makes this accident a police matter?"

Wojciechowski scanned a few more pages of notes and shut his notepad, dropping his pen atop it. He leaned back in his chair and crossed his arms. "Dr. Thorn found something when he cut her open."

"Less bone density than he expected, I know."

"More damage than usual for a fall."

"Like what?"

"I don't get all this medical stuff myself, but I understand he saw more than he expected, some damage to the bone that didn't show on the x-ray."

"Okay . . ."

"Like her hip had been traumatized from two different directions."

"At the same time?"

"Guess that would be hard to know, ma'am. But what tells me they were right to call us is what the doc calls the severe soft-tissue injury."

"Is that unusual in hip fractures? Seems you should expect some."

"Not on the victim's back," Wojciechowski said.

"Her back?"

"Dr. Berman, your mother has deep bruises on her lower back, one on either side of her spine."

"Maybe she landed on her back, or bumped into something trying to break her f—"

"No. Your mother was either driven to the floor by a flying two-footed kick, or someone jumped on her once she was on the floor."

Why in the world . . . ? "You're sure?"

"I wouldn't know how else to interpret what the doctor described. Would you?"

Nicole sat shaking her head.

"If you don't mind my sayin' so, ma'am, you look athletic enough to be able to do something like that."

"To attack my own mother with some sort of martial arts move . . ."

He stared at her. "Any training in that kinda stuff?"

"Never," she said. "Volleyball was my game, but that was more than fifteen years ago."

"Bet you can still jump."

"I can still do a lot of things to hurt a senior citizen a foot shorter than I am. But I wouldn't. I treasure her and always have."

Wojciechowski rested his chin on his fist. "How about your dad?"

"What about him?"

"He have any reason to want to harm your mother?"

"No way," Nicole said. "If you think I treasure her, she's his whole world."

"He wouldn't pay someone, arrange for something to happen . . ."

"Absolutely not."

"When's he expected?"

"Sometime after noon. He's on an eight a.m. to LaGuardia out of de Gaulle, which is two a.m. here."

"I'll meet the plane."

"That would help me. I was going to pick him up, but I'd rather not leave Mom. I appreciate that."

"Wish I could say I was doin' it out of the kindness of my heart, but I need to question him."

Nicole shook her head. "He'll be an open book."

"That so?"

"He always is."

"You sure about that?"

"I know him better than anyone but Mom."

"No vestiges of PTSD?"

"Sorry?"

"He's not exactly a private citizen, ma'am. Your own foundation website says he's a wounded vet."

"That was a long time ago. He's achieved an awful lot since then."

Wojciechowski shrugged. "Saw some action. Came back with only half a one of his hands. You never know how that stuff plays out. He talk about it at all?"

"No, he doesn't. He says guys who talk about the war are probably lying. That for the guys on the front lines, it's the last thing you want to talk about. Anyway, he's an entirely different person now."

"How would you know? You weren't born

till, what, years after he got back?"

"Nineteen Eighty, but I mostly know from Mom. She met him when he got back, sullen and angry. But you'll see it. Smart, funny, engaging, a man of faith. And like I said, he adores my mother."

"Prone to anger?"

Nicole had to think. "No. That's not one of his faults."

"What is?"

"I'm not going to sit here and psychoanalyze my own father. Especially with you probing for —"

Wojciechowski held up both hands. "Hey, I'm trying to clear him, not nail him. But I hafta ask you something hard."

"You already have."

"You're gonna want to be in touch with him when he lands, right?"

"Of course. He'll want an update on Mom."

"I need you to have no more contact with him until I bring him here."

"You think we're going to conspire on a story?"

"Just protocol. I'd rather he not even know we're involved until I tell him."

"He's likely to call or text."

"Just let him know someone will pick him up. I'll question him on the way back, so by

57

the time we get here, you should have him all to yourself."

"I hope you're not asking me not to talk with my mother as soon as she's conscious."

"Not without one of my people in there with you. I assume you'll just be asking her what happened, what she remembers . . ."

"Well, I won't be telling her you suspect my dad or me. That would devastate —"

"C'mon, Doc. You're a smart lady. You hafta know we don't suspect either of you, and I sure wouldn't *want* you or your father to have had anything to do with this. We have to clear you, that's all. I got a family too, ya know. Two families, actually. Two kids with the first wife. Two more now. I like to see close families."

"That's what you're going to see here, Detective."

He stood and reached for her hand. "I'm gonna get me some shut-eye before heading to the airport."

"And one of the uniformed officers will be with me when I talk to my mother?"

"No, I'll send a matron from the precinct, in street clothes so we don't alarm your mother when she comes to. My gal'll probably look like a hospital staffer. She won't be askin' any questions. Just taking notes. I want to talk to your mom myself."

CHAPTER 8

Ur

Terah trudged down from the roof, wishing it was daytime so he could pray to the sun god Utu and change his request from a son to a daughter. He believed Utu left heaven from the east every morning and soared through the skies in his chariot to observe everything that occurred each day, returning to heaven in the west at night after meting out divine justice and saving those in peril who called on his name.

Terah helped Ikuppi strap his sword back on and saw him off. He slipped inside and knelt before his table full of idols. They were lesser gods than Utu and even the king, but still, in tears, he quietly implored them to keep him from having to abdicate his position and flee with his family.

Terah's wife emerged from behind the curtain that separated the kitchen from the great room. She lay her hands gently on his shoulders. "A son will be the end of us," Belessunu said. "Where would we go? I'd not be ready to travel for several days, but even then, we are not young people. And Nimrod has allies all over the kingdom."

"We are now praying for a daughter," Terah said. "But the king himself is praying we'll have a son."

"Or so he says," Belessunu said. "Wouldn't he prefer *not* to have to murder the son of his senior officer?"

"I should hope. Regardless, he deceives me — telling me he also longs for a son for us. We must beseech the gods for a dau—"

"Truth be told," Belessunu said, turning Terah's face to look him in the eyes, "I will not pray for a daughter. And you know I do not pray to your handmade rubbish."

"Do not blaspheme, wife! If you anger the —"

"Terah, I am praying the God of our forefathers will bestow upon us the child He chooses. May His will be done."

"And if his will costs us our child?"

"If I bear a son, I would never allow you to offer him up to the will of a self-proclaimed mighty man who fears a new-born."

"You won't allow? Have I not been humiliated enough by your remaining childless

60

until we're old?" Terah immediately regretted the pain his words wrought in her eyes.

"I won't have to oppose you, husband. I know you. You would not do such a thing anyway."

"No, I would not. But you know as well as I do that defying Nimrod would cost us more than a son."

"Still, I will trust the one true God," she said.

Terah turned back to his idols. "Perhaps we do well to pray to our own gods."

"Will you still pray to the king too? Does he remain a god to you, one you admit deceives you?"

Terah sighed. "I hold out hope that Ikuppi is mistaken."

"Hope could cost us our child and land us in the dungeon — or worse. We must escape."

"From here?" Terah said. "From Amraphel? As you said, the entire kingdom is his. Where would we go?"

CHAPTER 9

Manhattan

Detective Wojciechowski's referring to Officer Julia Martinez as a matron had given Nicole an entirely wrong expectation. Friendly and talkative, Martinez was a striking twentysomething in a fashionable suit. "You know those security guys downstairs tried to talk me out of my sidearm?" she said.

"This *is* a gun-free zone," Nicole said.

"Not if you got a badge it's not. And you better be glad I do. Otherwise you got only bad guys with guns. You don't want that, especially if somebody's after your *madre.*"

The uniformed officers stood on either side of the door to the recovery room where Mrs. Berman had been delivered, unconscious and peaked, as if in a coma. Nicole and Officer Martinez sat across the hall awaiting word that her mother had awakened. A nurse said it would likely be at least half an hour.

It proved longer.

At 1:15 in the morning, Nicole got a text from her dad: "Boarding. news?"

She hesitated, telling herself a brief reply would not violate the letter of Detective Wojciechowski's instructions. "Recovery room. Still out. Have a safe trip. Love you."

"Luv u2"

When Nicole was finally summoned, she asked Martinez if she had her notebook ready.

"Notebook?" the officer said, producing her smartphone. "Do I look like a dinosaur?"

The nurse whispered, "Your mother is not communicative yet, but she's conscious. Take anything she says with a grain of salt. She won't remember much of this, if any."

"How long before she's, you know, lucid?" Officer Martinez said.

"Maybe an hour."

Her mother squinted against even the low light. She blinked sluggishly and seemed to slowly scan the recovery room. Logy and confused as she appeared, fear loitered behind her heavy eyelids.

Nicole was impressed that Officer Martinez immediately slipped into a chair outside her mother's range of vision. No way could her mother have detected Julia was a cop, but this way she didn't even have to wonder. Her mother's gaze finally reached Nicole but lingered only briefly.

"Hi, Mama," Nicole said quietly, taking her hand — the one free of IVs. Limp. Zero response. "You look good. Just rest. You're okay."

Her mother closed her eyes again but grimaced. Nicole stroked her hand. "Remember the prayer you taught me when I was little? 'I thank You, living and eternal King, for returning my soul within me in compassion. Great is Your faithfulness.'"

"Beautiful!" Julia Martinez whispered. "What is that?"

Her mother's eyes opened at the sound of a new voice, and Martinez immediately covered her lips with a hand.

"A Hebrew blessing," Nicole mouthed.

Martinez pulled her hand away and said, loud enough for only Nicole to hear, "Of course, you're Jewish. I'm Catholic."

"Messianic."

"What's that?"

"Messiah. We're Jews who believe in Jesus."

"No way! Cool!"

Nicole turned back to her mother when

she squeezed Nicole's hand. "I'm here, Mama."

The older woman's lips moved.

"Just rest, Mama. No need to talk."

"Talking to your father?" her mother slurred.

"No, just a friend."

She tugged Nicole's hands as if she wanted her closer. Nicole leaned in. "Where's Ben?"

"On his way from Paris. He'll be here in several hours."

"I'm dying."

"No, Mama. You're going to be fine. You just broke your hip."

"We have to — have to forgive each other, Nic. Recon — reconcile."

"No, no, we're fine."

"You thought I didn't care."

"Mom, relax, please. You're confused. That was twenty years ago."

"I'm sorry!"

"I was sorry too. We forgave each other. Remember?"

"Want us . . . want us to love each other."

"I couldn't love you more, Mama. Now you rest. It's all good between you and me."

"Don't hate me."

"Oh, Mama. I could never hate you. I never did." Nicole put a hand under her mother's neck and kissed her cheek, then spoke directly into her ear. "We're besties, remember? I had to tell you what that meant."

Tears rolled down her mother's cheeks.

"Mama, don't, please. I'm here for you, and I always will be."

CHAPTER 10

Ur

Belessunu winced and reached to steady herself, toppling one of Terah's idols. The ten-inch carving rolled into the one next to it, causing it to fall into the next. Terah scrambled from his knees to stop the tumbling and rolling idols, causing all the more to fall. "Look what you've done!" he cried.

When he finally stopped the avalanche, more than half the icons lay in chaos on the table. He turned to glare at his wife and saw her expression had changed from pain to mirth. "Your gods can't even keep themselves from falling! How are they going to save us from King —"

"You dare to laugh in the face of —"

"Objects? Yes, I dare."

"If we lose their favor and have a son, Belessunu, it'll be your fau—"

"The God of our forefathers has blessed us, and He will give us the child He —"

"Your god made Amraphel the king and me his lesser," Terah said. "How is that just?"

"Nimrod made *himself* king, and you made *yourself* inferior!"

"Leave me!" Terah bellowed. "I must pray you bear a daughter."

"Pray for what you will to these blind and deaf and silent images. I will pray for wisdom. I hope we do have a son, just to show you the folly of these carvings. But then we will need the mind of the one true God to know what to do."

"You'd better hope your god answers, Belessunu, because you have lost *your* mind."

"All I ask is that you return to the faith you showed when we married," she said.

Terah dismissed her with a wave, calling after her, "That was a long time ago." But as he rearranged the idols and prostrated himself before the table, he found himself unable to utter one prayer, not even silently. He still believed in the gods, except for Nimrod-Amraphel — not anymore. But Utu! Oh, when the sun reappeared from heaven in the morning, he would be able to pray with confidence to the god of truth, morality, and justice.

Perhaps while Utu slept, his twin sister, Inanna, the queen of heaven, would perform

68

a miracle on behalf of Belessunu. Terah cradled the image of her he had reverently created and dipped in gold. "Goddess of love, beauty, and fertility, if Belessunu carries a male child, change it to a female, I pray!"

From the other side of the curtain that separated the kitchen from the great room, Belessunu whispered emotional prayers Terah could not make out. And almost as suddenly as she began, she stopped. "Thank You, Lord," she said. "Terah!"

CHAPTER 11

Manhattan

"Don't worry, ma'am," the recovery room nurse said. "She doesn't know what she's saying, and as I told you, she won't likely remember —"

"I know," Nicole said, unable to control her own tears. "But whatever she's feeling right now breaks my heart."

"It's like a dream, Dr. Berman. Not even a real emotion."

Officer Martinez had her phone out, causing Nicole to give her a sharp look. "Not recording yet," Julia said. "She's not makin' sense."

A quiet knock announced Dr. Thorn. "How's our girl doing?" he said, flipping on the lights and taking her chart from the nurse. "Daughter can stay. Have the visitor step out."

"Ain't no visitor," Officer Martinez said, producing her badge.

The surgeon put a hand on her mother's shoulder and spoke loudly. "You with us yet, dear? Soon as you're up to it, you can eat, okay?"

"Not hungry."

"You will be. Surgery went long but well. I'll check in on you again tomorrow afternoon — well, this afternoon, actually."

Her mother nodded, but Nicole read frustration on her face. As the doctor began to pull away, Virginia held on to his wrist. "Daughter . . ."

"Yes! The one you were telling us about. She's been watching out for you."

"Hates me."

"Mama! No, please!"

"Need to forgive me."

Dr. Thorn turned his back to Nicole's mother and whispered, "You've been told this is the sedation talking, right?"

"Yes, but —"

"Let's talk outside," he said.

Officer Martinez followed them into the hall, phone out. "Gotta tell the detective what you found, why we're here." She recorded as he talked with Nicole.

"I found less bone density than —"

"Get to why you called the police," Nicole said.

"I had no choice."

71

"I'm not disputing that. What made it so obvious that her injuries were inflicted by someone else?"

"We were told the housekeeper found your mother on her stomach on the floor, unconscious, with a rug burn on her forehead. Paramedics determined her vitals were good, but when they examined her for internal injuries, they suspected the broken hip. That determined how they positioned her for transport here. MRI technicians found the back bruises and noted them on her chart, but when I got in there I saw the extent of the damage — besides the hip fracture, lower back soft-tissue damage, broken ribs, and spinal trauma. It's simply not possible for this to have been accidental, let alone the result of a fall — even a bad one. I could conclude only that my patient had been brutally attacked."

Nicole shook her head. "I can see you had no choice but to make that call. 'Course now I have a problem."

"Ma'am?"

"I've never known my mother to have an enemy. Not one. This had to be a home invasion, maybe a robbery."

"Obviously that's beyond my purview. But you have a more serious problem, don't you? Even if this officer had not been here, the nurse and I would be obligated to inform the police of what your mother said."

"That? She's recalling some childish spat from more than twenty years ago when I was a know-it-all high schooler. And you said yourself she's confused, won't remember —"

"She said you hated her, Dr. Berman. That's not for me to evaluate, but it has to be included in any investigation."

"Indulge me just another second, Doctor," Nicole said, "please. My mother sounds delirious. Can she be expected to own what she says in the state she's in?"

Dr. Thorn shrugged. "Delirium is common with hip fractures among the elderly, but frankly, your mother is on the young side for that. Most of my hip patients are eighty or older. So I would ascribe any incoherence to anesthesia."

"Well, you did anesthetize her twice."

"That was necessary and wholly safe. If she's not more lucid when she becomes fully conscious, we can administer simple tests of concentration. But even if she does awaken with no memory of what she said about you, I can't rule out that she may have been expressing some very real but suppressed fear. I'm duty bound to report that."

"I got it, Doc," Officer Martinez said.

CHAPTER 12

Ur

Terah jumped to his feet at his wife's cry and whipped back the curtain to the kitchen. "Is it the baby?" he said.

But Belessunu did not appear in danger or pain. She was kneeling, face pointed to the ceiling, smiling beatifically. "The Lord speaks," she breathed. Her conviction startled him. She had always been devout, but he had never seen her this way or heard her say such a thing.

"He speaks?"

She nodded, apparently overcome. "Directly to my heart."

Terah wanted to mock her, to ridicule her prayers the way she had his. But she was so — earnest. Whether she had conjured this or was just imagining it, clearly it was real to her. He couldn't help himself. "What is he saying?"

Belessunu lowered her gaze, shut her eyes,

and bowed her head. Silent for several moments, when she spoke she emitted something less than a whisper and Terah had to lean forward to hear.

"Gaze throughout the cities and be amazed! For I the Lord your God shall act. I will exalt the faithful who worship the one true God.

"The Babylonians are a vicious people who walk through the nations to occupy cities they do not own. Their appalling pride emanates from within themselves alone.

"They come for violence, faces set, gathering captives, mocking every stronghold. Then, on a whim their despot changes his mind and ascribes his power to idols."

Belessunu paused, but Terah dared not interrupt. Her head remained bowed, and she appeared transfixed. She raised a hand toward her husband, as if signaling him to remain silent. *"But only I, the Lord your God, am from everlasting to everlasting. Only I am the Holy One. I have appointed the ruler for judgment, marked him for correction. I am of purer eyes than to behold evil and cannot look on wickedness. I will not look on the treacherous and hold my tongue when the evil one devours.*

"Shall he continue to slay nations without compassion? Make plain the vision that the just man shall live by his faith. But the proud

man is like death and cannot be satisfied. He gathers to himself all peoples. Woe to him who plunders many nations, who covets evil gain that he may set his nest on high.

"Woe to him who builds a town with bloodshed, who establishes a city by sin! For the earth will be filled with the glory of the Lord, as the waters cover the sea."

Terah felt locked in place. "These are the words of the one true God?"

Belessunu lifted her face and nodded.

"He speaks of Nimrod?"

"There's more," she said.

Terah shuddered. "More?"

"He speaks of you."

"Me? No! I do not know Him!"

"He knows you."

"No! You must not let Him speak of me!"

Terah scrambled to the entrance of their dwelling and cowered by the doorframe, trembling.

Belessunu bowed her head once more, speaking no louder than before, forcing Terah to creep back near her in order to hear.

"What profit is an image its maker can carve? Should that maker trust in mute idols? Woe to the one who commands stone to awake, wood to arise and counsel! Alas, even formed of silver and gold, in it dwells no life.

"But I, the living God, reside in My holy temple. Let the whole earth fall silent in My presence."

CHAPTER 13

Manhattan

Dr. Thorn left Nicole and Julia Martinez in the hall outside the recovery room and headed for the elevator. The uniformed policemen on either side of the door peered straight ahead, as if not listening. Nicole knew better.

"You're not going to keep me from seeing her now, are you, Officer?"

"Long as you know I gotta record everything from here on," Martinez said. "And I gotta let the boss know what she said — about you hating her."

"I'm telling you, she's confusing something from twenty years ago. I was a stupid, independent teenager, but even then I never said I hated her."

"C'mon," Martinez said. "Not even in anger like we all do? Just sayin' stuff to push our parents' buttons? I did that more than once. My mother was old-school, man. She said I could go out with my friends, long as my room was clean, ya know? When I got home she was waiting in my messed-up room, and she was mad. I told her I didn't know she meant it had to be done *before* I went out. She called me a liar, which I was, and I said the worst thing I could think of — that I hated her. And after that I *never* got to go anywhere till my room was cleaned up."

"And you grew up to be a cop . . ."

"Yeah, see? Sayin' stupid stuff as a kid don't make you a bad person. You never did that, ever?"

"Say I hated her?" Nicole said. "No. That was a line I would never cross, because it was so far from the truth. Mom and Dad were exasperating back then, and I did a lot of huffing and storming off and slamming doors. And, yes, I went out with an older guy neither of them liked and stayed out later than I was supposed to. But down deep I knew they were right and were only worried about me. Maybe I *acted* like I hated them, but I never said it."

"Maybe you just don't remember."

"I'd remember that."

"Then why'd she say it, Dr. Berman?"

Nicole shook her head. "I've told you. In fact, the nurse *and* the doctor told us both.

She's not aware of what she's saying. You said yourself she wasn't making sense."

"Yeah, but you know why I'm here and what I'm supposed to do. I can't ignore it when a woman who was attacked says her daughter hates her."

"If I hated her, I wouldn't be here."

"Just sayin'."

"If you must tell Detective Wojciechowski, at least say she was just out of surgery when she said that."

Nicole found her mother asleep again, despite the nurse in the room and the bright overhead light. Martinez again sat out of the patient's field of vision and began texting. Nicole wished she could approve whatever Julia was writing. Martinez looked up. "Don't worry, Dr. Berman. You're innocent till proven guilty, remember?"

The nurse writing on the patient chart, said, "Doctor always wants them to rouse fully after surgery . . ."

"I'm okay with letting her sleep," Nicole said, pulling up a chair and taking her mother's hand.

"I'm not," Officer Martinez said, eyes on her phone. "We gotta know what she remembers."

"Well," Nicole said, "so far she's living in the past and misremembering. I'm not about to wake her."

The nurse turned off the light, leaving the room dark except for the monitors and a small night-light over the sink. "I'll be at the nurses' station down the hall, and we monitor all these machines from there, so I'll know if there's a crisis."

Julia Martinez slipped her phone in her pocket and folded her arms. "You're not gonna rat me out if I get a little snooze then, are ya?"

"Feel free," Nicole said, finding it ironic that Martinez asked for that consideration while apparently not minding that her report would make Nicole look bad. Her mother squeezed her hand, and Nicole studied her face. *Had to have been involuntary. What must she be dreaming about?*

"Just don't let me miss anything," Martinez said.

CHAPTER 14

Ur

"You must rest, Belessunu," Terah said, his voice quavery. "You look spent."

His wife nodded, the long day having engraved weariness on her countenance. She reached for his hand, but he hesitated. "Will you not help me rise?" she said. "The wife of your youth who carries your child?"

He helped her up and led her to their sleeping mat beyond another drape that hung in the narrow doorway at the other side of the great room. She lay on her back in the darkness, hands clasped above her protruding torso. "Are you laboring to breathe?" he said, sitting next to her.

"I'll be fine now."

"Belessunu, do you believe that was your god speaking through you?"

"You believed it. I could tell."

Terah held his head in his hands. "I fear it, that's all I know."

She put a hand on his arm. "That's not all you know. You know truth when you hear it."

"I will test my gods," he said.

She sighed. "The ones you carved yourself?"

"They led me in the carving! I know they are just images, but they embody real gods."

"And you will prove this how?"

"I will ask them for wisdom, a plan, in the event we are cursed with a manchild."

"No child will be a curse, Terah. If God gives us a son, He will also show us how to protect him."

Terah rose. "Sleep, wife. One of us must."

"We both must. I will sleep the sleep of the blessed."

"I dare not," he said, "until I devise a plan."

As evening gave way to the wee hours, the night finally cooled and a light breeze wafted through the window, reaching Terah as he knelt miserably before his array of idols. He stretched forward and pressed his cheek against the cold clay floor. From the other room, Belessunu's breathing came rhythmic and deep. How he envied her! Had his gods spoken to him as hers apparently had to her, he would not have been able to sleep for days.

"Why do you not speak?" he whined, voice low so as not to disturb Belessunu. "I serve you as loyally as I serve my king, and this is how you respond? I need help, a sign, a plan. Nimrod has betrayed my trust. Will you do the same? Must I pray to my wife's god, the god of my forefathers? At least he is not silent."

That challenge seemed to work, as something stirred within Terah and he pushed himself up to his knees. The answer was in the wilderness! But what could it be? And was this from the gods? Or from his ancestors' God? Regardless, he must know and know soon. Now.

Alive with purpose, he stood. After a peek around the bedroom curtain to be sure Belessunu was fast asleep, he grabbed his cloak and ventured into the night, quietly closing the door. A hundred yards from his house, Terah passed the pen where two of his young servants tended sheep, goats, and cattle.

Wedum and Mutuum sat poking a small fire, but as he approached they stood, eyes wary, long staffs at the ready.

"It is only me, men," Terah said. "As you were."

"Master," they said and squatted again.

The pungent smoke swirled, making Terah cough despite the pleasant aroma that dulled the sting of the odor of livestock dung. "The animals are not settled?"

"Dogs are too close," Wedum, the taller of the two, said. "We had to chase away a pack."

"Good lads."

"Can we help you with anything, master?"

"Just walking," he said. "Carry on."

"Mind the dogs, sir," Mutuum said. "Hear them now?"

Terah held his breath and closed his eyes. "I do. How many?"

"Five or six, if it's the same pack."

"And you can handle them if they return?"

"They didn't put up a fight," Wedum said. "But they had to smell the fear in the livestock. They may approach quietly next time, if the fire doesn't keep them away. If you go much farther, you should take a stick."

"No, the gods are with me tonight, men."

"Glory to the gods," they said in unison.

"But should they fail me, you will hear my cry and save me, will you not?"

"Without question, sir," Mutuum said. "Absolutely."

"I'm joking! The gods will not fail me."

"Glory to the gods."

86

CHAPTER 15

Manhattan

Puffs from her lips with each exhale told Nicole that Officer Julia Martinez was deep asleep. The dark recovery room felt warm, and the humming, whirring, blinking, and wheezing of the oxygen supply lulled Nicole too. She monitored her mother's pulse, blood pressure, and respiration at a glance. Everything read normal, and her more than half full IV bag dripped steadily into the tube.

Nicole enfolded her mother's free hand in her own, lowered her own chin to her chest, and tried to doze. But her mind still purred. Surely the New York PD would find some evidence her mother had surprised a burglar. Who else had reason to attack her?

Yet the housekeeper — Bulgarian Teodora Petrova — had found her. Teodora was too new to be entrusted with a key, meaning Nicole's mother had to have let her in.

Admittedly, the Bermans enjoyed a ridiculously expansive place, but how could someone have brutalized her mother without Teodora seeing them, let alone hearing something? Had one of them let the perpetrator in, or had he overpowered one of them? Thank God for a doorman, front-desk personnel, and closed-circuit TV. The culprit should be easy to identify.

Was Teodora herself a suspect? Nicole's mother had described her as heavyset, a recent emigrant with a thick accent. "About my age," her mother had said. "I could barely understand her. But she had a very professionally prepared résumé and lots of experience. She wore a bulky overcoat, much too warm for the weather, and she refused to take it off. I could not get her to smile, but I just assumed she was not fluent enough to understand American humor."

She'd worked two weeks — Monday, Wednesday, and Friday mornings from nine to eleven. Nicole's mother had had no complaints. "In fact," Mom had told her, "she's a workhorse. Tireless and fast."

"And you're not missing any cash or jewelry?"

"Thankfully."

Her parents had fired the previous maid when it became clear she could not be trusted. She'd been solid for three years before they started to notice things missing. She never admitted to taking anything.

What about her? Was she strong enough, athletic enough, to exact revenge? Maybe she had co-opted a boyfriend . . . Nicole would have to remember to suggest that to Wojciechowski. At least her father had changed the locks.

Nicole peeked at the monitors every so often, but soon her eyelids grew heavy and she began drifting. Her breathing matched the cadence of the clicks and hisses of the oxygen generator.

Whether she fell asleep, or for how long, Nicole couldn't say, but she was jarred alert when her mother squeezed her hand and pulled. "Nikki, is that you?"

Had she heard correctly? Her mother hadn't called her anything but Nicole or occasionally her father's pet name for her, Nic, since she was a teenager.

"Yes, Mama," she said. "Let's whisper."

"Why?"

"So we don't wake my friend. You okay? Need anything?"

"I need to know where I am and why I feel so awful."

"Are you in pain?"

89

"Not exactly. Stiff. Uncomfortable." She seemed to be getting her bearings. "Was I in an accident?"

"You broke your hip, Mom."

"How?"

"You don't remember?"

Her mother fell silent. Finally, she said, "I don't even know what day it is."

"Friday. Well, Saturday now."

"Fridays I walk my mile-and-a-half route, stop at Schnell's, and bring a bagel home. Have to be there before Teodora arrives."

"Did that happen today, uh, I mean yesterday?"

When her mother repeated the question, this time as if in slow motion, Nicole's heart sank. The woman had morphed from articulate — albeit puzzled — to slurring again. She pulled desperately at Nicole's hand. "Hap— happen today? Nikki. Make Daddy. Make him. Tell you the truth before I die."

"You're not going to die, Mom. You're going to be fine."

"Make him . . . truth."

"About what? What do you want me to ask him?"

Her mother's eyes were wide in the dim light now, her grip fierce, as if trying to pull herself up.

"Careful, Mama. You're not to be moving."

Loud beeping made Nicole scan the monitors. Her mother's pulse and blood pressure had skyrocketed. Officer Martinez leapt to her feet. "What's happening? Do I need to get somebody?"

The nurse rushed in, flipping on the light. Nicole had to shield her eyes.

"Clear, Officer, please! Dr. Berman, give me access! She just waking up, is that it?"

"She's been trying to talk," Nicole said. "Still confused."

"Mrs. Berman! I need you to lie fully back. There you go. Deep breaths. I'm adjusting your oxy—"

"She was talking?" Julia Martinez said. "What'd she say?"

"Not much," Nicole said. "Still out of it."

"Officer!" the nurse said. "Dr. Berman! In the hall, please."

"Officer?" Nicole's mother cried. "Where am I?"

CHAPTER 16

Ur

Terah wandered out into the wilderness, far from his home and far beyond the livestock pen. He moved past rock outcroppings that blocked his view of the fire Mutuum and Wedum had lit to keep themselves warm and repel the wild dogs. The cool air and the silence refreshed him, and he prayed to Nanna, god of the moon. Indeed, Nanna was the creator, the god of all gods, father of Utu, god of the sun, and his twin sister, Inanna. Utu had become King Nimrod's — and the Babylonian Empire's — favorite deity.

Terah for years had prayed also to Nimrod when he knelt before his idols. But the king, who also called himself Amraphel, never mentioned even being aware of Terah's petitions. Well, no more would he pray to that deceiver. Belessunu was right about him, at least. Clearly Nimrod was only a self-

92

proclaimed deity.

The other gods were often silent, and when they did answer, it was often in ways Terah did not understand. But to his knowledge, they certainly had never deceived him.

Fear washed over Terah so quickly it nearly drove him to the ground. What was this? What vexed him? The silence! Invigorating as it was, the breeze was too gentle to emit sound, and none of the vegetation in this arid expanse bore anything resembling leaves that would so much as rattle in the wind. All noise had ceased. Even the yipping of the wild dogs so far away, sounds that carried long distances here.

Had the dogs circled back to attack his animals, Terah would have heard from far off the commotion of Wedum and Mutuum engaging them. So what was he to make of the silence? Had the gods not coaxed him out here? And to what end? Had the wild dogs caught his scent and begun to furtively track him? Should he have taken tall Wedum up on that offer of a stick? He tried to tell himself his imagination had merely gotten the better of him.

Terah stopped dead and envisioned dogs cunning enough to go silent as they connived to encircle him. Perhaps even now they were stealthily closing the distance until he would have nowhere to turn when they attacked. He set out again, moving farther and farther from home, fearing they lay in wait for his return. Plus, he vaguely remembered rock formations not terribly far away that might afford him a hiding place, provided he could secure a high enough spot.

There would be no outwitting the dogs or eluding their noses. Clearly they smelled animals from long distances. How much different could human scent be?

Terah walked faster, trying to invoke in his mind the silhouettes of massive natural stone formations he remembered on the horizon. That made him envision the dogs too, waiting in the rocks to ambush him. But the nearer he came to where he remembered crags that might offer haven, the easier it was to tell himself the dogs were only in his mind.

Of the boulders he was certain. The dogs had likely run off in search of other prey. Perhaps they had even bedded down for the night. There! A quarter mile west a jagged outline appeared clearly on the horizon in the moonlight — just as he remembered. Glory to the gods. They had led him here, restored his confidence. From atop the massive rocks he could assure himself no dogs blocked his way back home.

But when the moon slid behind a cloud, Terah lost sight of his destination. *Just keep walking,* he told himself. But he had lost his point of reference. He knew men who could walk a straight line in any direction based on the positions of the stars. The logic of that eluded him, but still he strode with purpose to where he believed — hoped — security lay.

Chapter 17

Manhattan

The nurse's efforts to calm Nicole's mother lowered her pulse, blood pressure, and respiration only a tick each. She appeared calmer, but the numbers didn't lie. "Should you call Dr. Thorn?" Nicole said.

"No, this isn't an emergency, and I ought to be able to manage her vitals with a sleeping pill."

"She does look like she could use more rest," Nicole said.

"Problem is, I can't prescribe." The nurse stepped into the hall and flagged down a colleague. "Can you find me a resident, stat?"

Soon a plump, dark-haired woman in scrubs knocked and strode directly to the sink. She washed her hands and pulled on latex gloves as the nurse held the chart where she could read it. "Is this *the* Mrs. Berman?"

"One and the same."

"What's with the cops out there?"

"Tell you later," the nurse said, nodding to Nicole. "Her daughter, Nicole."

"Hi, and who's this?"

Julia Martinez flashed her badge.

"My, my," the doctor said, approaching the bed. "Rock star treatment, Mrs. Berman." Nicole's mother eyed her, looking wary and puzzled. "All right, let's get this light off. How long ago was she anesthetized for surgery?" The nurse pulled up the page on the chart. "Any allergies to drugs?"

Her mother just stared. "None," Nicole said.

"Let's go with low-dose hypnotic sedative. Five milligrams zolpidem tartrate."

"That's enough?" the nurse whispered.

The resident nodded. "With her small stature and history. Repeat in thirty minutes if she's still conscious and her numbers are still elevated. But no more than that. You have it on hand?"

"We do. I'll be right back."

"I'm on all night if you need me," the resident told Nicole on her way out.

Nicole saw terror in her mother's eyes. "They're going to give you a pill so you can sleep, Mama. We can talk tomorrow."

"Have to — got to — talk now."

"No, we don't. It'll wait."

"Won't. Wait."

"Just try to relax, Mom."

"Nic! Listen!"

Nicole had never seen her mother so exercised. She'd always been the rock of the family, the one Nicole and her father confided in. Nicole sighed. "What is it, Mama?"

Her voice came slow and liquidy, making Nicole wonder how her vital signs could be so elevated. "Make y— father tell you," she said, and the effort appeared to leave her exhausted.

"Tell me what?"

"The box. Tell you wha's in the box."

"What box?"

Her mother lifted a hand and drew weak circles in the air. "Box. Gray metal box. Secret. Never tol' me. Doesn't know I saw."

"Saw what?"

"Picture. The — the picture of the . . ."

"What, Mom?"

"Of the thing. The thing. The lady."

"No idea what you're talking about. I've never even seen a box."

"Find. Got to find. Before he comes back."

The nurse returned with the medication, but Nicole's mother kept turning away from the pill. "We need to get your vitals back to normal," the nurse said.

"Make. Her. Find box. Find picture."

"Okay," the nurse said, turning to Nicole. "Can you agree to do that so we can get this pill down her?"

"All right, Mama. All right."

"Promise?"

"Promise."

The nurse whispered, "Should work quickly on her. I'm guessing ten minutes, and she could sleep eight hours."

"Good," Julia Martinez said. "If she ain't gonna be talkin', I don't gotta be here."

"Nor do you, Dr. Berman," the nurse said. "You can take a break, and we'll bring her to her room in an hour or so."

Nicole nodded wearily. With her dad getting in, the cops coming back, and whatever this was her mother was going on about, the day promised to be a doozy.

"How much stock can I put in what she's saying?" Nicole said.

"Very little," the nurse said. "Could totally be a figment of her imagination, or the drugs — hard to tell. If she remembers it tomorrow, maybe press her on it."

Nicole and Julia Martinez stepped into the hall and away from the two uniformed officers. Nicole said, "You heard her. No sense troubling the detective with any of my mother's gibberish, right?"

"Okay, listen to me, Dr. Berman. I've been all nice and friendly, right? But I gotta decide whether to let you stay here or book you downtown. I got probable cause."

"You're joking."

"I sound like I'm playin'? I got to answer to my boss if everything isn't locked down tight here. Your mama said damaging stuff about you and your dad. If I'm gonna go home and go to bed, I gotta be sure she's safe."

"Safe from me? You can't possibly think —"

"That's what I get paid to do, ma'am. I can only go on what I heard."

"What you heard from a traumatized woman full of sedatives and confused —"

"I could get you on obstructin' justice right now!"

"What are you talking about?"

"Tryin' to talk me out of telling my boss what she's been saying about you and your daddy."

"I wasn't! I was just trying to say —"

"And interfering with an investigation."

"You're reaching now, Julia. I'm not interf—"

"I heard you promise to look for your father's secret box."

"Which probably doesn't even exist! And I only said that so she'd take the pill."

"How do I know you ain't gonna go straight to their apartment and look for it?"

"First, because I'm about to collapse. But what if I did? I have a right to go there with my mother's permission —"

"You can't have it both ways, Ms. Berman. She's either talkin' nonsense or she's not. If the hatin' and the box and the secret are all just confusion and drugs, what's that make her permission?"

Nicole shrugged.

"Don't you get it? Their place is a crime scene. You can't be pokin' around in there."

"Fine," Nicole said. "Forget I said anything — anything about what you should or shouldn't tell your boss. And yes, I should have assumed their apartment would be off-limits till the investigation was over. You have my word I won't go there."

"Your word. You think I finished fifth at the academy by bein' stupid? You want me to just trust you 'cause you got a title in front a your name? Tell you what — you wanna stay here with Mama tonight, you can't be talking to her anymore without NYPD in the room."

"In the room? Even in Eleven West?"

"Especially there! I don't know when she's

gonna wake up, and neither do you. You goin' there now?"

Nicole nodded.

"Then one will go with you and the other'll come when she does. Now I gotta get your dad's secret box added to the search warrant."

CHAPTER 18

Ur

Terah could not make sense of it. Not only had the moon disappeared, but the stars too. What was Nanna up to? Until this moment, the moon god had illumined his path, something the stars couldn't do anyway. But any hope, any sense of where he was, left him no better than a blind man unless something shifted in the black sky.

So this was the answer to his fervent prayers? Had even Nanna proved worthless? He was at least a reluctant god this night. King Nimrod had proved worse than reluctant — he was devious. All Terah's hopes now lay in the lesser gods, also represented by idols he had carved. And while he had long prayed to them in earnest faith, now he wondered, doubted. Was there something to Belessunu's prayers? Had her god truly spoken through her? And if so, to him?

If his gods had not drawn him out into

the wilderness, who had? Terah dared not stop and ponder it. For this blackest of all nights to descend now was worse than foul fortune. If a pack of wild dogs considered him prey, his life was at stake. He had to keep moving, had no choice but to continue. But was he still pointed the right direction? No matter how hard he squinted or how fast he blinked, Terah detected nothing. His hearing and smell became acute. Or was it madness that made him imagine the breath of predators and the tangy mustiness of wild fur? Had these beasts run long distances to now sit on their haunches, waiting to pounce? He must neither show fear nor even move too quickly.

Hands before him like one who walks in his sleep, Terah felt for solid rock, prayed for it. But now even he didn't know to whom he was praying. The sleeping Utu? The bashful Nanna? The treacherous Nimrod? Or the lesser gods, the ones his wife called his handmade rubbish? Terah could not be choosy. He prayed to them all, and whichever deigned to answer would be fine with him.

Even stepping so carefully into the unknown, traversing a quarter mile should not have taken this long. Terah was convinced he had veered hopelessly off course and that his next destination would be the Euphrates — normally more than a week's journey from his home. The scent and sounds of the animals grew more real. He fell to his knees in despair, only to gash both shins on rocks. He rolled to his side, covering the wounds with his hands. But the blood seeped through his fingers. The dripping gore was sure to bring the dogs.

"I pray to the one true God of my ancestors!" he cried. "If You are there, if You are true, forgive my unbelief! Forgive my straying from You! Deliver me and I will serve You and worship You and make Your name known!"

It was all or nothing now, for his shouts would draw the dogs if the smell of his blood did not.

Deep in his being, Terah felt God speak to him. *"Arise and walk, for your salvation draws nigh."*

He rose and staggered on, still reaching, feeling, hoping, anticipating. The moon reappeared just in time to reveal before his face a wall of sheer rock. Had the God of Noah delivered him? Or did this mean that Nanna, the moon deity, was the god of all gods after all? In the radiance that came from the sky, Terah espied the mouth of a cave.

And from only yards behind him came the unmistakable growling, panting, barking, charging of wild dogs.

CHAPTER 19

Manhattan

"So you drew the short straw?" Nicole said to the officer accompanying her to her mother's room on Eleven West. She guessed him at 6'4" and 250 pounds, but the Kevlar vest under his uniform shirt made him look even bigger. The nameplate over his right shirt pocket read "D. Decker." Something tells me you're a rookie."

"Fourteen months on the job, ma'am. But I don't know what you mean by short straw."

"Make me feel old, why don't you?" she said. "Just means you got the job no one wanted."

"I'm to know where you are at all times, and also to protect you. I'll be right outside your door the rest of the night."

"I feel safe already," she said. Who'd want to tangle with this young man? "Any gunplay in your first fourteen months?"

"No, ma'am. That's not as common as on TV."

"Fisticuffs?"

"Don't know that word either."

"Fights. Fought anyone?"

He shook his head. "Not yet. We're s'posed to carry ourselves in such as way as to discourage that before it starts."

"Easier for you than most, I'm sure."

"Yes, ma'am."

"Listen, Decker, did you hear Officer Martinez mention adding something to a search warrant?"

"Yes, ma'am."

"Can you do that, get a warrant to search a crime scene for whatever you want?"

"If I remember what they taught us at the academy, the Fourth Amendment prohibits unreasonable searches. So even though this looks like an attempted murder case, we'd have to have a warrant based on probable cause. It's not like any search would be fair game. The warrant application has to be specific, so the crime scene guys don't violate privacy rights."

"So why would Officer Martinez want to add my dad's box to the warrant?"

"Sorry, I don't know enough to say."

Nicole hadn't allowed herself to consider her mother's apparent attack attempted murder, but she couldn't deny it. She could only imagine how her mother's mention of her father's secret box would sound to Detective Wojciechowski under the circumstances. He'd have to assume he'd stumbled upon a motive.

Nicole approached the registration desk at Eleven West. "I'm —"

"We've been waiting for you, Dr. Berman," a young woman said. "All settled in?"

"Just about."

"We offer room service any time of the day or night."

"Even for visitors?"

"Yes." She consulted her video monitor. "The order form is in the room, and for you it's complimentary." The young woman looked past Nicole. "And will you be here overnight, Officer?"

"Yes, ma'am. And when Mrs. Berman arrives, another officer will join me."

She handed him two meal forms. "On the NYPD account?"

He nodded, and she brought him two folding chairs from a back room.

"Done this before, Decker?" Nicole said as they headed down the hall.

"More than once," he said. "Happy to serve."

"What're you blushing about?" she said.

"Been out with that girl is all."

"You don't say . . . ."

He set his chair next to her door and tipped his cap. "Night, ma'am."

Nicole unpacked, filled out her breakfast order for six and a half hours later, and opened the door to hang it on the knob. Decker's form was already there. "Were you ordering for the both of us?" she said.

"No, ma—"

"A joke, son."

Nicole always prayed at bedtime, but she hadn't knelt in ages. Now it seemed the thing to do. She changed, knelt by the bed, and prayed for her father's safety, her mother's recovery, and her own peace of mind. She also prayed for Officer Julia Martinez, who had come across overzealous, confrontational.

"I don't know that she's intentionally persecuting me, Lord," Nicole said. "But You know. Answer me in the day of distress. May the God of Jacob fortify me. Send me help and support from Your mighty hand. Grant my heart's desire, and I will rejoice in Your deliverance from heaven.

"Some rely upon chariots and horses, but I invoke the name of the Lord my God — Yeshua Hamashiac, Adonai, my strong tower. Amen."

Curious as she was, Nicole found herself unable to pray about whatever her mother had been referring to — some secret box and its mysterious photo. She was convinced it had to be a drug-induced hallucination. Such talk was so strange for her mother, usually so precise and careful. She seldom speculated and rarely overreacted.

And her father a man of secrets? Nicole couldn't imagine it. While, yes, she'd had to do her own Internet search to discover when and how he was wounded in Vietnam, it made sense he wouldn't want to discuss that. What wounded vet wants to revisit the day he thought he would die? Those who had seen the worst of war, injured or not, were known for leaving it in the past. He was no exception. In fact, the few times she had tried to draw him out on the subject, he actually paled and shook his head.

But stories from her father's life before and after Nam showed him as plainspoken and straightforward as anyone she'd ever known. He seemed to have himself figured out and had come to grips with the man who had grown from that angry, rebellious teen.

His hiding anything from her mother didn't jibe with the man she knew. Anesthesia had to have caused her mother to concoct this story out of some subconscious fear that her husband couldn't possibly be all that he seemed because down deep she didn't feel worthy of such a man.

But she was! Her steady faith and love for him was largely responsible for the man he had become.

Nicole knew she had to stop worrying about what her mother said or what it revealed. The woman would not likely remember it in the morning, and they would both laugh about it someday.

The fatigue that had assaulted Nicole when she'd run home for dinner never really left her. It had been only camouflaged by worry and tension over what Kayla Jefferson had revealed upon her return to the hospital. Learning your mother had tripped, fallen, and broken a hip was one thing. Finding out there had likely been foul play, being suspected if not accused of it, being separated from her dad at such a crucial time, and then having her mother talk nonsense that would be reported to the police — well, that was something else.

Nicole was still on her knees, her head resting on the bed. Her trim, athletic body warm and feeling heavy and sleepy, she had no interest in moving a muscle. But her feet and legs would fall asleep if she didn't move, and so she forced herself to crawl onto the bed. Pulling back the covers and sliding between the sheets was beyond her capacity.

CHAPTER 20

Ur

Terah prayed to awaken from this nightmare, but he knew better. In this horrible dream that was not a dream, he felt rooted to the rocky soil. The core of his being screamed for him to lift his tunic, tug at the wool stuck to his shin wounds, and flee with the speed of a man fifty years younger. But by the time he even gathered his hem, the dogs closed in on him.

He dived toward the mouth of the cave, tumbling into cool utter darkness. That did not stop the dogs. They didn't need to see. His scent led them, and his gasps gave him away. Terah felt for rocks to see how high he might climb. But where could he ascend that the dogs couldn't follow? Still, he had to try. Standing still made him a human delicacy.

As the dogs reached him, he scrambled up as far as he could. Teeth bit through his tunic and sank into his backside. "Utu, god of the sun, save me!" he screeched, switching allegiances without a second thought. What good was the god of his forebearers if he had led him this far only to be devoured? As good as praying to the sun god in a cave black as pitch.

So Terah bellowed all the more, playing the madman as he felt everywhere for stones to throw. "Be gone!" he wailed and whipped three rocks toward the sounds of the pack. A high-pitched yelp told him at least one had found its mark, but when he reached for more, he found one too heavy to lift with one hand. He heard the dogs ascending again, so Terah twisted himself around and hefted the rock in both hands over his head.

It proved so weighty it nearly carried him off his roost, but this was his last hope. He had to swing the enormous stone at the first animal to draw near. But one locked its teeth into the flesh of his left shoulder, too close to hit with the rock. When another leapt onto his thighs, Terah brought the crude weapon down with all his might. Bone and tissue gave way as the animal slid off him and sounded as if it knocked other dogs down as it fell. Terah thrashed to the right, swinging into range the body of the dog attached to his shoulder. He bashed it with the rock and heard ribs break.

Dogs kept coming, and Terah knew that without a miracle, he was beat. He called on his last reserve of strength to again raise the stone above his head. He crouched, waiting till the next wave of mongrels came so close he could smell their foul breath. With a maniacal shriek he used all his might to bang the rock into the animals. His momentum launched him off his perch, and he continued to yowl as he hurtled down, the rock and his body slamming into dogs the whole way.

Terah landed with a thud, his head afire with pain, fingers raw, shoulder and one backside deeply bitten, the rest of his body scraped and torn. He knew bruises would show from head to toe in the light of day. But whatever had happened, whatever he had done, whichever deity had sent the miracle, the surviving dogs had gone, their plaintive cries filling the night.

"Glory to the gods," he intoned, voice squeaking in the chill of the cave.

As he lay trying to gather himself, Terah prayed Belessunu would not wake to find him gone, that the dogs would not return for revenge, and that he would somehow muster the strength to get back home. "Gula, goddess of healing, lead me to the salves and ointments I need."

Wheezing, Terah wondered how a man well past his prime could have fended off such an attack. Had the gods led him here just to test him, to see if he could survive? He had acquitted himself well, but how would he explain his wounds? And what had he gained from all this? "Help me, great gods of nature, to find the value in my ordeal."

Terah struggled to his feet and felt for the wall, quickly realizing he had severely damaged his right ankle in the fall. That must have also accounted for the deep puncture wounds in his face.

He had been turned around, his back to the mouth of the cave. Slowly turning until the entrance appeared, he found the moon shining on the desolate landscape. "Thank you, Nanna," he whispered.

Listening intently for the dogs, Terah waited before venturing out. He backed deeper into the cave, keeping his eye on the mouth. Soon he followed the formation behind him as it angled off, and he again lost sight of the entrance. Could this be his answer, the reasons the gods sent him out here — to discover the perfect refuge, must his family flee? This might make his torment worth all the fear and the pain. He couldn't wait to tell his wife in the morning, assuming he could make it home. But first he would have to explain why he looked the way he did.

CHAPTER 21

Manhattan

Nicole's mind had not really shut off all night. Everything that had happened since her father called from Paris the afternoon before dominated both her every conscious thought as well as her dreams. And it seemed every twenty minutes she roused, expecting someone to deliver her mother. As the night wore on, she kept promising herself she would call at the top of the next hour to see what had happened to the promise of moving her mother within sixty minutes of having left her in Recovery.

But each time the clock slowly rolled past the hour, Nicole told herself someone would wake her if her mother were in danger. Hopefully all this delay implied was that her mother was still sleeping — making it more likely she would awaken less hazy than she'd been right after surgery.

Awakened by the delivery of her breakfast,

Nicole called Recovery, only to learn her mother was back in Intensive Care. "But not to worry, Dr. Berman. The resident assigned to her advised against putting her into a standard room until she wakes — which they expect by no later than ten."

"But she's all right?"

"Her vitals look good. She needed only the one dose of Zolpidem and is expected to be lucid after breakfast for her interrogation."

After showering and changing and consuming — not really savoring — a continental breakfast, Nicole stepped into the corridor on her way to ICU. Patrolman Decker had already eaten as well and looked remarkably alert. "Don't suppose you were allowed any sleep," she said.

"Oh, no, ma'am. I sleep during the day. Soon as I get off I'll hit the gym and go straight home to bed."

"Show off," she said. "I use any excuse to skip my workouts."

"Daily battle," he said, returning his chair to the front desk and following her to ICU.

Decker's partner guarded the door, which bore a sign: No Admittance. Hospital Personnel Only.

"Surely I'm allowed in," Nicole said.

"Sorry, ma'am," the officer said.

"You can come in with me," she said, "or Decker can, but I need to —"

"Detective wants to question her first. Says you can be there, but —"

"Do I need a lawyer?"

"Up to you, ma'am, if you think you're gonna be charged with any —"

"I mean to get to see my mother!"

"No, a lawyer couldn't help you with that."

"Can one of you at least let her know I'm here and that I *want* to see her?"

"I could," the officer said, "but she's still sleeping."

"I need to talk to somebody. As soon as she's awake, my mother needs to know I'm here and that my dad will be here around noon."

Nicole started toward the nurses' station, but Officer Decker said, "I gotta stay with you wherever you go, and I'm already on overtime. They'll be replacing me soon."

She kept moving. "You've been most kind, but you or whoever replaces you is going to have to keep up."

As she approached the desk, a woman at a computer monitor looked up, then past her, and smiled. "Hi, Duane!" she said.

Decker nodded and smiled. "Christi."

Nicole raised a brow at him. "Her too? One on every floor?"

He shrugged. "Not *every* floor. Guess they like the uniform."

Christi confirmed that Nicole was not to see her mother before the police did. Nicole began to plead her case, but Christi held up a hand. "I know nothing about this except that Mrs. Berman is a VIP patient and it's my job if I don't follow the rules."

"Convenient," Nicole said.

CHAPTER 22

Ur

How Terah wished he had a torch! It might have held off the dogs, but it also would have enabled him to see the full dimensions of the cave. Just by feeling about in the inky blackness, he could tell it was huge. Small cavities here and there opened to larger areas — so many that Terah had to be careful to retrace his steps to find his way out.

When he finally returned to the mouth of the cave, he hesitated before emerging, listening for danger and assessing his injuries in the moonlight. No part of his body had been spared. He may have broken a left toe. The tops of both feet were deeply scraped. He worried that right ankle might be broken. The wounds on his shins now had counterparts on his calves. The first dog had bit deep into his left backside, drawing blood that stuck to his tunic. Each time he pulled the material away brought a stab of pain.

Terah's lower back ached as if it had taken the brunt of the blows on his fall to the cave floor. His arms bore nicks and tears that oozed. His shoulder had suffered the deepest bite, and a circle of blood on his garment had already grown as large as his head. Terah also felt pain in his neck, and his skull bore too many sores to count. Both cheekbones felt bruised, and he gently touched lacerations at his chin, both cheeks, and near his ears.

Terah crept out of the cave, steadying himself with a hand on the edge of the opening for as long as he could. Once free, he found himself favoring the painful ankle and knew he would not get far unless he found something to use as support. He prayed the moon god Nanna would stay free of the clouds so he could search as he labored along.

The scarce vegetation consisted largely of scrub, nothing that would yield a walking stick. Terah mince-stepped in agony, vigilant for anything he might use. If only he were closer to the river, he might find driftwood. Grateful as he was to the gods for having spared his life, he began to despair of reaching his own estate where he might receive help from his servants. At least he had diverted the marauding dogs from his own animals.

Terah's goal became to reach home before Belessunu rose so he could use her polished copper plate to evaluate and begin repairing his face. If Gula, the goddess of healing, led him to the right concoction, he could lessen his wife's shock at the very sight of him. He vaguely remembered that Nimrod, who suffered a face wound in an early battle, had been treated with a solution of turpentine from two types of trees, ground daisy petals, and tamarisk. The king's physicians had pounded the ingredients into the flour of inninnu and poured the mix into beer and milk. They applied this to his cheek and wound cloth around it. When the binding was removed a few days later, no hint of his injury remained.

Belessunu herself had treated the minor wounds of their servants with a solution of honey and myrrh mixed with alcohol. Surely Terah could rustle up something while his wife slept. But who knew when he might reach home, inching along in the desolate wilderness?

About two hours into his excruciating journey, Terah reached the halfway point between the cave and his house. The small fire his servants had built outside the livestock pen came into view, and he focused on it the way he would an oasis in the desert. He couldn't imagine enduring another two hours limping along, but neither could he consider the alternative.

A couple of hundred feet farther, Terah finally happened upon what appeared to be a post that may have once been part of a crude fence. How it got here was a mystery, but Terah chose to thank the gods. It proved too long to fit under his arm as a crutch, and he was too weary and sore to try to shorten it. Not ideal as a walking stick because of its weight, it was better than nothing. He couldn't swing it in cadence with his steps without gripping it with both arms, and his damaged shoulder made that impossible. So Terah trudged along, using his left knee to help push the post ahead and then carefully catching up to it.

That slightly increased his speed, and exhausted as he was, he kept his eyes on the fire in the distance. Stopping even to rest would render him unable to move again.

CHAPTER 23

Manhattan

Nicole Berman learned a hard lesson that fall Saturday morning, prohibited from seeing her own mother until she could be questioned by the New York Police Department. She found herself livid not over the injustice of Officer Martinez taking at face value her mother's comments while delirious but rather over her own passivity.

It made sense, of course, to eliminate both Nicole and her father as suspects in the attack on her mother. Anyone in the Berman family or circle of friends would find ludicrous the idea that her father or she would ever do anything to harm her mother. So, sure, let the cops recite all the clichés and mix all the metaphors they wanted, jumping through hoops, covering bases, dotting i's and crossing t's. It shouldn't take long to rule out her and her dad.

But something about having to do nothing but sit and wait and pace and pray and wonder, unable to do a thing, awoke in Nicole something she knew she had inherited from her father. Ben Berman seldom allowed life to happen to him. He was anything but a reactor. He embodied the very definition of *proactive.*

Nicole knew down deep she shouldn't be so hard on herself. She had rushed to Mount Sinai, micromanaged her mother's care as much as she was able, and even fought to temper Officer Martinez's report of Mom's barely coherent comments. Given the legal ramifications and the realities of the investigation, Nicole could have done no more.

But now the inactivity, her powerlessness, ignited in her a resolve that would change the way she attacked life. That would be a laugh to friends and colleagues who already teased her about being an overachiever — as if something was wrong with that. They looked at her résumé or her curriculum vitae and scoffed at her interest in adding one more achievement. "Two doctorates not enough for you? All those digs you've been on and now you want to run your own?"

Her father had always been her biggest supporter. Nicole once heard him berate a colleague who intimated that she had accomplished so much only through nepotism. Dad had said, "She's earned everything that's come her way. Her education stacks up against anybody's — including mine — and she's not even forty yet. Degrees from Yale, Princeton, Columbia, and the University of Berlin, and she's taught at Regent, Fuller, Brandeis, and Harvard. Okay, I gave her a leg up by taking her on digs since she was fourteen, but not every kid who does that gets licensed in Israel, Iraq, and Jordan. Some say archaeology is as much art as science. I say it's *more* art than science, and that's where Nic has it over me. She's as intuitive as anyone I've ever worked with on a dig."

As she sat fuming, Nicole tried to distract herself by imagining her father meeting Detective Wojciechowski at LaGuardia. The detective seemed a tough native New Yorker, and clearly his plan would be to poke and dig and unearth any fissures in the Berman marriage — anything pointing to a motive. Obviously her father had a perfect alibi, but Wojciechowski would look for his involvement, his masterminding the assault.

Knowing that could not be true made Nicole confident such a line of inquiry would lead nowhere. She just wished she could be a fly on the wall, or in the squad car, for the nine-mile ride into Manhattan. But even more, she was determined to take charge of situations, of everything she was after in life. Some accused her of being overbearing anyway, so they wouldn't be disappointed — or surprised.

Constructive assertiveness, that was her goal. No more letting life happen to her. Nicole would keep pushing for the best care for her mother, for full disclosure from the NYPD, and for them to find the assailant as soon as she and her father were cleared.

And that wasn't all. Regardless what she found in her mail from the Saudis, she would continue to force the issue, to push for her license to lead a dig there. If that meant insisting her dad quit playing games and commit to the financing, she'd do that too. She would even start lining up her volunteers so she could vet her team in plenty of time.

Nicole was about to burst from frustration as the morning wore on and Patrolman Duane Decker and his partner were relieved. The replacements — a man and a woman in their thirties — had apparently not been fully informed of what was going on. When Nicole tried to introduce herself, they looked wary. "Our job is to keep you out of here," the woman cop said. "So you might as well camp out somewhere else."

"Your job is to keep *any* unauthorized persons out," Nicole said, "since we don't know who attacked my mother."

"Not here to chat," the man said. "You wanna sit here quietly, fine, but you're not gettin' in."

Nicole was tempted to tell him she knew better, that Wojciechowski had already said she could be present when her mother was questioned. But saying nothing for now would make that small victory all the sweeter.

Nicole's phone chirped, and she opened a text from her father.

"Flt att just told me 2 wait til all else get off. Mom OK?"

Nicole hesitated. She could at least put him at ease about that, couldn't she?

"Mom's stable."

"U here?"

"No, you're being picked up."

"Who? Staff?"

Now Nicole had stepped in it. What was she supposed to say to that after having been warned not to tip him off?

"You don't know him."

"Whats going on Nic?"

"It's all good. See you soon."

CHAPTER 24

Ur

The longer he labored on, the more blood Terah lost. He grew light-headed. Though he continued to pray and felt grateful for having discovered the cave, thankful to be alive, and glad he'd found the post — awkward as it was — he could not imagine why one of his servants had not come looking for him. Had he not been clear he was just out walking and would be back? Where could they think he had gone?

The fire near the livestock pen still blazed, so they had not abandoned their posts. Could not one have stayed with the animals and the other ventured out to look for him? His servants were loyal. He was good to them, some would even say generous. They had no reason to treat him with such disrespect.

When Terah finally drew close enough that he should be able to be seen in the distance, he leaned the wood post against his body and waved with his good arm. One of his servants — he looked tall enough to be Wedum — appeared as if he was poking something into the fire. A stick? Some brush? It ignited, and the young man stood, waving back at his master.

Now Terah was sure it was Wedum. *Why would he mock me this way? Can he not see I am beckoning him?* The makeshift flaming torch continued to arc back and forth. *He dares summon me? And where is Mutuum? Surely the animals have not also been attacked by the wild dogs.*

Terah resolved not to give up so close to home. He'd made it this far, and clearly no help was coming. He hoisted the post, propelled it with his knee, and gingerly set out once more. When he finally came within earshot of Wedum, Terah called out, "Come to me, man! I am injured!" But his voice was weak, pathetic. So he resorted to just crying "Help!" with each step.

Finally his servant came running, the burning baton in his hand. "Master, what is it? What's happened to you?"

"Now you wonder, Wedum? Did you not worry when I had not returned in due time?"

"I did, and I was about to leave Mutuum

with the livestock and come look for you. But he was called away by the midwife. And I knew you would not want me to leave the animals, especially with the dogs —"

"The dogs nearly killed me! You favor my livestock over me?"

"A thousand pardons, master! I did not know!"

"And was the midwife for my wife?"

"No! Mutuum's wife is about to give birth. She might have already. Let me help you, master. The animals are safe for the night."

"Which midwife is tending to his wife?"

"Yadidatum, the one whose son is imprisoned."

"And likely to lose a hand."

"She is terrified, master. The last thief bled to death."

"Which I will do if you don't get me home."

"I'll leave the fire burning to ward off the dogs, and I'll take you the rest of the way in the cart."

"Very well, but we must be very quiet. I do not want Belessunu to wake and see me like this."

"Where did the dogs overtake you, sir?"

"In the plains," Terah said. The cave would remain his secret.

"And how were you able to overpower them?"

"I was imbued with strength from on high," Terah said.

"Glory to the gods you were not hurt worse."

CHAPTER 25

Queens, New York

LaGuardia was busy enough without this delay. Today of all days, Ben Berman had to let a jumbo jet empty all its other passengers before he disembarked? What was the point of his obsession with never checking a bag, even when traveling internationally, if the time he saved by not having to wait at baggage claim was devoured this way?

And why would Nicole send someone for him he didn't even know? It made sense she didn't want to leave her mother, and he wouldn't have asked her to. But no one at the foundation was available? Oh yeah. It was Saturday. Still, send a car. He would find the driver displaying his name at the airport exit, and off they'd go. How hard could that be?

But no. A flight attendant told him to wait, and Nicole was just as mysterious. Good thing she got back to him, though, because his mind had leapt to the worst scenario — something had gone terribly wrong and he'd lost the love of his life. "Thank You," he said silently, "Lord my God, King of the universe."

Was it just him or were people taking twice as long as usual to gather their belongings and get off the plane? Emptying first class alone seemed to take forever, but coach looked like the Triboro Bridge at five p.m.

Ben stopped the flight attendant who had given him the message as she rushed by. "I have to be last off, is that it?"

"Matter of fact, someone's coming on to get you."

"What, I don't look able to walk or — ?"

"That's all I was told, Dr. Berman. Sorry. Police procedure, I guess."

"Police?"

"A detective with a long, funny name." She pulled a scrap of paper from her pocket and showed him.

"And you have no idea what this is about?"

"Sorry, I don't."

Enough of this. Ben dialed Nicole. The call went to her voice mail. "Nic, why am I being picked up by a cop? You said your mom was stable. I want to know what's going on. Call me as soon as you get this."

CHAPTER 26

Ur

Terah's servant, Wedum, suggested his master sit and wait while he fetched the donkey-drawn cart from near the livestock pen. Terah tentatively lowered himself till he could reach the ground with his good hand, but as soon as he sat, sharp pain from the dog bite in his hindquarter drove him back. But he put too much weight on his bad ankle and toppled. Unable to cushion the fall with his shoulder-bit side, he hit hard, banging his head on the stony ground again.

He cried out in agony, but Wedum was jogging to the cart and apparently heard none of this. Terah lay motionless, wondering what he had done to so offend the gods and what more they had in store for him. He painfully rolled to his other side and struggled to his knees among sharp rocks. All he wanted was to rest a moment, supporting himself with any body part not raw with injury. That meant only his unbitten right buttock, however with a bleeding left shoulder and a broken or sprained right ankle — not to mention lacerations and contusions nearly everywhere else — Terah was unable to find relief in any posture but standing. So he fought to rise with only his left ankle. While the bottoms of his feet had been protected by his sandals, his legs were so weary they trembled.

So Terah stood, keeping as much weight as possible off his throbbing lower back. He felt on the verge of passing out when Wedum reappeared with his noisily shambling cart.

"There is no room next to you," Terah said. "And I cannot sit anyway. You must help me into the back."

Wedum situated the cart close, but the back of the wagon consisted merely of a shallow box intended to carry firewood or small game. No way would Terah be able to lie in it or sit on its edge. All he could hope was to kneel and steady himself with his one good hand. Awkward and uncomfortable as this would be, he welcomed anything that got him off his feet for the rest of this torturous trek.

Wedum tried lifting and guiding Terah into the back of the wagon. But after several attempts, Terah said, "You must get down and let me use you as a platform."

Wedum immediately dropped to all fours. Terah held tight to his servant's shirt as he forced his left foot onto his calf, then pulled himself onto the man's back. Desperately gripping the side of the wagon bed, Terah ordered Wedum to slowly rise. He felt as if he were about to fall, but as soon as the top half of his body was above the lip of the cart, he shifted his weight and somehow managed to drop into the wagon. He wouldn't have been surprised to see his own body parts strewn about. Wedum helped him kneel, facing the front. "Master, you're bleeding more."

"I know. We must hurry. And stop well short of the house. The cart is too noisy, and when you try to extract me, I might cry out."

With the donkey's first jolting step, the wagon lurched, Terah lost his grip, and he collapsed onto his back, lacerating the back of his head on the rear edge of the wagon bed. Dizziness and ringing in his ears made him fear losing consciousness. He was so exhausted he could not move. Wedum scrambled back to help him up. "This time hold my collar. I will do whatever I can to keep the donkey from jerking."

Terah, drained of strength and muscle,

felt like a hunk of flesh trying to keep from disintegrating into a puddle. All his weight again rested on his tender knees in the uneven cart, and he desperately gripped Wedum's shirt at the neck. The servant gently brushed the donkey's back with a twig and made clicking noises. The animal slowly stepped off, but even the gentle sway of the cart nearly pitched Terah back again. His death grip threatened to choke Wedum.

The cart jostled along like some giant wooden turtle, slowing wending its way toward Terah's house where a torch burned on the wall outside. About twenty yards from of the entrance, Terah patted Wedum's shoulder and said, "This will do."

Working together to get Terah out and to the ground took as long as loading him had. "I am sorry I cannot walk on my own," he whispered. "If you can get me inside without a sound . . ."

"Certainly, master."

Terah had no idea what spooked the donkey, but it brayed insufferably. "Oh no," Terah said. "You must keep him from doing that again."

Wedum propped Terah against the side of the cart and went around the front to face the animal. "He appears calm," the servant whispered. "Perhaps a lizard skittered past."

He placed his hands on the beast's jowls and turned its face directly to his. Wedum rested his chin above the donkey's nose and appeared to force the animal's head down. "You must be quiet," he said.

Terah feared that any second the donkey would use its brutal strength and powerful jaw to snap at Wedum and rip his face apart. But the man seemed to have a way with it. The donkey repositioned his forelegs and stood stock-still.

Terah was overcome with gratitude to Wedum for his help, but did not want to express it inappropriately. Wedum had no choice but to serve him, and yet Terah could tell he was more than willing, and that obligation seemed to play no part in his kindness. "Take me to the donkey," he said.

"To the donkey, master?"

"Yes."

Wedum looked puzzled. "Very well." He stuck his head under Terah's good arm and wrapped that arm over his shoulder, supporting him with his back. "Remember, he is not as familiar with you, so stay clear of those enormous teeth."

"Oh, of that you may be sure," Terah said. "Hold me up."

Wedum grasped Terah's waist and supported him as he leaned toward the donkey's long neck. He caressed the coarse mane and spoke soothingly. "I want to thank you, and your master, for your service to me in my distress. I appreciate it more than you know."

When he turned back to let Wedum help him walk again, the servant was chuckling. "That's the only time I have ever been called a master, master. I appreciate your compassion for my four-legged servant."

"You are welcome," Terah said. "Now let us fall silent until I am inside."

Chapter 27

Queens

Ben Berman didn't mind shabby. He appreciated people comfortable in their own skin — and clothes — and NYPD Detective George Wojciechowski was certainly that. The plainclothes cop kept having to hike up his pants, but he clearly knew his business and seemed to care not a whit what anyone else thought of him.

"My wife — ?" Ben said as soon as Wojciechowski identified himself.

The detective held up a hand. "Just got word she's awake, so you'll be able to see her soon's we get there."

"You know my next question."

" 'Course. What am I doin' here? Let's talk as we walk. My guy's waitin' at the curb outside baggage claim."

"And this is all I have," Ben said, indicating his computer case and the large soft leather bag over his shoulder.

"Hold on," Wojciechowski said as they stepped off the plane. "That's all you took to Paris?"

"I travel light."

"I'll say. How long were you s'posed to be there?"

"Six days. Till Wednesday."

Wojciechowski cocked his head. "Runnin' your big foundation, you must travel overseas a lot."

Ben nodded.

"You gotta know light travelers look suspicious."

"Yeah, but we drug runners know what customs agents look for."

"Gotta tell ya, Berman, now's not the time you wanna be cute."

"How would I know? My daughter tells me my wife's stable, yet you meet me at the airport. What am I supposed to think? Somebody break into the foundation? Embezzle from me? What?"

"You've been in touch with your daughter?"

"Of course. Had to know what was going on."

"What'd she tell you?"

"Texted me her mom was stable, that's all. Good to hear, but it doesn't explain, you know — you."

Wojciechowski filled him in as they moved through the crowded terminal. Eager to get to his wife, Ben weaved through slowpokes and those who spilled into his way from the crowds frequenting food kiosks. But he had to keep slowing to accommodate the stocky cop at least a decade his junior. "I can see where your daughter gets her height," the detective huffed. "Bear with me."

By the time Ben heard the full account, they were on the escalator down to the exit. As they passed baggage claim, Ben saw through the windows the squad car idling at the head of the taxi line, red and white roof lights flashing. "Cabbies must love that," Ben said.

As they emerged, Wojciechowski said, "I'm gonna sit in back with you. Security glass makes it hard for us to talk otherwise. And my guy's not a bellhop, so toss your stuff on the seat." As Ben opened the door, he waved apologetically at the line of cabs. Some drivers rolled down their windows and profanely insisted the cop car move out of the way. Wojciechowski waved at them too, but with only one finger.

When he slid into the other side of the back seat, the uniformed patrolman behind the wheel said through the Plexiglas, "Careful, boss, that could be on the Internet

147

already."

"You know what you can do with the Internet, Carl," Wojciechowski said, making the driver laugh. The detective turned to Ben. "When we get there, Carl's gonna have to let us out."

"I know. No inside handles. Learned that as a teenager."

"Bad boy, were ya?"

"Couple of back-seat rides, yep," Ben said.

"Only things on your record are misdemeanors. Kept your nose clean since, far as we can tell. Just wonderin' how you happened to be on the other side of the globe when your wife gets attacked."

"Well, I sure didn't plan it that way."

"You planned it?"

"You know what I mean, Detective. Any time I leave my wife I worry about her. We're careful. That's why we live in a secure building. This is the kind of news any husband dreads."

"Assuming . . ."

"Assuming what?"

"Assuming you had nothin' to do with it. If you didn't, help me clear ya so we can move on."

" 'Scuse me, boss," Carl said. "Gonna be just as bad going this way. At least an hour. Thanks, MTA."

"On a Saturday?" Ben said. "Usually takes me twenty, twenty-five minutes. What's going on?"

"Besides all the tunnel stuff," Wojciechowski said, "Mets got an early afternoon home game. But we can use the time. Talk this through with me."

Ben shook his head. "I watch true crime shows. I get what you have to do. I just always wondered how it would feel, having to prove your innocence."

"You always wondered about that?"

"Don't make it into something it's not. Just learning what's really happened to my wife and before I can process it, I have to defend myself. You must do this enough that you can put yourself in my shoes."

"Ha! I *wish* I was suspected of doin' away with my first wife!" Wojciechowski said. "I couldn't afford to have it done, so she's still drinkin' from the alimony spigot and leavin' me with barely enough to live on. I wish to high heaven she'd marry some other sucker and let me up, know what I mean?"

"Well, that doesn't happen to be the case with me. I met Ginny when I got back from Nam, and she was literally my salvation. I owe her everything."

"Wait, back up. Your dad owned The Berman Foundation before you, right?"

"Right."

"So what was a rich kid doin' in Nam? You that much of a patriot?"

"Hardly. At least not then. It was all about making a statement, sticking it to my parents, running from the family business."

"But now you run the family business! What happened? Losin' half your hand wake you up?"

Ben shook his head. "Ginny did."

"Tell me more. Where'd you meet?"

"Rehab center, not far from here, actually."

"And how long ago was this?"

"It was '74."

"We were still fightin' in '74?"

"Sure. Last battle was '75."

"Sorry, man," Wojciechowski said. "Some luck, getting injured that late, eh?"

"You play the cards you're dealt."

"So you meet Virginia . . ."

Ben told how he had been anything but religious, rather a nonpracticing Jew. "Ginny was a born-againer, you know."

"Got a few in the department," Wojciechowski said. "Pretty sure they see me as a project. I'm what they call a lapsed Catholic, so to them I'm a lost cause either way. That's how your wife saw you, did she?"

Ben nodded.

"Okay, so she's, what, a nurse in this rehab —"

"Volunteer, actually. Her church group came a couple of times a week just to read to us, talk to us, that kind of thing."

"You couldn't have been there long. I mean, you suffered a nasty wound, but they operate, you rehab, and you go home, right?"

"The hand was pretty bad. Just the thumb left, as you can see. It took more than one operation, and then there was the emotional thing."

"What's that mean?"

"Depression," Ben said.

"Got it. Suicidal?"

"Never actually attempted it, but I was heading that way. It was a dark time I don't like to think about."

"So how did Virginia get to you?"

"I'd never met anyone like her. I hadn't smiled for weeks, gave her no encouragement, yet she kept coming back. She'd pray for me, ask me about myself, try to cheer me up. I resented it, frankly, wasn't going to break, resolved not to cave."

"But you did. Why?"

"You won't believe it."

"Try me. People lie to me all day every

day, so I think I know the truth when I hear it."

"Well, see, I knew they were church kids and I figured I knew what she was about — saving my soul. So I played the trump card, told her if I wanted to talk religion, I'd ask for a rabbi. Thing was, that was the last thing I wanted to get into. But she immediately jumps on it, tells me she *loves* the Jewish faith and wants me to tell her all about my experience. Then I had to tell her I was only ethnically Jewish, and — like my parents — agnostic leaning toward atheism. I hardly knew a thing about Judaism really."

"That didn't discourage her?"

"She took it as a challenge! She starts in with the Jesus-was-a-Jew business, which I'd heard before. But because I was neither here nor there about being Jewish myself, what did I care what some religious figure was? Virginia's telling me how the whole Christian faith is rooted in Judaism and that they believe Jesus is the Messiah the Jewish Bible predicted thousands of years ago."

"But you're not buying it."

"Not caring is more like it."

"But you wound up marrying her, and you're trying to convince me life's been so peaceful ever since that you couldn't have had anything to do with what's happened to her. So you can't still be on opposite sides of the religious fence."

"Of course not. That's what I meant about her literally being my salvation."

CHAPTER 28

Ur

Terah put a finger to his lips and pointed to the door. Wedum silently manipulated the handle and helped Terah inside to a chair. He grabbed two candles and lit them from the torch on the wall outside. "Anything else I can get you?" he mouthed.

"Lots of water and a walking stick," Terah breathed, quieter than a whisper.

Wedum hurried off while Terah rested on his right cheek and flexed limbs and digits and felt for puncture wounds everywhere he could reach. His body was a disaster. All he wanted was to bathe, treat his wounds, and change into a fresh tunic.

Wedum returned with more than a huge pot of water. He had refashioned the wood post Terah found. Wedum had broken off the widest expanses of wood and shortened the rest to where Terah could use it as a crutch.

But that wasn't all. "I found Mutuum looking for me. He's outside and he has news."

Terah motioned to bring him in, but again put a finger to his lips.

The younger, shorter servant's eyes grew wide in the low light. "Oh, sir," Mutuum said, "what the dogs have done to you . . ."

"You and Wedum will help me, and I will be fine. Now, what news?"

Mutuum gleamed and could not seem to suppress a grin. "I have become a father," he whispered. "I have a son!"

Terah forced a weary smile and shook a fist at him. "Glory to the gods!"

"With your permission, master, we want to name him after you."

Terah was touched. "Are you sure? Are there not other servants' children bearing my name?"

"Only two," Mutuum said. "We would be so honored . . ."

"The honor is mine, son."

"You are still bleeding," Wedum said. "I must mix clay and mud for your shoulder. And I will find ointments."

"I also need a clean tunic and my wife's reflection plate." He pointed to the draped entrance to the room where Belessunu slept. "Just inside the doorway, but be very quiet."

155

Wedum and Mutuum looked at each other, terror in their eyes.

"It's all right!" Terah said. "You have my permission. Just do not wake her."

The servants finally agreed that Wedum would go outside to concoct a pack for Terah's shoulder while Mutuum would creep just far enough into the sleep chamber to fetch the items Terah requested.

Mutuum soon returned with a hand over his chest, as if he had barely escaped and could breathe again. "The mistress snores," he said, setting aside the shiny plate and the tunic.

Mutuum helped Terah disrobe and began gently dabbing at his wounds while Wedum applied the mudpack. It felt cool to his shoulder, though the pressure only increased his pain. The bite appeared to have nearly reached the bone, leaving gristly flesh in its wake.

Mutuum dipped a rag into the water and reached toward Terah's face.

"No, let me see first."

Mutuum positioned one of the candles so it illuminated Terah, and he finally dared lift the polished plate before him. Oh no! Worse than he'd feared. Much worse. Regardless what his servants did, there would be no masking this before daybreak.

Caked blood from gouges on his head and face stiffened his hair and beard. Bruises covered his cheekbones, and streaks of color had already begun encircling his eyes. His swollen nose and lips made him nearly unrecognizable. He could only imagine what Belessunu would think.

"We must do what we can," Terah said, knowing Belessunu would ask questions he didn't want to answer. "She cannot see me this way."

The servants spent nearly another hour washing Terah's hair and applying various salves to the punctures in his scalp and face. Yet every time he looked into the plate, his face looked only more dreadful. While they had removed the dried blood from his hair and beard and combed them out, the ugly colors continued to spread. By now the whites of his eyes appeared monstrously red with blood.

Wedum and Mutuum patted Terah dry and pulled the clean tunic over his head. He took a last look at his reflection. "I cannot believe I actually look worse than I feel," he said.

"You do not feel bad?" Mutuum said.

"I feel terrible!" he said and had to press a hand over his mouth to keep from bursting into laughter. "I don't know what will happen with this ankle, but I believe everything else will heal in time. But how long will it take for this face?"

The servants looked at each other. Two or three weeks, they decided. "Probably three," Wedum said. "You could stay with me, master. We could tell your mistress you have gone on a three-week lion hunt. Surely you will look better when you return."

"A lion attack would only improve how I look!"

Both servants held their sides and pressed their lips together. Finally, Wedum said, "Shall I prepare a place for you while you heal?"

"Thank you, but our own child is due soon. My wife will get used to my face in time, but she would never forgive my being away when she gives birth. Anyway, how would I explain my absence to the king?"

The men nodded. "I must get back to my wife and baby Terah," Mutuum said.

"Yes," Terah said, "and, Wedum, in the morning, can you get to the palace early and summon Ikuppi of the king's guard?"

"I don't know him."

"Any guard can point you to him. Tell him you bear a message from me. He is to inform the king that I will return to court as soon as our child is born. And have Ikuppi come here after first meal."

"I will, master," Wedum said, "and —" He stopped abruptly and held up both hands, pointing to the bedroom. It sounded as if Belessunu was rising.

"Douse the candles!" Terah hissed.

The light disappeared just before Belessunu came shuffling out, feeling her way to the kitchen. The men sat rigid in the darkness as she pulled a piece of bread from a loaf and poured herself a cup of water. She sat heavily and Terah heard her eating.

Belessunu stopped midchew and turned slowly, apparently aware of the men's silhouettes. "Lord God, spare me!" she said, her voice shaky and high. "Whoever you are and whatever you want, my husband will be home presently!"

"Calm yourself, wife," Terah said. "It is only I and Wedum and Mutuum. They have come to announce the news of Mutuum's new son. They have named the boy after me!"

"Oh! Oh!" she said. "Why are you sitting in the dark?"

"We didn't want to wake you," Terah said.

"You'd rather scare me to death?"

"Apologies!" Wedum said.

"Yes, so sorry," Mutuum said.

She stood. "Praise God for your child,

son. I must come and see little Terah soon."

"Perhaps after dawn," Mutuum said.

"Expect us," she said. "And tell my servant girls not to come here tomorrow but to meet me at Mutuum's house."

"Expect only her," Terah said. "I will not be able to rise so early."

"Been up praying to your carvings, have you?" his wife said.

"I did a lot of praying tonight, yes, love. Will you let me sleep?"

"Of course," Belessunu said. And she trundled back through the drapery to bed.

CHAPTER 29

Grand Central Parkway
Astoria, New York

Ben Berman's knee bounced as he sat next to Detective Wojciechowski in the back of a squad car glaciating toward the Robert F. Kennedy Triboro Bridge over the East River.

"You're jittery," Wojciechowski said.

"This is more free parking than traffic jam."

"Goin' as fast as we can," the detective said.

"Don't suppose he could use the lights and siren . . ."

"Yeah, no. Your wife's stable. This is not an emergency."

Ben turned away. "She wasn't fighting for her life when I left."

"Fighting for her . . . ? Thought you were an archaeologist, not some fiction writer."

"What am I supposed to think?" Ben said. "First I hear she's fallen, then rush back only to find out she was attacked. She's stable, she's talking nonsense, she's sleeping again, she's awake. My head's spinning. Let's just get there."

"Maybe you didn't expect her to be conscious. Maybe you need to get there before she says something you have to explain."

"So much for just trying to clear me. Why don't you use every resource to get me there?"

"I am, Berman. Look around. Carl flips on the siren, where does this traffic go to get out of his way?"

The shoulder was lined with construction barrels. "It's just that I flew all night —"

"And I'm just as anxious to get on with this as you are. Why don't we use this time we've got?"

"I don't know what else to tell you," Ben said. "You're going to have to talk to people who know us."

"I got somebody talking to your assistant right now. Olsen?"

Ben nodded. "Abigail. Good. She's known us forever. Nicole put you onto her?"

"She did. What's the deal between those two? I can tell from only meetin' your daughter that she and Olsen aren't exactly best friends. Nicole can't even say the woman's name without lookin' like she just smelled something."

"Okay, they don't click, but there's no bad blood. Nicole would tell me."

"Doesn't complain about Olsen?"

"She gets frustrated with Abagail, sure. Nothing serious."

"And what does Ms. Olsen say?" Wojciechowski said.

"Nothing."

"Knows better than to badmouth the boss's kid, I get it. Better hope Ms. Olsen backs up your happy marriage story. Or does she have a problem with your wife too?"

"No. They worked together a long time too. My wife kept the books for the foundation for years."

"And they got along?"

"It's hard not to get along with Virginia."

"How about Abigail? Not so easy to work with?"

"She's no Ginny, but no problems."

"And the bookkeeper bein' the boss's wife never got on her nerves?"

"Well, Virginia was pretty buttoned-down. Had to be with being audited every year. The family connection could look like a conflict of interest. But her books were so clean —"

"So clean she could get on your assistant's

163

nerves?"

"At times, sure. But Abigail knew better than to complain to me about my wife."

Wojciechowski seemed to study Ben. "So your office wasn't exactly Disneyland — happiest place on earth."

"We have a great atmosphere, actually."

"Uh-huh. Should we be looking at Abigail Olsen?"

"Oh, for Pete's sake!"

"Claustrophobic, Ben? You look like you want out. Hittin' a nerve here?"

"Why aren't we moving?"

Wojciechowski rapped on the Plexiglas. "Hey, Jeff Gordon, how you gonna get the checkered flag if you don't go over the top of this traffic?"

Carl reached for his radio. "I'll find out what's goin' on."

"Better yet," Wojciechowski said, "call your dad, *Commissioner* Gordon, and see if Batman's available."

Ben was not amused. Wojciechowski slapped him on the arm. "C'mon, lighten up. Just tryin' to do my job here. Go back to your love story."

"I don't see the relevance. Am I doing myself any good with this?"

"Here's the thing: Your wife was conscious between surgery and when she conked out for the night. During that time, one my officers — and even your wife's surgeon — heard her say things that didn't do your daughter any favors."

"Such as?" Ben asked.

"For one thing, she said your daughter hated her."

The squad car had sat idling on the Triboro Bridge over the East River for the last fifteen minutes, and impatient horns blared.

"Dispatch says there's a wreck on the other side of the river," the driver told Wojciechowski.

"Great," the detective said. "We got nothin' else to do today. Don't know why they call it a river anyway. You can smell the saltwater."

Ben was ready to burst. "That doesn't even sound like Virginia. Plus, it's not true. They're close. You're saying she was accusing Nicole of attacking her?"

"No. My officer says she was trying to get your daughter to forgive her and stop hating her."

Ben shook his head. "*Hate* is not even a word I've ever heard Nicole use, let alone about her mother."

"Your daughter claims the only time they even had words was twenty years ago."

"That's true. Nicole was anything but a

problem kid, and our disagreements never got ugly."

"Your daughter says her mother was delirious and didn't even know what she was saying. But she's not the medical expert here."

"So what does the doc say? He must have an opinion on her mental state."

Wojciechowski raised a brow. "He agrees with your daughter on that."

"So why are we still talking about this? You couldn't use it against Nicole even if she *was* guilty — and that's out of the question."

"I decide what's out of the question."

"I'd know if there was *any* problem between Nic and Ginny."

"And how about between you and Ginny?"

"I don't know how else to say it. Did she talk about me too?"

CHAPTER 30

Ur

Belessunu had returned to bed, Wedum and Mutuum were gone, and Terah sat in the dark on his uninjured side, hands in his lap, head bowed. The crude crutch Wedum had improvised from the discarded fence post stood propped against his chair. He felt every injury. Slashes, gashes, scrapes, punctures, bites, a broken toe on his left foot, at least a sprained ankle on the other.

Most important now, however, was waiting till he knew Belessunu was asleep again before he joined her. Otherwise she would wonder at the commotion, managing the crutch and stifling groans as he tried to stretch out next to her.

When finally he heard her soft snoring, Terah had to rock three times before he could get his aching body upright and reach for the crutch. It took all he had to hobble from his chair to the opening of the bedroom. He pushed aside the drapery with his head and surprised himself by noiselessly navigating the last few feet. He planted the crutch on the floor next to the sleeping mat and began lowering himself. When his seat reached the mat he couldn't avoid getting too much of his weight on the bite to his left side. He quickly shifted, whimpered, and lost hold of the crutch. It clattered to the floor loud enough to have awoken the sphynx.

Terah lay on his back and held his breath as Belessunu's gentle snoring stopped — then resumed. For the rest of the night he kept rousing, wondering if morning had broken. Belessunu had agreed to let him sleep, but if she got a look at him in the morning light, she would no doubt wake him to find out what had happened. He covered his face with a blanket, determined to break everything to her gently.

Sunlight invaded not only the window but Terah's face covering as well. He reached timidly for Belessunu, but her side of the mat was empty. He listened for clues that she was nearby and, satisfied she was gone, stiffly managed to sit up. If Wedum had accomplished his task, Ikuppi would be there soon. Terah hoped he would arrive before Belessunu returned.

CHAPTER 31

Parris Island, South Carolina
1971

Ben Berman had boarded the bus in New York twelve hours before, and there was no other way to say it — he was full of himself. Eighteen years old, two weeks out of high school, the night before he had told his latest steady not to wait for him.

In tears, she pleaded, promising to write several times a week. "I'll stay true to you!"

"Don't," he said, "because I won't do the same. A marine, on leave, in uniform? You think I'm gonna ignore all the possibilities?"

"Well, not if you don't want to!"

"I don't," he said. "Sorry."

"You're not sorry!"

Not only was she right, but Ben had also been just as cold to his own parents the next morning before leaving for the bus station. For months he'd been doing just enough to graduate, while in his spare time he and his best friend, Jimmy, worked out like mad-men to prepare for the rigors of marine boot camp. Clearly, neither parent believed he would go through with enlisting.

"You're not happy with us, fine," his dad said. "You feel guilty and want to turn your back on a life of privilege, okay, you've already done that. Three schools in four years, no interest in the foundation. But you don't have to commit suicide."

"Suicide?" Ben said. "Look at me! I'm gonna be a fighting machine."

His mother dissolved. "You get sent to Vietnam and you'll come home in a box!"

"I *want* to go to Nam! That's where the action is. We're about to wrap that thing up, and I can be part of it."

"Do you hear yourself, Ben?" his father said. "What adult says such things?"

"A patriot."

"Patriot-schmatriot," his father said. "You don't care any more about this country than you care about us."

"Well, one out of two ain't bad."

"That's cruel, Benz," his mother said.

He had no comeback. That had been meaner than he'd intended. Ben tried changing the subject. "Jimmy's as excited as I am."

"That's what you think," his dad said. "I

171

talked to Mr. Dunklebaum yesterday. He promised James a piece of the dealership, and the boy made the wise decision."

"Oh, bull!" Ben said. "The last thing Jimmy wants is to sell cars the rest of his life. Can't tell you the number of times he's said that."

"You've known him for what, one semester?" his dad said. "All you got in common is detentions and demerits."

"We're tight, Dad. Anyway, he couldn't bail out of the buddy system now even if he wanted to."

"Maybe if his father didn't know somebody in the recruiting office and already got it squared away. Probably gave the guy a car at cost. I'm telling you, Ben, unless you want to ride that bus alone, there's no sense going."

"Nice try, Dad."

"You don't want to go to boot camp by yourself, do you, Benz?" his mother said.

"I won't be going alone! But if it came to that, sure, why not?"

"You didn't even like boarding school."

"I was too young! You shouldn't have sent me. How was that supposed to make me feel?"

"You didn't even like summer camp," she said.

"I didn't like being *sent*," he said. "This is my choice."

"We're not taking you to the bus station."

"Seriously, Mom?"

"I told you and told you, I want no part of this. You want to delay college a year, work at the foundation. Then get your degree, and by then you'll want to take over the foundation some day."

"So I gotta take a cab?"

"You don't have to go at all."

"I'm going! I *want* to go. This is my life, not yours. Just for once, let me make my own decisions!"

"You haven't earned that right."

"I heard that, Dad. Too bad I've reached the age that gives me the right."

Ben's father waved him off, but his mother sat with a tissue pressed to her mouth as he called for a cab. "You don't have to do this, Benz."

Then he called Jimmy. "Hey, man! You bailin' on me?"

"Huh? Nah."

"You goin' or what?"

"Hmm?"

"You heard me. Should I have the cabbie pick you up?"

"Me, no. I'll find my own way."

"You don't have a ride yet?"

"Oh, you know," Jimmy said, "there's plenty of ways to get there. If Ma or Pa can't take me, I can take the bus, the train, you know."

"So I'ma see you in a hour, bro?"

"Um, yeah. 'Course. I told ya. See ya down there."

"*Semper fi,* Jimmy!"

"Yup. Buddies all the way. Boot camp, then Nam."

Ben hung up. "Told you! Jimmy's on his way."

"Care to put a wager on that?" his dad said.

"How 'bout a grand, Dad?"

"You don't have a thousand, son, but sure. I win, and you'll have to work for the foundation to pay me back. No way you'll make that much with the marines."

It turned out that the only thing close to a buddy on the Greyhound had been a middle-aged woman across the aisle who asked if Ben was a recruit and told him she was returning home to Beaufort after a family visit. Half a dozen dingy depot bathrooms and two stale vending machine sandwiches later, another dozen recruits had boarded here and there, but they were with family or friends — some with buddies —

and they offered Ben no more than a nod, a Semper fi! or a subdued "Oohrah" on their way to the back.

One poor sap who instead said "Hoorah" immediately got razzed by the rest — including Ben — who said, "You'll never live that down at Parris Island, man. Get it right!"

"What'd you say your name was, Ben?"

"Berman."

"What's that?"

"Berman."

"I heard you. I'm askin' you, what's that, Jewish?"

"What if it is?"

The kid raised both hands and moved on with the others. They sat playing cards, insulting each other, and talking too loud. But they never invited Ben back. The woman across the way jabbered on and on about her visit to New York and never took a hint when Ben looked out the window or even dug in his bag for a book.

The farther the bus rolled from Manhattan, the stranger the landscape. Ben had only read about the south and did not look forward to its legendary heat, stickiness, or bugs. He sat sideways, grateful he didn't have to share his seat, and that gave him a view of the guys behind him. He detected fear in their eyes and tight-lipped smiles. Wusses.

Once, he was sure he heard "Jew" and caught a couple of them glancing his way. Slurs had never really bothered him. They only exposed the limited intellect of the bigots. How a person could judge him for his origin, over which he had no control, was beyond Ben. If he had exercised his faith or came off somehow superior because of his heritage, he could see why others might resent him. But besides his name and bloodline, he didn't feel any more Jewish than the WASPs he'd gone to school with. Like Ben, they played sports, loved the Mets or the Yankees but never both, lied about what girls let them get away with, enjoyed drinking, and hated hangovers. But he got a taste of what his black friends suffered — they for the color of their skin, he for no more than his name and ethnicity. Ben's father even cautioned him never to insist on a kosher meal in public, as if he ever would. "We enjoy them because we enjoy them," Mr. Berman would say. "Not because we're observant. So we never draw attention to ourselves by insisting. If it's on the menu and you want it, eat kosher. Otherwise, partake at home."

The boys in the back of the bus ignited

the rebel in Ben, the part of him that triggered the biggest controversy during his last semester. He had demanded a kosher meal in the cafeteria. "All of a sudden you're Orthodox," one of the lunch ladies said, and the storm began.

"Of course I know you're Jewish," the headmaster had told Ben's father. "But at the beginning of his tenure with us, Ben declined the option of kosher meals. So why now?"

"I've become observant," Ben said before his father silenced him with a stare.

"It won't happen again," his father said, and on the way out of the school he grumbled, "Why, Ben? Why must you always —"

"I have to do everything they say, Dad. Here was a chance to make them do what I said. Why can't I —"

"Because you're not in charge, son. You're not even paying for school. You do what they say, and you do what I say."

"Not for long," Ben said.

And here he was, admittedly alone on the bus, but finally living the dream. Unfortunately, he had not been able to even doze as the Beaufort woman proceeded to bore him half to death. By the time Ben disembarked at Parris Island, he harbored a deep resentment — in fact, hatred — for his lying former buddy. As rough as marine basic training was supposed to be, he'd handle it with or without Jimmy.

Really, how hard could this be?

CHAPTER 32

Ur

The first of Terah's two meals each day was usually more substantial than bread and figs and water — all he could manage in his condition and with his wife away. One thing he could say for Belessunu: the woman could cook. Variety marked her daily first meals. Quantity was her second meal strategy. Terah had not gone to bed hungry for years. He allowed himself to hope she would add meat to his banquet tonight. By then perhaps she would be used to his horrific new face, and — he hoped — might even pamper him.

The day had emerged cloudless and windless, and Terah wished he could make his way outside and sit in the shade of the overhang to wait for Ikuppi. But if Belessunu preceded him, Terah would be unable to get back inside quickly enough so that revealing his ravaged face — as well as the rest of his injuries — could come in stages.

All he could accomplish, alone and crippled, was to limp to a chair by the window where he had a view of the road. Ikuppi would arrive in some sort of a conveyance — his own chariot or one appropriated from the palace. Belessunu walked everywhere, despite her age and how close she was to bearing her first child. The servants' hovels lay less than half a mile away, so Terah assumed his wife and servant girls would arrive before midday.

On the horizon looking toward the city of Shinar and the palace, rising dust signaled the approach of Ikuppi, not Belessunu, for only an animal pulling a transport produced such a cloud. As it rumbled into view, Terah was surprised his friend had secured the use of one of the king's own chariots. Ikuppi drove three giant steeds that seemed to enjoy running free with their lighter than usual load. He steered them under the overhang and leapt out, his sword clanging off the side of the chariot. As he reached the door, Terah called out to him.

"Ikuppi, give me a moment, if you please!"

"At your service," he said. "But I bring a message from the king."

"When I give you leave to enter," Terah said, "I beg you close the door and do not approach me."

"Are you ill, sir?"

"I will explain. Can you accede to my request?"

"Of course!"

"Enter."

Terah leaned forward and rested his elbows on his knees, pressing the fingers of both hands to his forehead and covering his face, peeking out.

Ikuppi's alarm was plain, and his hand appeared to instinctively go for the hilt of his sword. "What is it, friend? What ails you?"

Terah told him of the wild dogs. "You must not revile me when I reveal my face."

"Never."

Terah slowly lowered his hands, and Ikuppi gaped. Terah said, "Come, sit, and I will show you the rest of my wounds."

Despite that Ikuppi was an elite protector of the king, he seemed to approach timidly. "Glory to the gods you are alive," he said quietly. "Belessunu must be horrif—"

"You are the first beyond my servants to see me. When Belessunu returns, Ikuppi," Terah said, "I need you to intercept her and prepare her."

"Very well."

"And you say you bring a message?"

181

"From the king, yes. He wishes me to remind you how overjoyed he is with the prospect of your first child and to remember to bring the baby to him at your first opportunity. What response should I deliver back?"

"That I remain honored by his interest and support and will fulfill his wish in all humility."

Ikuppi leaned close and whispered, almost as if he feared he might be overheard at the edge of the wilderness. "But you will do no such thing."

"Of course not."

"What will you do, then, Terah?"

CHAPTER 33

Randalls Island, Manhattan

"Once the looky-loos get their gawk," Wojciechowski said, "this thing could open up and we'd be at Sinai in minutes."

"Sorry to pop your balloon, boss," Carl said. "S'posed to be like this all the way to the FDR and even over to Madison."

"Must be some wreck," Ben said.

But when the squad car finally crept past the accident, it was little more than a fender bender still waiting for a wrecker.

"So you and Virginia," Wojciechowski said. "What'd she do to win you over, way back then?"

"First tell me if she said anything that's supposed to incriminate me," Ben said.

"I wouldn't say it incriminates you — yet."

"But like what she said about Nic, it didn't do me any favors?"

"Fair enough," Wojciechowski said.

"She thinks I hate her too?"

"No, she didn't say that, that I know of."

"Whatever it was," Ben said, "she had to be loopy from the meds. Ask anybody who's ever known us and they'll tell you we've been crazy in love since day one. I'm not sayin' we agree on everything, and she can be a tightwad, but I'd tell a polygraph machine I love her more every day and the needle wouldn't even twitch."

Wojciechowski snorted. "C'mon, man. You're not on the Hallmark Channel. I'd love to believe you got a fairy tale goin' on, but get real. Nobody's that happy. Not in my world anyway."

"You find an iota of anything that shows I would even dream of hurting Ginny, and you won't find one person who'd believe it."

Wojciechowski smirked. "You've never strayed?"

"Not once."

"Tempted?"

"You're asking if I notice other women? You've got me there. But I wouldn't so much as cross the street to disrespect my wife."

"Whoa, that's gotta be boring!" the detective said. "Who wants to live that way?"

"People who want to stay married."

The driver turned and smiled. "He's right.

Most people married that long, it's been to two or three different people."

Wojciechowski laughed. "How many times for you, Carl?"

"Three! And I been married thirteen years, total!"

Wojciechowski turned back to Ben. "Okay, so you're Dudley Do-Right and she's the virgin Sunday school kid with the name to go with it."

"She was, you know."

"What — a virgin? What're the odds of that?"

"No idea, but I know her."

"And you believed her."

Ben narrowed his eyes at the detective. "Careful."

"Okay, Berman, let's say if you believe her, I believe her. Should I believe what she said about you in the wee hours this morning?"

"Depends on what it was. When she's fully conscious, you can take to the bank whatever she says."

"And how 'bout you, Dudley?"

"I tell the truth," Ben said.

"No, I'm sayin', you married a virgin — but did she?"

"What's that got to do with this?"

"In my business we call that a nondenial denial," Wojciechowski said.

"I'm not denying anything. I just don't see how my past is relevant. I don't talk about it. I was an entirely different person before I met Ginny. That's my whole point. Haven't you ever heard 'Old things have passed away and all things have become new'?"

"What's that, Robert Frost?"

"C'mon," Ben said. "Good Catholic boy like you ought to recognize Saint Paul in Second Corinthians."

"Aah, shoulda known. But fair's fair. I don't talk about my former life either. It's been a long time since I been to church."

"Never went to Sunday school?"

"We called it Parish School of Religion, somethin' like that. But back on point. How'd Virginia turn a, what'd you call yerself — nonpracticin' Jew — into a guy who quotes the saints? You didn't even wanna talk religion with her, right? Played the I'm-Jewish card?"

"Exactly. And I was watching to see how she'd get around that, like sales people are trained to do. That's how I took it at first — her trying to sell me something. But I never expected her to appeal to my intellect."

"Like how?"

"She tells me she's disappointed I'm not more into my heritage because *she's* so

186

curious about it. Says there's all these Messianic prophecies in the Old Testament — pretty much the Jewish Bible, you know — and that they've all clearly been fulfilled in Jesus. So I say, 'Whoa there, I may not know much, but one thing I do know, in fact one thing everybody knows, is that Jews don't believe in Jesus. The Messiah the Hebrew Scriptures talk about, that's not Jesus.' And she says, 'He sure fulfills all those prophecies.' I tell her no, she's got it wrong, and she says, 'Prove it.' I tell her you don't prove religious stuff, that's what I don't like about it — it's based on faith and you either believe it or you don't, and I don't."

"But she got in your head," Wojciechowski said.

"She was so earnest! But naïve. I mean, everybody knows Jesus isn't the Jewish Messiah, right? Even Gentiles know that. It's the difference between Judaism and Christianity."

"That's what I always thought," the detective said.

"Well, now I was going to have to prove it," Ben said. "She told me she'd send me a list of all the prophecies written hundreds and sometimes even thousands of years before the birth of Jesus, and I could look them up. Then I had to show why even one of them did not apply to Him. That was a challenge I couldn't blow off, plus her smile was growing on me and I wanted to see more of her.

"Now, I'd never been that great a student. Not because I didn't have the smarts. I tested off the charts, which was why I was always in trouble for being a screw-up in high school. I couldn't pretend I was incapable of a lot more."

"Website says you've got two doctorates, just like your daughter."

"Yeah, that's what's required to do what we want to do — lead archaeological digs. And I went from barely graduated high schooler to marine, to wounded vet, and finally to a whole lot of education — and it all started with what Ginny assigned me. Once I dived into it, I couldn't deny that Jesus fulfilled every Messianic prophecy in the Jewish Bible. I became a believer, what's called a Messianic Jew. And I fell in love."

Wojciechowski affected a game-show host tone. "And that's made you who you are today . . ."

"She got me hooked on historical texts and ancient civilizations. You see why it would be impossible for me to do anything to hurt the love of my life?"

"Why is it, then," the detective said, "that your wife's convinced you keep secrets?"

CHAPTER 34

Ur

"You must have a plan, Terah," Ikuppi said.

"That depends on gender. A daughter I would present to the king straightaway."

"We both know no danger lies there."

Terah nodded miserably. "Should the gods curse us with a son, the three of us must flee."

Ikuppi shook his head. "Flee the king?"

"I will not sacrifice my own flesh and blood to him."

"Yet you yourself say a manchild would be accursed."

"And so I should offer him up? Belessunu would never forgive me."

Ikuppi appeared to measure his next comment and find himself unable to utter it.

"Speak!" Terah said. "Something troubles you."

The man stood and paced. Finally he said, "When I delivered your message to King

Nimrod this morning, he called in his stargazers. He asked whether if Belessunu bore a son, it would portend the end of his reign."

"And?"

"They were unanimous that your son would not only depose him but would cost him his life. They said everything pointed to this as a decision of the gods. He railed that he too was a god but had not foreseen this. Now he wants to test the gods themselves!"

"What does that mean, Ikuppi?"

"He would trick them with a substitute king. The imposter would dress in the king's robes, be assigned a queen, and live in the palace — even occupy the throne while Nimrod and his family go into hiding."

"To what end?"

"That the gods would mistake the substitute for the real king, strike him dead, the peril to Nimrod would disappear, and your son would not have to be slain."

"But knowing that," Terah said, "what madman would agree to become the substitute king?"

"King Nimrod was hoping you would."

"Ha! That's insane!"

"There is a strange logic to it, Terah."

"How can you say that, as my friend?"

"I'm not suggesting you consider such a

thing," Ikuppi said. "I'm just saying that Nimrod would view such a choice as sacrificial. You would give up your own life for the sake of your son. Otherwise, he will ask that you show your eternal loyalty to him by willingly offering your son to him to be eliminated."

"You must help me, Ikuppi."

"What can I do?"

"Help me kneel and then bow with me before my gods. And when we have prayed to all of them, help me outside to kneel before Utu, who rides high in the sky even now."

"But are not all these the same gods Nimrod is plotting to trick?"

"We must expose to them his evil plan and beseech them with all our might for a daughter."

CHAPTER 35

Mount Sinai Hospital
Manhattan

Ben strode ahead of Detective George Wojciechowski.

"Hold up, Berman!" the cop said. "Young gal named Jefferson is gonna take us to Recovery . . ."

"I know this place like my own home."

"I bet you do," Wojciechowski said. "But let her do her job."

Kayla found them at the elevators where Ben had already pushed the call button three times. Twice he had tried to enter an empty car, only to have Wojciechowski insist he wait. "I know you're a rock star here, but —"

"I don't need my hand held," Ben said.

"You don't even have a visitor badge yet, but the way everybody's pointin', I guess they know you."

Kayla introduced herself and took Ben's

bags, telling him she would get them to the room on Eleven West after she took him and the detective to Recovery. She handed them each a badge. Wojciechowski said, "I'll use my own," patting the gold shield on his belt.

Ben shoved his visitor badge into his shirt pocket.

"Uh, sorry, Dr. Berman," Kayla said, "but you'll need that to —"

"No, I won't, because I've got you. You'll get me anywhere I need to go."

"Yes, sir, I will. And may I just say, on behalf of the medical center executive team, how grateful we —"

"Not now, Ms. Jefferson, please. Just get me to my wife."

CHAPTER 36

Ur

Terah regretted his request of Ikuppi as soon as his friend helped situate him before his table of carved idols. If anything, he felt worse now than when his injuries and wounds were fresh. It was all he could do to remain on his fragile knees. And his idols emitted no more an aura of divinity now than they had the night before. They bore the look of his own handiwork — clever carving that produced a measure of beauty but that were, as Belessunu had said more than once, blind, deaf, and mute.

Regardless how Terah cried out to them, beseeching them to hear him, he felt nothing, sensed nothing. No truth or insight was impressed upon his heart. Did he lack faith? On the contrary! He believed with all his being. He had to. He was without options.

Perhaps his gods were silent because of Ikuppi's unbelief. "Do you trust in the gods, my friend?"

"I always have."

"But do you now?"

"I think I do."

"That's not good enough, Ikuppi. They will not hear the pleas of unbelievers!"

"Terah, I'm trying! You are my friend. I want what's best for you and Belessunu."

"Do not pray for her! She opposes my gods."

"But it is she who is to deliver your child. Do we not want to pray she gives you a daughter?"

Terah settled onto his throbbing rear, causing him to yelp and roll to his side. "Take me outside, Ikuppi! We must pray to Utu!"

Merely getting there proved agonizing, and Ikuppi suggested they kneel near the horses in the shade of the overhang. "To pray to the sun?" Terah said. "Are you mad?"

"I'm just thinking of you, friend."

"Get me out where I can face him in the sky and make him listen."

"Let's pray to his sister too," Ikuppi said, guiding Terah into the open. "She is a mother. She will understand."

"Oh, god of morality, truth, and justice," Terah began, eyes nearly shut from the brightness in the sky, "see your servant's plight and bestow mercy upon me! And to your twin, Inanna, queen of heaven, if the child Belessunu carries is a male, change it before it comes forth!"

Terah pitched forward on his face and wept bitterly. "No one hears me!"

"Terah, let me help you up," Ikuppi said. "Someone approaches."

CHAPTER 37

Parris Island

Despite that it was midnight when the bus disgorged the marine recruits, Ben Berman emerged into heat and humidity he had never experienced in New York City, even in the middle of the summer. His reflection in a bus window showed his long hair instantly curling, the back of his shirt puddled with sweat. He found it hard to breathe.

Ben knew he would be assigned a narrow bunk in a dorm or Quonset hut, but he actually welcomed that. He didn't need comfort — simply somewhere to stretch out. He'd also been warned that boot camp days started before dawn, whenever that was down here, so he might get only a few hours' sleep. He'd take whatever he could get after excitement had kept him awake the night before and the woman on the bus had cost him any rest on the trip.

Any hope he harbored that the lateness of the hour might spare him the fabled verbal hazing newcomers expected was dashed when a full contingent of drill sergeants met him not ten feet from the bus. He had been the first off, the other dozen following.

"Name, longhair?" a marine bellowed at him.

"Berman, sir," Ben said, proud of himself for knowing how to address his superiors and wondering what kind of abuse the other guys — with much longer hair — might face.

"I can't hear you, maggot!" the man said. "First and last name, age, and hometown!"

"Ben Berman, sir! Eighteen, Manhattan. Sir!"

"Kansas or New York, sweetheart?"

"New York, sir!"

"Drop and give me twenty, ladybug! Gentlemen, we have a preschooler from New York City who doesn't know his own name!"

Ben dropped his bags and reeled off twenty perfect push-ups.

The marine ran his finger down the top page on his clipboard and stopped. "Try that name for me again, sister!"

"Benzion Berman, sir!"

"Those twenty didn't take you long

199

enough, Benzion! Give me twenty more!"

Ben shot through another twenty as the other recruits were screamed at and assigned their own push-ups for infractions as varied as being too tall, too skinny, too fat, speaking too softly, forgetting to add "sir" to the end of every sentence, and an endless list of other things none of them could have anticipated.

"What kinda name is Benzion, Berman?"

"First name, sir!"

"Twenty more, son, for knowin' that's not what I was askin'. You're gonna be the first to visit our Jewish chaplain, ain't you?"

Ben didn't know how to respond, and his third set of twenty was not so easy.

"I can't hear you, Berman!"

"Sir! Yes, sir!"

The recruits were to grab their bags and run, following a set of painted yellow footsteps to a processing center where they stripped and stood next each other, a thermometer popped in each mouth. They'd had one chance to throw away anything they'd brought that even looked like a weapon. One guy pleaded to keep a small jackknife he said was an heirloom from his grandfather.

"Your choice, pissant!" a drill sergeant screamed in his ear. "You have it on your

person past this point, you will be arrested!"
Shoulders sagging, the recruit dropped it
into the trash.

One coughed and complained of asthma,
which made him a target for abuse. Those
not in Ben's shape — which meant most —
stood awkwardly, obviously embarrassed
about their bodies.

Ben distracted himself by looking forward
to a little sleep. Some of the guys looked
panicky, and a heavyset kid appeared to
fight tears. He was berated unmercifully and
asked by several if he planned to start bawl-
ing, which resulted in just that. But to his
credit, when they asked if he was going to
run home to his mama, he shook his head
and did whatever was asked.

After cursory physical exams and multiple
shots to each arm and both backsides —
followed immediately by more push-ups —
one barber shaved all thirteen heads in less
than two minutes. "Come in a hippie, go
out a skinhead," he said over and over.

The guys were issued boots, socks, under-
wear, undershirts, trousers, shirts, and caps.
The three slowest to dress were made to
drop for more push-ups, then sent outside
to run.

Ben had read enough to know that this
was all about stripping every would-be

marine of his individuality, his identity, and making him part of a unit. He hadn't expected it to make any more sense than that, assuming that — if anything — the institutionalism of the military might even be less logical than that of the Ivy League and its prep schools and universities. He wasn't escaping bureaucratized lunacy; he was choosing the opposite of what his parents wished for him. So far so good.

With their personal belongings locked away for safekeeping ("You won't be needing them here!"), the recruits were herded outside again for calisthenics. One fainted, was doused with water, and razzed unmercifully. One of the drill instructors crowed, "I don't see one here likely to survive!" and made the entire group run for not responding, "Sir, yes, sir!"

Finally sent to their bunks in a Quonset hut, Ben could not believe how long it had taken to process — and humiliate them. It was already well past two in the morning, and sunrise this far south had to be at around six. If they were to be awakened before dawn, he was going to have to sleep fast.

Fat chance.

The welcoming committee found reasons to bellow instructions and reminders to the recruits even after they were in bed, hauling some out for more physical activity if they had violated rules they could not yet know. Ones who hid their faces in their pillows and even appeared to be crying were rousted out for more attention.

Ben was forced outside to run for going to bed without his boots on, but when he returned he was assigned two more sets of twenty push-ups because he went back to bed with them on. Illogic was all part of the milieu, and he was determined not to crack under it. But when he was finally in his bunk for good, fully dressed so he could hit the ground running at reveille, it was four in the morning.

He was in better shape mentally and physically than the rest of these guys and would survive this. Many had. But he had not expected his bunk, and the harassment, to transport him right back to his first trip away from home, at age nine, to a boarding school in Massachusetts.

That was going to be fun. No parents. Beautiful campus. Lots of guys to make friends with. Perfect for an only child, right? He'd been warmly welcomed, shown around the place, introduced to staff and teachers. He'd been helped storing his clothes and supplies, setting up his schedule, directed to the dining hall, and enjoyed the first dinner . . .

But when he'd finally gone to bed and began chatting with the guys near him, the announcement came. No talking after lights out. In the silent darkness, Ben had found himself awash in grief. He could only wonder why he had been sent away. Dad and Mom had talked this up for two years — the privilege, the advantages, the benefits to his future.

It had all looked and felt great, even when he'd been dropped off and they drove out of sight. Why then, the first time he had to just think, was he so homesick? So heartsick? Was he too young to be sent away for nine months out of the year? Nine months! And this would be his life until high school! The years loomed before him like eternity. Nothing could make it anything like what his parents had promised it would be and what it had at first seemed to be.

In the night, alone in bed, Ben felt abandoned. Unloved.

But marine boot camp should have been different. He was an adult now, wasn't he? No surprises yet, not really. Maybe it had all started a little quicker than he'd expected, but he'd heard the stories. Sure, Jimmy had lied to him, bailed on him, which only showed what kind of a buddy he would have been anyway. Good riddance. They wouldn't have necessarily been running or doing push-ups side by side anyway. It might have been good to know a friend was nearby, going through the same stuff he was, but it wouldn't have made that much of a difference, would it?

The barracks were, finally, mercifully quiet for perhaps ten, maybe fifteen minutes before Ben felt himself fading. How much sleep could a guy get before predawn, anyway? It was already predawn if he thought about it. But Ben couldn't think about it. Because all of a sudden he was that lonely nine-year-old again, sent to and abandoned at boarding school.

This was supposed to be different because he had chosen it. Enlisting was his idea. No way was he going to turn tail and admit defeat. He'd invested too much into this. Why, then, did he bury his own face in his pillow and have to fight with everything in him to keep from crying? Wuss!

And what seemed only ten minutes or so after he drifted off, drums badgered him awake. Drums! What happened to the famous bugle? All around him guys staggered out of bed and squinted at their watches. It was 4:25 a.m. Or as he would learn to say, oh-four-hundred-twenty-five hours.

CHAPTER 38

Ur

The dot on the road in the distance could easily have been Belessunu and her servant girls. Terah dared not take the time to make sure. He couldn't risk anyone, especially her, seeing him in such a state. He didn't want even random sojourners — most of whom would know him from the king's court — to be repulsed by his face, or worse, spread the word about him.

"Worry more about haste than whether I protest," he told Ikuppi, who all but dragged him, moaning, back into the house. He collapsed into a chair and felt as if he could sleep for a week. "Bring me water and then see who is on the road."

As he sipped and Ikuppi leaned out the window, Terah felt disgust for his idols. What a travesty that they would answer the prayers of a wicked king and ignore a devout supplicant.

"Belessunu should be home by now! I need her."

"It's a man driving a donkey-pulled cart," Ikuppi said. "One of your men? Maybe he knows what's become of her."

"If it's Wedum, he'll know. You don't think she's abandoned me, do you, Ikuppi?"

"Because you do not worship the same gods?"

"Because I pray for a daughter."

"She's not doing the same?" Ikuppi said. "Surely she knows what the king would do —"

"She says her god would never give her a son only to snatch him away."

"Terah, I cannot imagine Belessunu forsaking you after all these years, especially now when she's about to deliver."

The donkey skidded to a stop, and three raps came on the door. "Master, it is I," Wedum said. "If that is the chariot of the king himself, I will withdraw, but otherwise you must come!"

Ikuppi opened the door. "The king is not here."

Wedum rushed to Terah's side. "The gods have smiled upon you, master! The midwife was with Mutuum and his wife and son when Belessunu came to visit. And now your wife herself is in the throes of child-birth."

209

CHAPTER 39

Manhattan

Nicole knew her mother was awake, yet still she had not been able to talk to her. She'd seen her mother's alleged lunch — soup, Jell-O, crackers, and ginger ale — and was sure she'd heard Mom ask for her when it was delivered.

She found it maddening to have to sit in the hall until Wojciechowski showed up. But at least he was bringing her dad. Nicole looked up every time she heard the elevator doors. The most recent one had brought the surgeon, Dr. Thorn, and she stopped him before he went in. The uniform cops slid in front of the door as she approached the doctor. She could only shake her head. Protecting a mother from her own daughter?

"This is ridiculous," she told Dr. Thorn. "I get why you had to report what you did, but couldn't you have tempered it with what you told me? It wouldn't take five minutes to clear my father and me if you just stipulated that nothing my mother has said so far has any credibility."

"That'll be in my full report in the end," Dr. Thorn said. "They tell me she's much more articulate now, which is encouraging."

"She *was* agitated and looked like she needed more rest," Nicole said.

Dr. Thorn nodded. "She needed to be calmed to reduce her pulse."

"Did the medication hurt her?"

"No. It just delayed the waning of the anesthesia. I'll administer some simple cognitive tests to find out where she is mentally."

"May I join you?" Nicole said.

"No, you may not!" the woman cop said.

"If it were up to me, sure," the doctor said. "Guess you have to wait for their detective and take it up with him."

As Dr. Thorn entered her mother's room, Nicole heard the elevator again and whirled to see her father with Detective Wojciechowski and Kayla Jefferson. She had a niggling feeling she owed Kayla an apology. She hoped the young woman hadn't taken anything personally and understood Nicole's stress over her mother.

She and her father embraced fiercely, and he whispered, "How's this for an unplanned weekend?" He turned to the detective. "Can we get in there now?"

"We can," Wojciechowski said, "but do me a favor. Ask her anything you want, but don't talk to each other. Got it?"

Nicole nodded. "Afraid we're going to conspire?"

Wojciechowski clearly didn't find that funny. "Remember, I don't have to let you in yet. This is a privilege."

Kayla said, "Dr. Berman, I'll be delivering your father's bags now, but I just wanted to tell you I was serious about what I said yesterday. About joining a dig team some-day?"

"Oh, yeah, okay."

"Sorry, I know you have other things on your mind right now."

Good thinking.

Nicole felt as if she and her father were following Wojciechowski into the Forbidden City. As soon as her mother saw them, she burst into tears.

CHAPTER 40

Ur

"Glory to the gods!" Ikuppi said. "What good fortune has been bestowed upon your wife, Terah!"

"Yes, glory to the gods, but I cannot go! I can barely move. How soon does Yadidatum think the baby will come?"

"This afternoon for sure," Wedum said.

"Ikuppi, you must go now and bring them here."

"Who?"

"Belessunu and the midwife! She must have the baby here."

"Oh, Terah, no! That would be foolhardy."

Terah scowled at him. "It is not a request, Ikuppi. Wedum will lead you and also fetch blankets and pillows to make her comfortable for the journey back."

"Terah! There is nothing comfortable about a chariot ride over this terrain."

"It's less than half a mile, man. But do

not bring her servant girls back. I want no one else to see me."

"Your wife was in great distress, master," Wedum said. "I don't know if we would get there in time to —"

"Then go!"

"Yadidatum may forbid —"

"The midwife is also a servant, is she not?" Terah hissed. "And with her son in danger for his life, she dare not cross me. She will do what I say! Be gone!"

As the men hurried out the door, Terah called after Ikuppi, "Prepare them both for what I look like!"

As soon as Ikuppi and Wedum charged off in the king's chariot, regret overwhelmed Terah. What had he done? He could not abide losing a newborn, even if it was a male who would be sentenced to death anyway. And Belessunu! Regardless of their disagreements, even over matters as weighty as what gods they believed in, she meant everything to him. Serving the king had become profitable, and Terah was known, respected, even feared throughout the realm. But Belessunu was his whole life. He would give up all the rest for her. But now he risked her life, and for what?

CHAPTER 41

Manhattan

"Benz!" Nicole's mother reached for her father.

Nicole and her father shared a knowing glance. That was what her grandmother had called him, not what her mother had ever used for him.

"You're back already? Weren't you to be in Paris for another —"

"With you in here, Ginny? Wild horses couldn't have kept me away."

"Oh, I spoiled your trip."

"Yeah, you know how I *love* to travel."

"Tell me you've both come with news!"

"News?" Nicole said.

"Don't tease," her mother said. "Nicole's license has come through, hasn't it?"

"Still waiting, Mom," Nicole said. "Believe me, you will be the first to know."

"Sorry," Dr. Thorn said, "let me finish up here, then she's all yours."

"Will I be in the way if I hold her hand?" her father asked.

"Not at all. Now, Mrs. Berman, can you count backward from one hundred for me in a series of sevens?"

"Backward from one hundred in sevens. Sure. One hundred, ninety-three, eighty-six, seventy-nine, seventy-two, sixty-five, fifty —"

"Very good, that's fine."

"She's a numbers gal, aren't you, babe? That was easy."

Dr. Thorn sighed and raised his brows at Nicole's dad.

"Sorry," her father said.

"Now, Virginia, if you could tell me the months of the year in reverse order . . ."

"December, November, October, September, um, August —"

"Good. One more. Spell *world* backward for me."

"W-O-R-L-D-B-A-C — I'm teasing you, Doctor. I knew what you meant. D-L-R-O-W."

"Very funny. Now, just tell me what you remember about coming here. What happened, why you're here, what we've done for you, anything you can remember."

"Okay, ah, what's today?"

"You don't know what day it is?"

"Well, I feel as if I've lost a day."

"That's not unusual, Virginia. Do you remember what day it was when you arrived here?"

"Friday."

"Correct. What do you remember about Friday?"

"I woke up in an ambulance with no idea what I was doing there. My hips hurt and my legs felt numb. I kept wanting to sleep and people kept asking my name, date of birth, that kind of thing. Someone said Teo had called them and said I broke my hip."

"And Teo is?"

"Our new housekeeper."

"Teodora," Nicole said.

Dr. Thorn glanced at her. "Let her answer, please."

"Sorry."

"Teodora Petrova," her mother said. "I guess she found me on the floor. I don't remember any of that. They did a bunch of tests that really hurt, and I remember thinking that at least my legs weren't numb anymore and I kind of wished they were. Then I met you, I think. Did I meet you?"

"You did. And I explained that I was going to operate on you. I tried to tell you everything and what you might expect. You recall any of that?"

"Sorry."

Nicole's mother looked embarrassed, perhaps worried.

"Don't let that concern you, Virginia," Dr. Thorn said. "Anesthesia often acts as an amnesiac. Some of what occurred between your MRI and x-rays may or may not come back to you in time. Tell me whatever you can recall, from meeting me until right now."

Nicole's mother appeared to concentrate. "It seems that was the day before yesterday. Was it?"

"What do you think?"

"I think it probably wasn't. If you operated on me the day I got here, and I woke up in time for lunch, today is probably Saturday."

"Very good. Anything else from surgery till now?"

Her mom sighed and let her head fall back on the pillow. "Not really. Just . . ."

"Take your time."

"Well, it wasn't anything that was said or that actually happened."

"That's all right. What was it?"

"I just recall hoping Nicole would come to me. I wanted to ask if anyone had called her, but I don't think I did."

Nicole said, "You don't remember that I —"

She caught herself when the doctor looked sharply at her.

"I'm so glad you're here now, Nic."

"So you remember waking in the ambulance, getting a couple of painful tests, meeting me but not recalling what I said . . ."

"And waking up here, seems like about an hour ago."

Nicole was heartbroken that her mother was unaware that she had rushed to her side as soon as she'd heard. But she was also relieved her mother seemed to recall nothing of the nonsense in the middle of the night.

Dr. Thorn told Nicole's mother that he would be releasing her to her private room where her family could stay with her and that he would be checking in on her periodically.

When he was gone, Detective Wojciechowski handed her his card and said, "My turn, Virginia — may I call you Virginia?"

She squinted at the card and asked for her glasses. "Sure. And you are?"

A nurse produced a white plastic bag, and Nicole's mother rooted through it. As she was slipping on her glasses, Wojciechowski said, "I go by George, or GW. Some of the guys call me G-Dub."

Smooth. He had hammered Nicole like his prime suspect and now he was sweet-talking the victim.

CHAPTER 42

Ur

Terah fretted, unable to pace, his injuries having left him stiff and sore. He chose not to rise from his chair even to retrieve his cup of water a few feet away. And he needed it, his throat parched from desperately praying aloud. Was it sacrilegious to pray to his idols from where he sat? Could they understand he would kneel before them again if he were able?

What kind of a man am I, insisting my beloved wife be delivered here on the verge of giving birth? "Oh, gods of the universe," he cried out, "forgive me and spare her, and if you give us a son, I will accept it as my just punishment."

Time seemed to crawl as Terah assessed how long Ikuppi and Wedum had been gone. Surely their only hope of getting Belessunu back safely was to gather her up quickly and set out at once. The less than half mile from the servants' dwellings to his home should take only minutes in one of the king's own chariots pulled by three powerful horses and led by a master charioteer. But of course Ikuppi would have to drive carefully.

They should have been here long ago, Terah knew, and he descended into morbid imaginings. He envisioned Belessunu giving birth before they even got to her. Would they then not let her rest, fearing his wrath, and bring her, the baby, and the midwife back?

Or had she fought returning and they felt obligated to take her by force? "Please, worshipful gods! Not that! Do not let my folly bring harm to her or the baby!"

The longer Terah waited, the worse became his anguish. He heard nothing, saw nothing out the window, his angle not allowing a view far down the road. He felt he would go mad if he did not somehow will himself upright so he could step outside and peer all the way to the horizon. When his wife arrived, in whatever condition, he would beg her forgiveness, pledge himself to her anew, and do whatever was necessary to protect his family, whether that included a son or a daughter.

He forced himself up onto the crutch,

swayed, wobbled, and finally stepped haltingly to reach his cup and drink greedily. But now the door was even farther away, and three strides when he was healthy became an ordeal he did not relish.

With leg and crutch sharing the load, Terah dragged his mangled ankle into position but couldn't let it even touch the floor without agony. It took several minutes to reach the door, and the complicated dance of managing the crutch, protecting the ankle, and opening the door nearly ended him.

Finally Terah was able to lean against the doorframe and position himself to see all the way to the horizon. In shimmering heat waves that rose from the packed-down wheel lanes built up from all the travel, Terah conjured images that simply would not materialize. He saw a cloud of dust that had to be caused by the chariot, but it faded. Was that a group walking? Regardless what his mind invented, nothing was really there. He told himself that not as much time had passed as he feared, but he knew better. Something must have gone terribly wrong.

Terah turned to try to make it back to his chair, but somehow his bad ankle had angled wrong. He found himself between the door and the frame, unable to move unless he put weight on the ankle. Dizzy and angry, he had to act despite the agony.

He set his bad foot as flat as he could on the clay and twisted himself to where he could quickly shift his weight back to his other leg and the crutch. Pressure on the ankle would be brief but excruciating. His sandal had grown tight on the swollen foot, and Terah hated to even look at it. Finally he mustered all his resolve and executed the maneuver.

He shrieked at what felt like a sword driven from the sole of his foot to his shin, but when he caught himself on his good leg, the crutch hit the clay at the wrong angle and slid from under him, rolling away. Terah hopped, desperate to keep pressure off the ankle, and lunged to keep himself upright by grabbing the door, but it swung shut on his hand, smashing his fingers.

He yanked his hand away, which threw him off-balance and toward the floor. Terah's bad foot involuntarily shot out to catch his fall and took all his weight. His leg gave way, pain forcing his eyes shut as he crashed to the floor, smashing his nose flat.

CHAPTER 43

Manhattan

"Wojciechowski," Nicole's mother read from the detective's card.

"You pronounced it right!" he said. "Nobody does that."

"My husband has Poles in his background," she said. "That's not an unusual name in Poland."

"Well, my great-grandfather came to this country from Danzig. Story is, he absolutely refused to let 'em mess with his name at Ellis Island. He wound up in Chicago, so that's where most of our family is. Except his oldest son, my grandpa, somehow got back to New York."

Nicole's mother still stared his card. "And you're with the police department. Have I done something wrong?"

Nicole noticed a twinkle in her mother's eye that Wojciechowski clearly missed. "Oh, no, ma'am. But I need to tell you, someone did something very wrong to you."

"To me?" The gleam had disappeared.

Wojciechowski told her what the doctor had reported. "No doubt you were assaulted, Mrs. Berman. Your injuries don't match a trip and fall."

" 'Senior Services and Domestic Violence Unit,' " she read. "George . . ."

"Yes, ma'am."

"Grant me a bit of vanity, will you? You know I only barely qualify as a senior citi—"

"I'm aware, Virginia. But I'm honored to serve as lead investigator on your case anyway."

To Nicole her mother seemed herself again.

"But I gotta ask you somethin'," Wojciechowski said. "I just told you you'd been assaulted, which I'm gonna assume was news to you."

"It certainly was."

"And your response — if you don't mind my sayin' so — was you tryin' to be funny. You know what that sounds like to me?"

She shook her head, looking suddenly sobered.

"That sounds like deflection. You seem like a smart, uh, cultured lady. I know your daughter and your husband now, a coupla smart people."

"Oh, yes, they're —"

"And I'm tryin' to clear them as what we call people of interest in this attack, so we can start look —"

"Oh, no, they would never —"

"Routine, ma'am, standard operating procedure. Now, call me overly suspicious, but I been doin' this for a lotta years and I'm guessing you've never been attacked before."

"Correct."

"So it's gotta be a shock to find this out."

"Well, yes."

"But instead of reacting like you're even surprised, you crack wise about vanity and bein' a senior citizen. That's strange. That's deflection."

"Deflecting what?"

"My job makes me wonder. I'm thinking maybe you want me laughin' at your comments — funny, don't get me wrong — so I quit looking at your husband or your daughter for this."

CHAPTER 44

Ur

Terah lay sprawled on the clay floor, blood gushing from his nose. Angry with himself for thinking he could accomplish something beyond his strength, he also dreaded that Belessunu would see him like this at the most vulnerable time of her life. He attempted to get to his knees, but now nothing worked.

He tried holding his nostrils shut, hoping the blood would clot, but no. Terah hunched himself into a position where he could support his ravaged face in the crook of his arm, but all that served was to soak his sleeve with blood. It was all he could do to stanch his tears. Chief officer of the king of the realm, in authority over everyone but Nimrod himself, and here he lay, decimated and blubbering in an expanding puddle of his own blood.

Terah looked bad enough before this last

disaster. He could have calmed his wife, assured her he would heal in due time and return to full health. But now he couldn't be sure. And would she ever be able to erase from her memory the sight of him lying here?

Terah simply could not move. If Ikuppi and Wedum ever did arrive with Belessunu, she would have to be their top priority until Yadidatum could superintend the birth. Only then would they be able to somehow collect him from the floor and get him cleaned up again. The last thing he wanted was to distract his wife from her own ordeal. He just hoped he hadn't already caused her some irreversible trauma.

Terah tried to slow his breathing and his heart, which seemed to thunder against the floor. He raised his chin so he could see his entire array of idols on the table. "So this is what you have wrought? Your servant lies here in abject humiliation, despite that only hours ago you told me my salvation drew nigh. I should curse and reject the lot of you!"

But he couldn't bring himself to do it. Did they not have the power to put him to death for such blasphemy?

What was this now? A rumbling beneath him! Did that portend the return of the chariot with his cherished one? Terah heard no wheels, no hooves. He felt only the movement beneath him. The idols began to wobble and pitch, then to topple. This was their answer to his profane challenge? Must he humbly beseech their forgiveness yet again? He was already prostrate!

But then it struck him. When the promise of his deliverance had been impressed deep in Terah's soul the night before — and proved true when he discovered the cave that saved his life — it had come not in response to his prayers to the gods. He had been praying to the God of his forefathers and his wife, the deity she referred to as the one true God.

The shifting of the earth deepened, and the idols knocked into each other and rolled off the table, shattering as they hit the floor. "Is this You, God of Noah?"

And Terah was transported to the same conviction he'd felt in the night when it seemed God had spoken directly to him. Now, deep inside, he sensed, felt, a pronouncement, as if God Himself said, *"You shall have no other gods before me."*

"Unclean!" Terah keened. "Unworthy! Lord, forgive me or strike me dead!"

The earth stopped quaking. The idols lay in waste like Terah. For an instant he had believed. Had God forgiven him, proved by the fact that he remained alive? He couldn't be sure. And as quickly as his faith in the one true God came, it also fled. Terah felt guilty about the state of the idols in pieces all around him. He must be careful not to further offend them if he had allowed another god to invade his home.

Terah prayed to the shards on the floor. "I will repair each and every one of you and return you to your places of reverence."

The chariot rattled to a stop and from outside came the frantic voices of Ikuppi and Wedum.

CHAPTER 45

Manhattan

Nicole wanted to defend her mother, to explain her to Detective Wojciechowski. But the truth was that he had read her fairly well. Humor was her go-to deflector mechanism. But she would not have even dreamed her husband or daughter could be suspects in a crime — let alone one perpetrated on her. What she was deflecting, Nicole was sure, was the reality that she had been a victim at all.

"I apologize, George," her mother said. "Forgive me. I didn't mean to take this lightly. Frankly, I'm having a terrible time accepting that someone, anyone, would even want to hurt me, let alone actually try."

"Got it," Wojciechowski said. "But you understand, somebody didn't just try. They did."

Nicole's mother suddenly sounded exhausted. "I guess that's not reaching me. I got it into my head that I had tripped and fallen and broke my hip. That became my reality."

"Back up, Virginia. Who told you you'd tripped and fallen, and what did they say you had tripped over?"

"I don't know," she said. "I think I heard that in the ambulance or the emergency room. Someone told the EMTs, or more likely they told the ER people, because I don't recall being put into the ambulance. Anyway, someone told someone that. Even that didn't make much sense to me, because I walk every day, do pretty well for someone my age. I've never fallen before, and certainly never tripped in my own home."

"You don't have loose rugs or a carpet that's developed a raised edge?"

"No. I'd notice something like that. I don't remember tripping, don't remember falling, don't remember getting this rug burn on my forehead, don't remember Teo finding me, helping me, calling 911, being carried out, any of that. Just the ambulance, the ER, and whatever they call that room where you meet the doctor before surgery. So you see why it's hard for me to even accept that this was more than what I first heard it was."

"A trip and fall."

"Exactly."

"Let me tell you, ma'am, I've seen the photos of your back, and I've even seen the x-rays. 'Course, the doc had to explain what I was lookin' at, but once he did, boy . . ."

"What?"

"Lemme just say, if you injured yourself that way by fallin', you musta done it on purpose. You didn't just break a hip. You also broke ribs, and those bruises on your back would convince even you that you've been assaulted. I mean, the housekeeper says she found you lyin' facedown, consistent with that abrasion on your forehead, but it doesn't explain the bruises on your back. It looks like someone jumped on you with both feet, either to knock you down or after you were already down." Wojciechowski sucked in a long breath. "Now, Virginia, I hafta ask you some difficult personal questions. So I'm gonna ask your family to excuse us now."

"Oh, I prefer they stay," she said.

"Trust me, I'll give you that option, promise. But I need you to tell me that privately."

"I won't be saying anything without them here, I can tell you that right now."

"And all you have to do is tell me that without them here and I'll bring 'em right back in. Dr. Berman, and, Dr. Berman, would you mind?"

Nicole's father rose. "Be right outside," he said.

"You'll be back in a second," Virginia said.

Her father followed Nicole out, and before the door was shut, her mother insisted Wojciechowski let them return. "Happy to," he said, speaking quickly. "But this is your chance to tell me with a look, a squeeze of the hand, or just say it if you have anything at all you wanna tell me, just between the two of us."

"I would do that," Virginia said. "And if I need to talk to you in the future, I'll let you know. But I have no secrets from my family. There's not a chance in a million they'd have had anything to do with this."

"Got it."

"And I'm not saying another word without them here."

"I hear you, ma'am, and hope you know I'm just doin' my job."

Nicole was amused that her mother did not even respond to that.

CHAPTER 46

Ur

Terah stretched to try to cover the tarn of blood that had streamed from his demolished nose, and he buried his face in his sopped sleeve. It was futile to try to hide the extent of the carnage, as if Belessunu would not notice. But maybe he could appear unconscious and make her wonder whether he was alive. Unless Wedum or Ikuppi had explained his injuries, she would have no idea what had happened to him.

But even as he lay there, with them marshalling at the door, he hated himself afresh. She plainly had not given birth yet or there would be cries or at least women cooing at the baby. Yet here he was, trying to slow his breathing so his back wouldn't heave and he might look dead.

"Belessunu," Ikuppi said, "you must not be alarmed at your husband's face. He had an accident in the night and wants you to know it looks worse than it feels."

"What are you saying?" she said, her voice constricted as if in pain. "I was talking to him last night, and, oh! Oh, get me to my bed!"

As the entourage noisily entered, someone stumbled over Terah's bad ankle and he screamed. His ruse over before it began, he took another tack. "Did the earthquake delay you?"

"Earthquake?" Wedum said. "Master, your idols! What has happened?"

Ikuppi ran to help him sit up, but still Terah kept his face turned away. "The earth shook and threw me to the floor. I think my nose is broken."

"An earthquake struck only here?" Belessunu whined as Wedum and Yadidatum guided her past the drape into the bedchamber. "Husband, the only thing that delayed us was your insistence that we come here! I could have had the baby in the king's chariot."

"I am sorry!" he called out as they moved her to the mat and lowered her.

"Now leave us and close the curtain!" the midwife said, and Wedum fled into the great room.

"Wait!" Ikuppi said. "Give Wedum clean clothes for the master!"

"I am occupied!" Yadidatum said. "Come and get them yourself and then be gone!"

Ikuppi backed into the bedroom, feeling for a clean tunic, his sword banging the doorframe. Wedum rushed out to draw water.

With Belessunu deep into labor and caterwauling between instructions from the midwife, Wedum and Ikuppi pulled Terah from the floor and somehow got him back to his chair. It was not lost on him that he was getting twice the attention his wife was.

"Yadidatum knows more than babies," Wedum said. "When she is free, she can minister to you as well."

"I would not even ask," Terah said. "I cannot allow myself to become beholden to her."

Ikuppi held a wet cloth above Terah's upper lip and pressed his thumb and forefinger to the bridge of his nose. The bleeding finally stopped, but the pressure was so painful that Terah had no doubt the nose was broken. Somehow the men succeeded in wiping the blood from Terah and the floor and getting him into the fresh tunic.

"What do you want me to do with this mess?" Wedum said, indicating the fragments of idols.

"Save every piece and return them to the

table. And then let's pray Belessunu brings forth a daughter."

"We can pray to broken idols?" Ikuppi said.

"I don't know," Terah said. "I never have. But we would not be praying to the pieces. We would be praying to the gods, and they know my intentions."

Belessunu called out from the mat in the other room, "Do you hear yourself, Terah? You yourself admit that the idols are just pieces! Your shaping them into images changes nothing!"

"Concentrate on delivering our daughter!" Terah said. "The gods are listening."

Wedum had just moved all the remains of the idols to the table when the midwife grew excited and Belessunu screamed.

"That's it!" Yadidatum said, but for a long moment nothing more.

"What is happening?" Terah said. "Shall I come in?"

"No!" both women yelled in unison.

"What of the baby? Is it all right?"

"It will be!" Yadidatum said. "Master, you have a son!"

And as Terah broke into sobs, the baby wailed.

CHAPTER 47

Parris Island

Ben Berman had painted himself into a corner. By day he kept his head down, pasted on a game face, and endured whatever his drill sergeants hurled his way. He was as close to quitting as anyone, but he had left himself no choice. Clearly in the best shape of any of his fellow recruits, Ben found that allowed him only to survive. Some days he was within seconds of throwing in the towel and storming back to freedom.

He would hardly have been the only one. Every day two or three recruits seemed relieved to take the walk of shame, suffering no end of ridicule for drubbing out and running home to Mama. But unless they literally escaped, the Corps stalled the processing of their paperwork and made their lives miserable. Some simply shut down, refusing to follow orders, execute drills, or even move — desperate attempts to force the hands of the Marine Corps. But the longer the USMC could hold these washouts, the more they could berate them for reneging on their contracts, reminding them they would have been the worst choices for the Corps anyway.

Ben wondered what the deserters would say when they finally staggered back to loved ones who had seen them off to become marines. Nearly every day he believed that humiliation would be preferable to the relentless torture of mind and body he suffered at boot camp.

But Ben had left himself without that option. He had done too much, said too much, had irrevocably turned his back on his parents' lifestyle and priorities. He had arrived in South Carolina expecting to bear up under unpleasant training, get himself shipped to the front, and do whatever he had to do to prove to his parents he was a gung-ho patriot. Which, as his father had observed, was anything but the case. Ben's aim proved more transparent than he wished. He had made the ultimate play to exert his independence — and while that goal still seemed worthy, accomplishing it loomed light-years beyond what he expected. There had to have been a better way to achieve the same result, but he couldn't rerack now. He had to play this out to its conclusion, and if that meant giving his life for his country in Vietnam, so be it.

Only he knew such a sacrifice would have nothing to do with his love of country and everything to do with establishing his own identity. And every day that priority hit him as more and more misplaced. Stupid, really. Having no options somehow focused Ben on the task.

He made a name for himself as a potential leader, but he never really got with the program — not inside. By day, he was the macho marine, quietly making his statement about values. By night, he pressed his face into his pillow and silently cried himself to sleep, his resentment of his parents slowly eroding while he vowed never to admit that. He planned to make his own way in life, not even inviting them to his graduation or official induction ceremonies.

Ben wrote his parents twice, each time with a brief note on a souvenir postcard designed to give them a hint of his new geography and daily routine. His mother wrote him at least weekly, while his father responded only to the postcards. Both simply expressed their love for him and pleaded for information about where he might be deployed. Naturally Vietnam became the elephant in the room.

As Ben excelled in weapons training and marksmanship, he became a favorite of the leadership and was lauded as a future rifleman who would make his country proud. He played the game but couldn't have cared less. He wished he'd thought of another way to assert his independence and take a stand against elitism. Ben hated everything about the military except how he looked in uniform.

It was unhealthy, he knew, but he found himself fantasizing over the prospect of dying overseas.

CHAPTER 48

Ur

The midwife Yadidatum delivered the placenta and had Wedum dispose of it. She helped Belessunu begin nursing the baby and sat quietly instructing her in newborn care. Terah remained in misery, longing to see his son while dreading what it all meant. His career, his life as he knew it, was over. There would be no declining the king's insistence on seeing the child, whom he would surely kill, perhaps with his own hands.

Terah wanted to pray, but the idol bits strewn on the table could do nothing now. What if he promised to recreate them from fresh, unspoiled materials and offered them his unwavering loyalty for the rest of his days? Might they then impress upon him what he was to do?

"Help me kneel before the table," he said, whimpering.

Wedum and Ikuppi, who had sat avoiding his gaze, leapt into action, each taking an arm and struggling to position him on the floor. Terah moaned when Wedum put too much pressure on his damaged shoulder, but soon he was on his knees, leaning on his crutch. The odor of his own blood sickened him. He leaned as far as he could reach and ran his fingers over the bits of ivory and wood and precious metals splayed before him. He detected no power, no aura, and couldn't shake the feeling that Belessunu's assessment of the icons was correct. Could it have been her god who had forced these to collapse and scolded Terah for putting other gods before him? Terah didn't want to consider the consequences if that were true.

As the night before, when he prayed to whatever god seemed available and willing to rescue him, Terah wanted to cover himself. Pray to the gods but then also pray to his forefathers' God? Or the other way around?

Despite the fact that in the moment it seemed clear that Belessunu's God had provided haven and delivered him from the dogs, as well as shaken his idols to the floor and warned him, Terah cast his initial lot with the gods he knew. He couldn't deny they had ignored his desperate plea for a daughter, but could that mean they also had a plan for what he was to do now? Or was this their plan — to have his son murdered at the hands of the king. He bowed his head and wept as he prayed, "Is this my destiny, my calling, to prove my loyalty to you and even to the king?"

"Terah!" Belessunu cried out. "Do you not know I can hear you?"

"I am not praying to you, wife!"

"That's wise," she said, "because I can do no more for you than can the residue of your carved trash. I have made you a father, but I cannot allow you to offer our son to the gods — especially to the king."

Her voice suddenly changed, causing Terah to painfully turn, alarmed. Wedum and Ikuppi looked frightened as well, and it sounded as if the midwife herself had begun praying to the gods. But Terah knew what was coming, because he had experienced the same thing from Belessunu the night before.

"The one true God speaks," she said in a monotone, the only other sound the baby's suckling. *"The Lord your God sits high above the nations, My glory beyond the heavens. Who is like the Lord your God, Who lives on high and stoops to behold things in the*

heavens and in the earth?"

She fell silent, and Terah trembled. He was overcome with longing to see his son and yet felt drawn to — to what? To what seemed the safety of his idols, despite their state. Was he mad? What god had cursed him with a manchild? "May I see the lad?"

"Yes," Yadidatum said. "Come."

"I need assistance."

"You are all welcome."

Wedum and Ikuppi muscled Terah past the drapery into the sleep chamber where Belessunu sat on the far end of the mat with her back to the wall, the ruddy child in her arms. The midwife immediately rose as the men entered, and as she moved to stand behind them, Belessunu wiped the baby's mouth. One chubby hand reached for her face from within his wrappings. Terah's wife looked exhausted, her hair heavy and matted, but she also appeared as happy as he had seen her in months.

Terah approached haltingly, working his crutch with both hands. "Help me down," he said. The two men lowered him to the mat at Belessunu's feet, and the baby turned and seemed to look directly at him. "Leave us," Terah said. Wedum, Ikuppi, and Yadidatum moved to the other room.

Terah knew the newborn couldn't have

any concept of who or what he was looking at, but his dark eyes appeared to study his father's face — so deeply battered and bruised that he looked other than human. Terah found himself speechless, breathless.

"Take him," Belessunu said.

"Oh, I couldn't. My shoulder . . ."

"Hold him in one arm if you must." And she held the boy out to him.

Terah ignored the pain and gathered him in. So tiny. So delicate. And those deep, searching eyes . . .

My son. At long last I am a father. "I'll not always look this way, little one," he cooed, and almost as if the baby had been waiting to be reassured, his little hand slowly relaxed and his eyes closed. Terah snuggled him closer, knowing he would never, could never, allow this child to be put in harm's way.

And with a shudder, an idea came to him. "I shall name him Amraphel, as King Nimrod himself wishes to be known."

"You shall do no such thing," Belessunu said.

"Hear me, wife. The king could never slay his own namesake. It's a brilliant idea —"

She sat, shaking her head. "You're daft. Nimrod wants to kill him to keep the throne from him, and you would give him a king's name?"

Still gazing at his son, Terah whispered, "I don't know what I was thinking."

"You weren't," she said. "The Lord God has given me a name for him."

"That is not your place . . ."

"It is if it's of God," she said. "He would have us name him Abram."

"Abram," Terah said softly, letting it roll off his tongue. "Abram?"

"Its roots hint at strength and protection," she said. "But it means, 'exalted father.' "

"A prophecy that my son will himself bear sons?"

"Or daughters," she said. "Or both."

"Which means he shall not be eliminated by a fearful king."

"Of that you must make certain, husband."

"Belessunu," he said gravely, "I shall allow no one to touch this child."

Terah bowed his head, straining his painful neck, and gently pressed his swollen lips to Abram's downy cheek. He handed the boy back to her and called out, "Come take me to the other room!" which startled the baby. His eyes and mouth opened and his hand shot out, but before he could make a sound, Belessunu held him close and rocked him. And he immediately fell asleep again.

Once the men maneuvered Terah into the great room, and Yadidatum returned to Belessunu, Terah signaled that he wanted to kneel before the table again. While he could live with the name Belessunu believed had come from her God, Terah was not ready to entrust the safety of the boy to him. Again on his knees, shakily supported by his crutch, he prayed silently.

"Gods of the sea, the earth, and the sky, I pledge to you my life and worship and obedience if only you bestow upon me a plan to protect my family from the wrath of the king."

The earth shifted beneath him yet again, rattling the table, as if the God of his wife and forefathers was reminding him that it had been He who had intervened when Terah's gods had failed. But at the same time Terah received a message deep in his soul, and while it was brilliant, it was also diabolical and so did not strike him as having come from his wife's Lord.

It may come at deep cost, but Terah knew it would work.

CHAPTER 49

Manhattan

Wojciechowski emerged and motioned Nicole and her father close. "One tough woman."

"You bet," her father said. "Why do you think she had to be attacked from behind?"

"Dad!" Nicole said.

The detective shook his head. "Gallows humor's all the humor we cops got. But do you find this funny?"

"I'm being serious," Nicole's father said. "Anybody trying to pull something on Ginny had better try it when she's not looking."

"I got more questions," Wojciechowski said, "but they wanna move her to her room. I've gotta check with my people on alibis, havin' someone talk to this Bulgarian woman, CCTV footage of the foundation, and where you live, all that."

"Where I live?" Nicole said.

"No, your parents. You said you were in your office when your father called from France."

"That's right."

"Just need someone to confirm that. And, Mr. Berman, they say your home's a fortress, nobody in or out without bein' seen by the doorman, the desk staff, or the cameras. We oughta know soon who was in and outta your place around the time of the attack."

Nicole took her father to Eleven West to make sure the room was in order before her mother arrived. She tidied all her own stuff and tucked her belongings in a cabinet while he sat between his bags, staring at the floor.

"You all right, Dad? Need some help?"

He shook his head. "The idea that someone would . . ."

"I know."

"It just doesn't figure. I can't think of anyone for any reason. Frustrates me. Makes me angry, but at whom?"

She put a hand on his shoulder, then began unpacking his bag and hanging his clothes. It wasn't like him to let her do that, but he seemed dazed. Besides the stress of the horror, she assumed jet lag was also catching up with him.

"I can do that, hon," he said finally.

"Just set up your computer, Dad. Knowing you, you'll be here around the clock."

"And you?" he said.

"Debating. I want some alone time with Mom, but you and I don't both need to be here overnight, do we?"

"Suit yourself. You're in the homestretch with the Saudis, aren't you?"

She nodded and told him about the piece of mail she hadn't opened. "I just can't concentrate on anything but Mom."

"You told her you were still waiting to hear from them, Nic."

"I know. But she's got enough on her mind. If she knew, she wouldn't let it go until I opened it. But then she'd likely be as disappointed as I am."

"Wish you'd brought it so we'd know," he said. "But it does sound like a preliminary turndown."

"I'll check it tonight. But you know what comes next. If it's still pending, I need to be able to assure them I have team member names they can vet and that the funding is in place."

"How much of it do you need the foundation to put up?"

"Seriously, Dad?"

"What?"

"We've danced around this for so long I'm dizzy. You know as well as I do that unless you finance the dig, it's not going to happen."

When Nicole's mother was delivered to the room, along with the two uniformed cops who set up outside, she was sound asleep and Detective Wojciechowski was nowhere to be seen. The nurse said she had told Wojciechowski not to wake her. "So he said he'd be at the plaza cafeteria and hoped Mr. Berman could join him."

"I'll stay with her," Nicole said. "I wanted to order her some flowers anyway." The nurse pointed her to a card with the number of the hospital gift shop.

"And the cafeteria's in the pavilion, right?" her dad said.

The nurse nodded. "Guggenheim atrium. First floor."

When the nurse left, Nicole's father said, "I've got unfinished business with the detective anyway."

"Oh?"

"Something about your mother thinking I keep secrets. You hear her say anything like that?"

Nicole hesitated.

"What, Nic?"

"I've been told not to discuss that with you."

"Seriously?"

"It was as much a surprise to me as it is to you," she said, "but I guess Wojciechowski wants to get your initial reaction, without having been tipped off."

"But come on. I deserve to know —"

"Then you shouldn't have raised me to respect authority."

CHAPTER 50

Ur

Terah slowly rose from his knees, with help, and turned with a start when Yadidatum appeared. "If I am no longer needed here, master, I should get back. Naturally, I am at your service whenever you need me."

Cordial words were on the tip of Terah's tongue, thanking her for her help and apologizing for the harrowing trip at the most dangerous time before the birth. But they would not come. In fact, he was tempted to say, "Of course you're at my service," but he resisted. In truth, the plan he believed the gods had impressed upon his soul had so flustered Terah, he wasn't sure how to carry it out.

What he did say gushed from him unrehearsed. "I regret I was unable to make the trek with Belessunu this morning to see Mutuum's child."

"He is a beautiful boy, like yours, master.

And he is your namesake."

"I know. How many children do they have now?"

Yadidatum looked to Wedum. "I should know. I delivered them all. Four, is it?"

Wedum nodded. "One more than we have. Mutuum is a happy man."

"I would love to see the child," Terah said.

"I'm sure you would be most welcome," she said.

"Oh, yes," Wedum said. "They are proud of the child. Most proud!"

"But I am not able to travel . . ."

"I am sure they would welcome you as soon as you are able," Yadidatum said.

"But I want to see him today! Wedum will take you and bring you back here with the baby."

"But, sir, little Terah is only hours older than your Abram, and —"

Terah stopped feigning geniality. "Bring the child to me."

"Yes, sir," she said. "I'll ask Mutuum to —"

"No, I wish you to bring the baby."

"But if Mutuum insists on accompanying me, there is no room in Wedum's cart for another adult."

"The child will not be gone long before you return him."

"If you might indulge one more idea, sir."

"You have your instructions, Yadidatum."

The midwife nodded but looked downcast. Now was the time to initiate his plan. "What then? What's your idea?"

"I merely thought that if the king's guard could take us in the chariot, we would have room . . ."

Ikuppi said, "I would be happy to —"

"No!" Terah said. "I have other duties for you."

Yadidatum nodded but did not move. Terah had her where he wanted her. "Was there anything else?"

"I would be happy to tend your wounds, master."

"I am fine, thank you."

Still she seemed to stall. He raised his brows at her. "Master," she said, "I'm sure you're aware of what's happened to my son."

"What's *happened* to him? I'm not aware of anything having happened to him except that he was caught —"

"I am not asking for a pardon, sir. I'm begging for mercy. He is a young man, his whole life before him —"

"And our laws, the consequences, insure that offenders do not repeat. In fact, they regret what they've done for the rest of their lives."

"He already regrets it, master! No excuses, he takes all responsibility. But to maim him before he even marries or has a family —"

"Most such men are unable to wed."

"I was going to say that, sir. For a mistake, an error in judgment . . ."

"It's not as if he did not know better, Yadidatum."

"No! We have raised our children to honor the gods."

"Then must you not accept this punishment as from them?"

"I would take it as my own sentence," she said, her eyes filling. "I wish I could take his consequence."

"What good would a midwife be with only one hand?" Terah said.

"If it would leave my son whole, I would gladly —"

"You would?"

"On my life I swear, master. I would do anything to spare my child this horror."

Terah stepped closer and whispered, "Anything?"

He detected a wariness in her eyes, but she nodded solemnly.

"I will keep that in mind, Yadidatum. Now go and do as I have ordered."

As Wedum drove off with the midwife in the bed of his donkey cart, Terah told Ikuppi his scheme.

The guard looked stricken. "Terah, sir, I cannot be party to this!"

"What are you saying? You would have me subject my child to the king?"

"No! I am the one who informed you of his intentions, at the risk of my own life! But this would be wrong!"

"If it's wrong, I will pay the consequences. But the gods have given me this plan."

"This is not of the gods," Ikuppi said.

"You dare blaspheme in the home of an icon maker? You do not tell me what is or is not of the gods. I have decided, and this is what we will do."

"Can you do it without me, Terah? As a father myself, I cannot have this on my conscience. I will not!"

"You dare tell *me* what you will or will not do? I can trust no one else! You owe me your career, your life!"

Ikuppi sat heavily. "Your request weighs too heavily upon me."

"Have I not been clear, man? I trust you and I need your help! You must keep my confidence, and I will keep yours — of that you should have no doubt. But do not mistake my directive as a request."

"Oh, sir! I recognize that I am your subordinate but —"

"*You* are my subordinate? Everyone in the realm but the king is my subordinate! We are no longer discussing this."

CHAPTER 51

Guggenheim Pavilion
Mount Sinai Hospital
Manhattan

Ben Berman found Detective Wojciechowski alone at a table for four. The detective's trench coat and suitcoat lay draped over one of the chairs, and he had loosened his threadbare tie.

"They got kosher stuff here, Doc," he said.

"I forced myself to eat everything offered on the plane," Ben said, "so I'd better just have a salad."

"You don't gotta follow any food rules?"

"No. But I was raised on a lot of kosher food, and I like it."

"So you're not still Jewish?"

"Actually I'm more Jewish now than I was. I mean, I always will be ethnically, of course. But I've learned more about Judaism since believing in Yeshua than I ever knew before that."

When his salad arrived, Ben asked Wojciechowski if it would embarrass him if he asked a blessing.

"You mean pray?"

Ben nodded.

"Out loud?"

"Not so anyone else can hear."

"Either way, heck ya, I'd be embarrassed."

"No worries," Ben said. "I can do it silently."

"That doesn't help. What'm I supposed to do while you're doin' that?"

"I think that customarily, if a Messianic Jew is praying silently, a Gentile is required to stand on the table and dance — in any style you choose."

The detective squinted. "Here I'm tryin' to clear you of a crime, Berman, and you're a laugh a minute. I don't get it."

"Truth is," Ben said, "humor is my defense mechanism. Always has been. Even when I was a rebellious teenager, I tried to be funny."

"What you got to be defensive about? You hidin' something from me?"

"Of course I am. Don't look so shocked. I have zero fear you're going to clear me, and not just because I was across the Atlantic when this happened. I'm guessing by now you and your people have talked to enough

263

friends and associates of mine to know I'd have no motive, no reason, no anything that would cause me to have anything to do with hurting my wife."

"You're right, Doc. So what're you hidin'? You said it, I didn't."

"I'm hiding how I feel about all this."

"See, why would you do that?" Wojciechowski said. "You gotta know I do this almost every day. I look into some crime and I start clearing everybody I can, startin' with the people closest to the victims. And no matter how many of these blessed cop shows people watch, there's a typical response. They're horrified by what happened, they're insulted we would imply they coulda had anything to do with it, and that makes 'em angry. We take a lotta heat for doin' what we have to do, and we accept that. Only I don't see that from you."

"What do you see, Detective?"

"I see smart. I see earnest. I see helpful, as far as I can trust you. But I don't see the pushback I've learned to expect. You're always quick with a quip."

"All right, I don't mind telling you how I feel about all this. I *am* angry. Nobody's ever gone after Ginny before, at least not that way."

"What way, then?"

"Oh, when she handled the books for us, she could be tough on vendors and debtors. She expected them to be as precise and timely as we were, and she would not allow them to take advantage of us. But if I caught wind that anybody even raised their voice to her, I got involved. She didn't want me to and tried to keep all that stuff from me."

"Why?"

"Because she wanted to fight her own battles, and one of the big reasons she wanted the job — and you know she volunteered, saved the foundation a lot of money — was to take the burden off me. I mean, I couldn't have done it myself anyway; that's not in my wheelhouse. I would have had to hire somebody full-time or work with some outside firm, but she rightly wanted to free me to play to my strengths."

"So I'm back to what you're hidin'."

"Maybe I don't want you to see how terrified I am. I don't want Nicole to see that either. I know *she's* scared. She doesn't need me to be."

"You're ignoring your salad and haven't even done your prayer thing yet."

"Not hungry. I'll have 'em box it up."

"Men like to be macho. Heroes. But you think I'd be surprised or think less of you if you showed a little anger or fear? I never

265

had anything like this come close to either of my families, but I can put myself in your shoes. I'd be scared to death and wouldn't care who knew it."

"Well, now you know, Detective. And if it makes you feel any better, making light of it doesn't help me either. In fact, it makes me feel guilty."

"You *are* guilty, aren't you, Doc?"

"Sorry?"

"Just sayin' I'm not the only one you hid your real self from. You been keepin' stuff from the missus, haven't you, Ben?"

"Like what?"

"Why don't you tell me?"

"Because I have no idea."

Which wasn't entirely true. But Ben couldn't imagine how Ginny would have a clue, let alone Wojciechowski.

CHAPTER 52

Ur

Terah limped in to check on his wife and the baby. Belessunu had laid Abram next to her and they both appeared asleep. He tried to imagine the tiny lad as a toddler, then a youngster, then a grown-up. That last he found nearly impossible. Abram lay so still that Terah leaned close on his crutch to make sure he was breathing. Belessunu had freed his arms from the enveloping cloth, and he had them pressed against his little body, tiny fingers interlaced as if on purpose.

Sure enough, Abram's tiny chest rose and fell ever so slightly. Terah reached tentatively, careful to keep his balance, and laid his palm lightly on the boy's torso, his hand seeming to cover half the child. That caused the baby to jerk, both arms shooting straight out. Terah pressed lovingly. "Shh, little one. I'm here." And the wee hands settled over his own.

Terah could have stood soothing his son that way forever, but his only good leg grew weary and began to shake. He had to reposition himself, but pulling his hand away made the boy start again. So far, Terah had not been much of father. *But I will be, Abram. I will save your life this very day.* Especially if his plot had indeed come from the gods.

Terah slowly made his way out of the bedroom and found Ikuppi kneeling before the table of broken idols. "You do well to pray, my friend," Terah said, settling into a chair. "The gods will assure you we are doing the right thing."

"Don't say 'we,' sir. They offer me no peace about this. I am not part of it."

"You are whatever I say you are, and you will do what I say you'll do."

"But it doesn't even make sense, Terah! How will you explain —"

"It is not your place to judge the sense of it, man! All you must do is what I ask. Don't judge my wisdom."

"With all due respect, sir, it is more than your wisdom I judge. I question your morality."

"How dare you?"

"How dare I, Terah? How dare you?"

268

"Come close so we can hear each other without waking mother and child."

Ikuppi joined him. "You're going to regret this the rest of your life, Terah."

"I shall not! Even Belessunu's God says our son will become an exalted father. That's why we named him Abram. And to ensure that, I must protect him from the king."

"But if you do it the way you say you will, *I* will regret it the rest of my days. In fact, I don't know if I could live with myself."

"How can you say that, a father yourself!"

"And my family needs me. They do not need a man so weak he would violate his own conscience."

"If it is so distasteful to you, remember that you are merely doing what you're told and don't be so hard on yourself."

Ikuppi closed his eyes and shook his head, patting the long bronze sword at his waist. "I have killed many with this blade in the service of the throne. I have even flayed rebels strapped to walls. But never have I murdered an innocent."

"You will not be murdering anyone," Terah said. "You will only be doing what your superior tells you to do."

"But how can I make Mutuum and his

wife, or anyone, believe such a preposterous tale?"

"They don't have to believe it, as long as they accept it."

"I don't know how to be convincing."

"You don't have to convince them. You serve their master, so you will be speaking for me. They have no recourse regardless what they believe or don't believe."

CHAPTER 53

Vietnam, 1971

Ben Berman's resolve to simply keep his head down and do everything required of him at Parris Island resulted in his completing his field training at nearby Camp Lejeune and excelling at individual combat training. By the time he was deployed to Vietnam, he had learned bivouacking, navigation, camouflage, tactical signaling, sanitation, and navigation, among several other skills that made him an effective rifleman. He was assigned to the security force at a military hospital in a central coastal city, the name and location of which he was forbidden to reveal, at the risk of a court-martial.

At first Ben was disappointed. Working security at a hospital? How exciting or dangerous or fulfilling could that be? He found out fast. Jet-lagged and dragging when he arrived in the middle of the night, he was to report at dawn and work till mid-afternoon. He was assigned a bunk and given a sixty-second history of the US military presence there. About half the size of the better known Naval Support Activity Hospital far to the north in Danang, Ben's assigned facility covered fewer than twenty acres on the coast of the South China Sea, well within reach of enemy artillery.

Fortunately, Ben was able to sleep — which had not been the case on the interminable flight. And if he feared his role would involve hanging around hospital corridors and checking visitors' credentials, he was quickly disabused of that notion in the morning.

The place constantly buzzed with corpsmen running stretchered patients from the airfield out front to the receiving ward of one of the largest casualty treatment centers in Vietnam. Ben was told that most of the wounded had been helicopter evacuated right from the battlefield within fewer than two hours of when they had been hit. The injured and the ill consisted of American and allied troops and even Viet Cong.

Ben's first look at the receiving area nearly paralyzed him. Patients incapacitated, blown apart, or in the throes of some horrific disease were laid across a vast phalanx of what looked like sawhorses. Here they were quickly evaluated by admitting corpsmen who prioritized them and dispatched them to be treated by nearly four hundred professionals, both enlisted men and women and officers. Another more than three hundred Vietnamese nationals worked as nurse assistants, laundry hands, or general laborers.

So many patients poured in around the clock that during his first hour of duty, Ben was pressed into carrying one end of a stretcher — his M14 strapped over his shoulder — and once he was ordered to pull a sheet over the face of a young soldier who expired right before his eyes.

Ben's commanding officer told him that in just two years during the previous decade, the hospital had grown from fewer than fifty beds to more than three hundred. And the afflicted were not just military. Some were press, some medics, some Vietnamese civilians. Once admitted, even prisoners of war received equal treatment.

Ben was one of more than forty enlisted marines and army personnel there to support the navy forces. On his first day alone, he saw all five operating rooms, the fourteen-bed intensive care unit, and the steady stream of patients delivered directly from ambulances or from marine helicopters.

Ben could not get over the cacophony. Constant screaming, moaning, gasping from every room, corridor, and hut — doctors and nurses and orderlies shouting instructions. It simply never stopped. He saw more blood and severed body parts than he had in all the war movies he had ever seen, as well as exposed brains and internal organs.

That afternoon, trudging back toward his meager quarters after the shift he thought would never end, Ben stopped outside where a harried middle-aged nurse was taking a smoke break. "First day, soldier?" she said, introducing herself as Red.

Ben nodded. "How many people does this place take in anyway?"

"A few thousand a month. Not all of 'em need surgery, but a lot need more than one operation. So we average over five thousand operations a month."

"You're serious?"

"I got here just before the Tet offensive in '68, but that was a whole different animal. For nine months I'll bet we averaged closer to ten thousand admissions a month."

"Bullet wounds mostly?"

"I wish," she said. "Those are easy compared to a lot of what we see — victims shredded by booby traps, land mines, grenades, that kinda thing."

"Thought I wanted to see action over here, but this is rough to look at. And you've been here since '68?"

She shrugged, smiling. "Third tour. What else am I gonna do?"

"I can think of a million things I'd rather do. Don't know how I'm ever going to get this out of my head."

"Forgetting is a fantasy here, son."

"How do you handle it, ma'am?"

"Handle it? You don't handle it. You just keep at it."

"You ever get away?"

"Every chance I get if I can stay on my feet," she said. "Be glad you didn't get assigned to Danang. Everywhere off base is off-limits up there."

"Where do you go?"

"Into town, but since I don't carry a weapon, I gotta take a soldier with me. There's not much to do, but it's better than this, even if only for an hour or two. Walk around, have a drink, get a bite. Just don't trust anyone."

"I've got to get away from the noise," Ben said. "Never heard anything like it. Does it ever stop?"

She shook her head. "Dissipates a little

just before dawn sometimes. But I've worked every shift, and mostly it's constant."

Ben sighed. "I just feel so bad for them, and helpless."

"That's not all bad, Marine. Can't do this job if you don't care, and if you don't, you're finished. You'll be able to tune out the racket eventually, but it won't be easy. It took me months." Red peeked at her watch. "Gotta go, hon. You gonna be all right?"

"I don't know," Ben said. The truth was, he was haunted by more than the noise. End of day one and he'd seen inside more bodies than most civilians would in a lifetime.

CHAPTER 54

Ur

"I am miserable, Terah," Ikuppi said as they sat waiting at Terah's home.

"I have utmost confidence in you, friend."

"I may not be your friend in the days to come."

"Certainly you will!"

"I cannot guarantee I will regain my respect for y—"

"Are they coming?" Terah said. "Is that what I hear?"

Ikuppi made his way to the door. "It is them. And the midwife does not look happy."

"Why do I care what Yadidatum — ? Just get out there. You know what to do."

Ikuppi stepped out, leaving the door ajar so Terah could see and hear. "No, please stay in the cart and quiet the baby. The master does not want to awaken Belessunu or Abram. I will bring him to meet you by the animal pen."

"The animal pen!" the midwife said. "Of all the places . . ."

"Keep your rig quiet, Wedum, until you're clear of the house."

Wedum leaned forward and nudged the donkey, clicking with his tongue until the animal stepped off. Mutuum's newborn fussed in Yadidatum's arms, then began to cry as the cart moved away. The infant wailed as the donkey picked up speed. Ikuppi returned to help Terah to the chariot, but before they even reached the door, Belessunu spoke from the bedroom. "Terah?" she whispered.

He urged Ikuppi with a nod to keep moving, but he stopped when she sounded more urgent. "Come here so I don't wake the baby! Who was that outside?"

Terah steadied himself on his crutch and pointed to the bedchamber. "You know what to say," he mouthed.

Ikuppi set his jaw but tapped on the wall next to the curtain. "Begging your pardon, ma'am, may I help?"

"Ikuppi, where is Terah and who has arrived?"

"Wedum and Yadidatum have brought Mutuum's baby, little Terah."

"So soon? Whatever for?"

"Terah wanted to see him."

"How nice. Have them bring him in here."

"He is crying, and Terah did not want to bother you or Abram, so I will take him to meet them at the livestock pen."

"Oh no!" Belessunu said. "The dung, the flies. Spare the newborn that for now."

"Ma'am, you know the livestock pens are not removed from the servants' dwellings the way yours is. That baby is already used to whatever he will encounter here."

"Still, I hate to see . . . On the way back, if little Terah is quiet, I'd like to see him again."

CHAPTER 55

Guggenheim Pavilion

"I'm listening," Ben Berman said.

Detective George Wojciechowski set his dishes aside and thumbed through his notebook. "Let me tell ya what my matron says she heard your wife say last night in the recovery room. And in case you're wondering, she played me this off her phone. Your wife told your daughter that they had to talk right then. Nicole told her no, it could wait. Mrs. Berman said it wouldn't wait. Your daughter told her to just relax, and your wife insisted she listen. So Nicole said, basically, 'Okay, what is it?'

"My officer says your wife told your daughter to make you tell her what's in the box."

Ben felt the color drain from his cheeks.

"A gray metal box," Wojciechowski said. "Says there's a secret in there you don't know she saw — 'a picture of a lady' is how she worded it." He looked up at Ben.

"A lady," Ben said, more statement than question. He forced himself to hold the detective's gaze. How could she have found that? And when? Why hadn't he put it in a safe deposit box?

Wojciechowski peeked back at his notes. "And to calm Virginia so the nurse could give her her meds, your daughter promised."

"Promised what?" Ben said, his voice weak.

"To make you tell her the secret."

"Secret?"

Wojciechowski sighed. "Doc, this is Interrogation 101."

"I don't follow."

"More than thirty years ago I was taught that when somebody starts parroting back your questions, they're stalling, pretending they have no idea what you're talkin' about. But you do. You know the box, and you know the picture. And you know the lady, don't you?"

Ben hesitated. He hadn't even considered needing a lawyer.

"Listen to me," Wojciechowski said. "This is where I play your best friend and urge you to do the right thing for your own good. Maybe the box, the picture, the lady have nothin' to do with what happened to your wife. But if she found the box, you know it didn't take my CSIs long to find it. And it points to motive, Ben. How do we know you didn't find out your wife discovered the box and you couldn't think of another way to keep from havin' to come clean?"

"Another way than having someone scare Ginny?"

"Or worse. Maybe they didn't finish the job you gave 'em."

Ben folded his hands and rested his chin on them, closing his eyes. "I didn't. I wouldn't. Ever."

"One a my guys talked to your assistant, Olsen, and says she corroborates your claim of a blissful marriage — but he also said she kinda did it begrudgingly."

"What's that mean?"

"That maybe she wasn't thrilled about admitting that."

"That's a weird speculation," Ben said. "And you need to know this is the first I've heard that Ginny knew anything about the box."

"If that's true, you got no reason *not* to tell me what we're gonna find in it and why it has nothin' to do with this case."

CHAPTER 56

Ur

Terah hoped he might sit in the chariot, but he would have had to lodge himself on the floor and press his back against the rear of the carriage — which he could not manage. He had to stand next to Ikuppi, stay clear of the reins, support himself on one leg, grip the lip of the conveyance with one hand, and keep his crutch lodged under his bad arm with little but his weight to keep it in place.

Even the light jostling when the horses walked toward the pen a hundred yards away made the tip of the crutch dance on the floor and forced Terah to press it to his body under his dog-bitten shoulder. He could not imagine also holding a baby on a trip to the palace, and Ikuppi would certainly not allow the horses to pull them all the way at such a slow gait. That could take hours.

When they reached the pen, he found the midwife still in the bed of the cart while Wedum spoke with another servant tending the animals. He had built a small fire. The man ran off, and Wedum told Terah he had assigned him to busy himself gathering kindling until the master and his guests left.

"Good man," Terah said. "Now let me see this baby."

Ikuppi suggested Terah sit in a corner of the chariot so he could support himself and hold the child. Yadidatum handed the baby to Wedum before she climbed out of his cart. The child began squawking, so she took him back.

Terah told Wedum to hurry back to the servants' settlement and tell Mutuum and his wife that they would bring the baby back as soon as Belessunu was awake and had a chance to see him, now that she was no longer in pain as she had been when he was born.

Wedum rode off in his cart, and Yadidatum glared at Terah.

"What is it?" he called down to her.

"If you'll forgive me for saying so, sir, this is not fair to the child."

Who had told her? Only he and Ikuppi knew the plan, and the guard had not been out of his sight. "What is not fair, ma'am?"

284

"Carting him here and there. He should be at his mother's breast."

"He'll be back to her soon enough, and you would be wise to watch your tongue. I would not tolerate such cheek from even your husband."

Fear flashed on her face. "I apologize, master! I am thinking only of the child."

"You would do well to think of the welfare of your own son."

She cradled little Terah in both arms. "My son is all I think of."

"Tell her, Ikuppi."

"The king's chief officer has the power to have a servant executed — or slay you himself, without consequence or having to even give cause. Do you not know that?"

"I know it, sir. I was speaking only for the child I delivered."

"Do not talk about me when I am standing right here!" Terah said. "You delivered my son too, and it earns you no privilege. You will speak to me with the deference I deserve, especially from someone of your station."

"Yes, my lord. My apologies."

"Don't let it happen again."

She nodded. And the baby howled.

"Can you not quiet the child?"

"He may be hungry, sir."

"Was he not fed before you set out?"

"He was. But newborns . . ."

"I don't need to hear it, and I don't care to hear his caterwauling either."

Yadidatum rocked the baby and touched a finger to his mouth. His tiny lips locked onto the tip and he sucked. "Do you wish to hold him, master?"

"I do not."

"You wanted only to see him?"

"I wish to show him to the king."

"I don't understand. What interest would the king have in the child of a servant?"

"You question me again?"

"I mean no disrespect, sir. I ask sincerely."

"It is not your place to ask. It is your place to do as you are told. And I am telling you to secure yourself and the baby in the chariot for the ride to the palace."

CHAPTER 57

Eleven West
Mount Sinai Hospital
Manhattan

Nicole grew restless, obsessed by even the idea of some mysterious box her mother was so convinced she must find and about which she had promised to confront her father. If it was at her parents' place, the cops would have already found it and figured a way into it. They knew what she didn't — whether such a box even existed, and if there was anything to what her mother had said.

Nicole regretted her decision to ignore the letter from the Saudis, despite how certain she was that it bore bad news. She had to know where she stood, what was still needed to land her dig permit and her ID as lead archaeologist. She hated still being dependent on her father, but she was convinced that if she found in Saudi Arabia what she suspected she might, she could become independently wealthy and evade the nepotism charges she'd faced for so long.

Of course, personal profit was not her goal and never had been. But that was certainly better than the alternative, and Nicole couldn't deny she was jealous of those who had become wealthy or celebrated by others in the profession because of what they'd discovered in the ground. She could never pay back her father regardless, and he certainly didn't need her to. But to become financially autonomous for the first time . . . well, she could barely conceive of it. The Saudi dig, she feared, was only an impossible dream if her dad didn't come through with the funds.

Much as she wanted to prove or disprove her mother's wee-hours claims, Nicole could not let the Saudi thing rest. If she were ever to realize this ultimate goal, she had to stay at the task, find out what the authorities needed from her, and deliver. But she would not leave her mother alone, and neither would she ask a nurse or an aide to sit with her. She was ready to go as soon as her dad and Wojciechowski returned from lunch and the detective had finished questioning her mother. And while they had already taken longer than she expected, she hoped Mom would rouse before they returned. Nicole wanted time with her alone to assure herself once and for all that everything she'd said in the night had been some muddled dream from her anesthesia-affected subconscious.

Nicole sat tapping a text to her father, asking how long he and Wojciechowski might be, when footsteps approached outside. Had her plan to speak with her mother alone already failed? No. She heard "gift shop delivery," and opened the door to the police woman. The other cop blocked the delivery boy from the door. "Can't let him in," the female officer said. "You order those?"

"I did."

"Just give 'em to me," the blocking cop told the kid, who looked relieved and hurried off. "Want me to inspect 'em, ma'am?"

"I'm sure they're fine," Nicole said.

As soon as she brought them in and shut the door, her mother roused. "Oh, Nic, let me see."

Nicole removed the noisy cellophane from the bouquet, which consisted of white and yellow daisies and yellow roses in a smiley-face cup.

"My favorites!" her mother said, reaching. "Let me just smell them and you can put them right here."

She seemed to drink in the fragrance, which Nicole found overwhelming. It reminded her of a funeral. "You sure you want them this close, Mom?"

"Absolutely!"

Nicole asked how she was feeling and whether she needed or wanted anything. Virginia said she still felt exhausted. "But I can't imagine why. I've been in bed since I got here. I'd love a Coke and an ice water."

"That I can find right here. When are you going to be hungry again?"

"No idea."

Nicole rushed to get her drinks, not wanting to miss her own opportunity. "Mom," she said, "I need to ask you something."

CHAPTER 58

Shinar

The chariot ride to the palace proved agonizing. Terah had intimidated Yadidatum into silence, or so he hoped. But little Terah screamed the entire trip, as did big Terah's tender wounds. He insisted Ikuppi maintain at least a moderate pace, but Terah had to fight to keep his balance, and every bump and sway tortured him all the more.

"Silence that child!" he shouted at the midwife.

Yadidatum pressed the baby to her chest and turned away, mumbling, "You ask too much of a newborn."

"You are going to regret —"

"Sir, I apologize, but the child is hungry and probably wet. And after having been safe in the womb for so long, he is being shaken about over an unforgiving road. Anyway, may I ask what business a servant's baby has at the palace?"

Terah glowered at her and turned his face toward the city, willing it to appear on the horizon. "Careful you don't write your son's death sentence, woman," he murmured over the piercing cries of the child. He leaned toward Ikuppi's ear. "You will corroborate my account of her insolence."

"If you report it to the king, Terah, he will demand to know why you have not slain her yourself."

"I'll tell him I did not want to upset my wife, who does not yet know my decision on behalf of the throne."

Ikuppi said, "You know that anyone involved in this — including Belessunu — will be put to death as soon as it is found out."

"That is a risk I must take. My son is to be a father, that's all I know, all I care about."

"Even over Belessunu's life?"

"She is no threat to the throne. He will assume she left me when she learns what I have done."

"He will pursue Abram, Terah! Will he not find Belessunu with the boy?"

"Don't underestimate me, Ikuppi. The king will never find them."

"I pray you are right."

"You are a true friend."

"No," Ikuppi said. "I have told you, I can

no longer be your friend if you insist on carrying out this evil."

"Ikuppi! I am saving my son! What else can I do?"

"This deceit will curse you. I cannot support it."

"Do today as I instruct you, and I will ask no more."

"I could do no more anyway. I told you of the king's intentions so you and your family could cast yourselves upon the mercy of the gods."

"Nimrod himself is one of the gods."

"I pray you will not force me to go through with this, Terah."

"Do not forget whom you serve."

"I will never be able to forget."

Mutuum's baby continued to wail as Ikuppi slowed the chariot to maneuver through the city gate. Terah covered his own face as people stared.

"Park in the paddock behind the palace and be sure Nimrod is holding court. And bring me a cape."

"A cape?"

"You see how people look at me, man! I must explain my condition when I enter court, before I let the king see me this way. Your own cape would fit me."

293

"It will be the first thing the king notices."

"I'm taking a servant and a baby in there, and you think Nimrod will care what I'm wearing?"

"You can't cover your head in the presence of the king."

"Better than his seeing my face before you have prepared him."

"Wait!" Yadidatum whispered desperately. "You're taking me before the king? Servants are not allowed in the court!"

"It will be all right," Terah said. "Do as I say and not only will you be spared, but I will look into your son's case as well."

She looked as if she was about to cry. "I will do anything you ask."

"Tell the king you delivered this baby."

"I did!"

"That I am the father and —"

"You!"

"— that Belessunu is the mother."

"What?"

"That we named him Amraphel."

"The king's name? But Mutuum and his wife named this boy after you!"

"Do you want my help or not, Yadida-tum?"

"Of course I do. While we're here, might we be able to see my son?"

"Let's see how you perform."

The baby stopped crying and went limp. She repositioned him over her shoulder and he sighed. "Wore himself out, poor thing," she said.

Terah sent Ikuppi off and motioned Yadidatum close. He spoke softly, earnestly, trying to set her at ease. "Give me no reason to have you executed or your son mutilated. As Ikuppi told you, I don't even need cause, and if I did, I could say anything I wanted. The king will not want to be bothered with a case involving a servant — you or your son. I can make this turn out as you wish, but you have two stories to tell."

"Two?"

"One in the king's court, and one to Mutuum and his wife."

CHAPTER 59

Guggenheim Pavilion

"Detective," Ben Berman said, "you have my word that the woman in the picture has nothing to do with what happened to my wife."

"Oh, I have your word, do I?" Wojciechowski said. "How lucky for us both! Case closed, then, eh?"

"C'mon," Ben said. "If you're as good as you think you are, you know neither Nic nor I had anything to do with this."

Wojciechowski looked at his phone. "How long's your wife gonna sleep, anyway? Listen, you're right — our people are findin' pretty much what you said they would. No one sees a lick of trouble in your marriage . . ."

"See?"

"Yeah, I see, and you're not far off when you try to guess what I'm thinkin'. But you know I gotta follow every trail. Just telling the DA I cleared this guy 'cause I found him funny and easy to talk to is not gonna cut it. Tell me about the lady in the picture, and if I agree it doesn't relate, maybe I can even help put your wife's mind at ease. How's that?"

Ben shook his head. "I don't know how she knows about it, but since she does, I have to tell her. I should have a long time ago. Either that or gotten rid of the picture."

"Or hidden it better," Wojciechowski said.

"That too."

"But there's a reason you didn't, and a reason you never told your wife. I gotta know those reasons, Ben."

CHAPTER 60

King Nimrod's Palace
Shinar

Terah and Yadidatum waited behind pillars at the far end of the king's court as Ikuppi approached the throne from a side portal and bowed.

"Yes, guard?" King Nimrod said, peering down from the elevated dais. "What business have you this day for the throne?"

"Your servant, the chief officer wishes a private audience, my lord."

"And why does he not ask for himself?"

"You will see, oh King."

"Aah, does this portend good news? You yourself reported that Terah would be absent from court until his wife gave birth. Am I to meet the blessing the gods have bestowed on him and Belessunu in their old age?"

"He wishes to share the tidings with you himself, my king."

"Very well." Nimrod turned to an aide. "Dismiss all members of the court save this guard. Summon my wife, and also my stargazers and wise men. They have prophesied this and so deserve to rejoice with us."

"Something else the king should be aware of before Terah enters your presence," Ikuppi said.

"Carry on."

"Your chief officer begs leave to enter the court with his head and face temporarily covered."

"What?"

"He will reveal himself after he has explained injuries he suffered in a fall just before the birth of his child."

"How did this happen?"

"He was tending to business on his estate when word came that the midwife had been summoned. The servant driving him back to his home hit a rut that pitched Terah out at some speed. He has suffered multiple injuries, none life-threatening but all painful, causing a limp, requiring a crutch, and resulting in bad bruising, especially to his face."

"How ghastly! And so unfortunate at this time of joy."

"Quite. And due to his injuries, he is unable to carry the child and wishes the midwife to accompany him."

"A servant?"

"Yes, my lord."

"Before me in the court?"

"Correct, sir."

Nimrod sighed. "I'll allow it."

The court was cleared, Ikuppi positioned himself near the portal that led to the guards' quarters, and soon the king's stargazers entered in full regalia — three positioning themselves behind the throne to the right, three to the left.

CHAPTER 61

Eleven West

"Mama, the detective has more questions for you, and he and Dad will be back soon, but —"

"Oh, Nicole, I'm about questioned out. I know only what I've already said. It's all so fuzzy. I don't know what else I can tell him."

"Just do the best you can. But right now I want to know what you remember about last night."

"That's hazy too, Nic. Bits and pieces of getting here, lots of attention, doctors, nurses, tests. They think I was attacked, didn't just trip and fall. I can't imagine either one, but I know I hurt myself somehow."

"You *were* attacked, Mom."

"I'm getting the idea. But I had a hard time waking up after surgery, recall some activity in the night and sleeping again. I should be as rested as I've ever been, but

301

there's something exhausting about lying around doing nothing."

"Remember talking to me in the night?"

She hesitated. "Vaguely."

"Do you?"

"Those flowers, dear. Lovely . . ."

"Focus, Mom. What did we talk about in the night?"

Her mother looked past Nicole and appeared to be thinking. "I remember being agitated, maybe scared. Hoping you'd stay with me, that you'd be there when I woke up."

"You were eager to tell me something, Mom — afraid you weren't going to make it."

She grimaced and nodded. "I remember that."

"What was it?"

"I don't know, Nic. Thought I might die."

"But that made you want to tell me something important."

The frustration on her mother's face tempted Nicole to stop pushing. But she had to know.

"That I loved you, I guess. To be sure you knew that."

"But I know that, Mama. You've shown your love for Dad and me in so many ways."

Her mother sighed and nodded. "Hope

so. Was worrying about that, making sure I said a proper good-bye."

"Mom, you said something about my hating you."

"Oh, surely not."

"You did."

"I don't remember that at all, Nic. I know you love me."

"I sure hope you know that because I do. But you did say it, and others heard it. They think you and I may not have the relationship I say we do."

"We have a wonderful relationship! When friends tell me about their squabbles with their grown kids, I can't identify and I feel so blessed."

"Then why would you have said something like that? Could you have been confusing something from the past when you thought I hated you?"

Her mother paused and seemed to be thinking. "You were a rascal for a while in high school, weren't you? When you were a junior or a senior?"

"Junior. But I never hated you and hope I never acted like I did."

"You never said you did," her mother said. "I would have remembered that. I might have wondered if you did when you were disrespectful, but you never really got ugly with me."

"And didn't I eventually apologize?"

"Of course you did."

"That's a relief. So there's nothing between us, is there? You'd tell me, wouldn't you?"

Her mother let out a long sigh. "You and your father are my best friends . . ." Her voice trailed off.

"Mama, you also said in the night that you wanted me to talk to Dad about something."

Another long pause. "Did I?"

"Remember?"

Her mother shook her head. "You said something, Nic, about his trying to get here — and if I was going to die, I sure wanted to see him first. Maybe I was telling you something I wanted him to know, in case he didn't get here in time."

"You know you're not in mortal danger, right, Mom?"

"I think so."

"You're not. You were hurt, bad, but it's just a matter of getting better now."

"I hope so."

"I'd tell you straight, Mama."

"I know."

"But that wasn't what you wanted me to talk to Dad about — that you loved him in case you didn't make it."

"It wasn't?"

"No."

"Remind me, Nicole."

"I need you to tell me, Mom — to remember it yourself."

Her mother ran her fingers lightly over the ugly scab on her forehead and scowled. Was she struggling to recall what she'd said, or did she know full well and did not want to admit it?

"It was important to you, Mom. I told you it could wait, and you said it couldn't. You made me promise I'd ask him about it."

Her mother nodded. "And did you?"

"Did I what, promise or — ?"

"Did you talk to him?"

"Not yet, Mom. I wanted to be sure you weren't just confused because of your meds or all you'd been through."

Her mother grew fidgety, wouldn't meet Nicole's gaze, and busied herself reaching for the bouquet. "So lovely," she said.

"Mama . . ."

"Um-hm."

"Do you still want me to talk to Dad about something? Anything?"

She nodded.

"You do?"

"I do."

"About what? Tell me."

"I already told you."

"Last night you told me?"

Her mother nodded again.

And Nicole heard her father and Detective Wojciechowski at the door.

CHAPTER 62

The Palace, Shinar

The stargazers bowed when the king's wife entered the court, but she stared — visibly puzzled at the man hidden in a hooded cape standing with a servant woman holding a baby.

Nimrod had not only not stood when Ninlila arrived, but he also did not even acknowledge her. Despite that she was dressed in elaborate regalia and even wore a jewel-studded crown, she had never been referred to as the queen of the realm. Terah attributed this to Nimrod/Amraphel's vanity. Apparently he feared even his own wife's designs on succeeding him.

Ninlila carried his scepter, which he reached for without looking at her. Pressing it to the floor, he repositioned himself and draped one leg over the arm on the throne. A favorite pose of the king, the slouch elevated the hem of his robe and exposed nearly the full length of one thigh. Terah had long wanted to caution him against such a casual appearance, but he himself had been tasked with imprisoning other advisers who dared critique the king. Nimrod would do what he wished, which, of course, was his right.

Ninlila stood with her arm over the back of the throne, appearing expectant, perhaps perplexed at having been summoned.

"Terah, approach," the king said.

Terah laid a hand gently on Yadidatum's shoulder. She trembled, but thankfully Mutuum's baby remained asleep. "Stay one step behind me, but do not hide yourself from the throne."

"I am about to faint, master," she squeaked.

"Do this for your son. You must not fail."

Terah leaned heavily on his crutch to take as much weight as possible off the mutilated ankle on the long walk to the base of the steps leading to the throne. He swung his free hand more than normal to give him the most speed of which he was capable, but each step stabbed with such pain that he had to fight to keep from moaning aloud.

When Terah lost sight of Yadidatum in his peripheral vision, he turned to find her lagging ten feet behind. "Stay with me!" he hissed, painfully slowing. But when she caught up, he noticed Ninlila whispering to the king and the stargazers scowling.

"Relax," Nimrod said dismissively. "I have permitted this." The stargazers whispered to each other until the king shouted, "Enough! Silence!"

Terah reached the steps, and when Yadidatum arrived beside him, he whispered, "Stay where you were." She took one step back.

Nimrod smiled. "Terah, remove your hood."

All on the podium seemed to recoil at the sight, but Nimrod appeared to take it in stride. "I trust you don't feel as bad as you look, my friend."

"I have seen my reflection, my lord, and I doubt anyone has ever felt as bad as I look."

"Well said. But this too shall pass. Please, introduce your guests."

"Great King, I am proud to present to you my wife Belessunu's midwife, Yadidatum, and our son, Amraphel."

Yadidatum shakily held the baby out. The stargazers looked horrified.

The king let his scepter fall, swung his leg down from the arm of the chair, and sat forward, elbows on his knees. The clank of the scepter made the baby start, but Yadidatum gathered him back into her chest and quieted him.

"You have named him after me, Terah? I'm touched!"

"My wife's idea," Terah said, fighting to maintain his composure. He looked to Yadidatum, who nodded.

"Ninlila," Nimrod said, "fetch the child for me and let us rejoice over how the gods have blessed my chief officer and his wife."

But as Ninlila moved to descend the steps, Yadidatum started up to meet her.

"Do not ascend, woman!" the head stargazer roared as the rest appeared ready to flee. The shout so startled the midwife that she nearly tumbled backward, and Terah reached to steady her. That put pressure on his bad ankle and he cried out in pain, grabbing the crutch with both hands to keep from falling.

The baby erupted into frantic wailing, clearly frustrating the king. Ikuppi quickly explained, "Woman, you are in court only by imperial consent, but no commoner, let alone a servant, has ever mounted the royal podium."

"I beg your forgiveness, Highness!" Yadidatum said.

"Just quiet the child," Nimrod said, waving.

She rocked the baby, holding him close, but it took several minutes to calm him. Ninlila finally took him, but Terah thought she looked as if she were extracting something from a tar pit. When she handed the baby to her husband, the stargazers stepped back as if petrified.

Nimrod looked surprisingly comfortable with the boy, cradling him and smiling. "My namesake," he said.

But as soon as the baby fussed again, Nimrod gave him back to Ninlila. She approached the steps, reaching him out to the midwife. "No," the king said. "I believe Terah offers this child as a gift to the throne."

The head stargazer stepped to the king, keeping a wide berth between himself and the king's wife. He whispered desperately in Nimrod's ear. The king nodded and dismissed him, and the man ushered his fellow soothsayers out.

"Am I not right, Terah?" Nimrod said. "You present your son as an offering?"

"I — I serve at your pleasure, my King," Terah said, trying to sound stunned.

"What does this mean?" Yadidatum said.

Nimrod glared. "It is none of your concern, midwife."

"He's *giving* you this child!"

311

Terah held up a hand. "Yadidatum, difficult as this is, everything I have belongs to my sovereign."

"But what will become of him?"

Ikuppi interrupted, "The king does not answer to us, woman, and certainly not to you."

"I don't mind, guard," Nimrod said. "It is a fair question. Amraphel will be afforded whatever he deserves from the dominion."

"Why were those men so afraid of him?"

"Yadidatum!" Ikuppi shouted.

Nimrod smiled again. "I'll have to ask them, won't I? And now you are dismissed. Terah, you may share the good news with your wife and pass along my deepest gratitude."

"I don't understand!" Yadidatum said.

"I said you were dismissed, servant."

"The parents of this child must surrender him to you?" she cried as Ninlila carried the baby away.

The king stood, and Ikuppi rushed to hand him his scepter. "They named him after me, woman. They do this willingly."

"*They?*" the midwife spat. "The mother of this child does not even know —"

"Think of your own son," Terah whispered. He turned to the king. "Belessunu may indeed be distraught over this. She

312

might even leave me."

"This is not right!" Yadidatum yelled. "Master, I thought you merely wanted me to —"

Suddenly Ikuppi was at her side. "Do not make things worse," he said. "Give this up and I will take you to see your son."

She fell silent.

"Terah," Nimrod said, "should your wife unwisely punish you for this selfless show of loyalty, I will make available to you your choice of companions from throughout the kingdom — perhaps even your insolent midwife."

CHAPTER 63

Eleven West

"Well, Detective," Nicole's mother said, "I have an alarm clock set at six every morning."

"Okay, so your alarm goes off Friday and —"

"Oh, no, sir. My alarm hasn't gone off in, what, thirty years?"

"So you're one a those who wakes up before the alarm goes off . . ."

"Every time."

"And yesterday?"

"I was up about ten minutes early.

"So by the time I've got my walking suit on, the coffeemaker I set the night before has done its job. I don't like to eat before I walk, so I have my QT."

"Your . . . ?"

"My quiet time. I pray, read my Bible, sometimes a devotional."

"You do this every day?"

She nodded.

"So lemme back up. Your walkin' suit?"

"A burgundy sweat suit kind of a thing, except I don't walk fast enough to sweat. I'm not working out per se, just getting in my walk. I don't rush. Mondays, Wednesdays, and Fridays, I have a mile-and-a-half route. Tuesdays and Thursdays I do three miles. Take my time. And take weekends off."

"But the short route every other day . . ."

"Right. I've always liked the housekeeper to come by eight, and I never know how long it's going to take me. I stop at Schnell's at the corner and bring home a bagel. You just never know when the bakery is going to be busy."

"Know if they got a CCTV camera?"

"No idea," her mother said.

"They do," Ben said. "Every shop in the neighborhood does."

"So yesterday," Wojciechowski said, "you're out walking by . . ."

"Between six twenty and six thirty."

"So you get to Schnell's when?"

"Between seven thirty and seven forty-five. They were busy, so I stood in line for a while. But still I wound up talking to one of the girls for several minutes, maybe ten. Then I had to get going to make sure I let

Teodora in. Yesterday was the end of only her second week with us, so her sixth time cleaning."

"And there's enough for her to do three times a week in an apartment with just two people?"

Nicole's mother looked sheepish. "It's too big a place for us, and 'apartment' doesn't do it justice. The kitchen and the bathrooms get most of the attention, but she gets to the whole place every week."

"And you got back in time to let her in?"

"In plenty of time, actually. She arrived right at eight if I recall."

"No one followed you, looked out of place, made you uncomfortable?"

Nicole's mother shook her head. "Everybody knows me. Watches for me. You don't get much of that in New York anymore. We're blessed."

"And yet here we are," the detective said. "Anything unusual about the housekeeper yesterday?"

"No. I've always found it amusing that she seems overdressed for our weather, but she's new to the US, doesn't have much."

"Overdressed?"

Nicole's mother shrugged. "She dresses as I would in the dead of winter. We're just starting to get a little nip in the air in the mornings and when the sun goes down. But she wears a parka, boots. Carries her work shoes in a bag, changes when she gets to our place."

Nicole's mother sipped her Coke and then her water. "Pleasant enough, but not a conversationalist. She understands me enough and I can understand her, but it's rough."

"Okay," Wojciechowski said. "I already had someone interrogate your former housekeeper. Rock-solid alibi, but she didn't deny why she got fired. Said she finally yielded to temptation and took some stuff. But somethin's not adding up for me here with the new housekeeper. Ben, you said you heard from your assistant" — he thumbed back through his notebook — "Abigail Olsen, sometime after ten thirty p.m. in Paris, that your wife had been admitted to Sinai. So that was after four thirty p.m. here."

"Right."

"And the people at our 911 control center say the call came in from your home land-line a little after four o'clock. The caller identified herself as the housekeeper. But she's not the one who let in the EMTs."

"No?" Nicole's dad said.

"She was there and seemed distraught,

they said, but on their way they had called the desk in the lobby of your building and told 'em they were gonna need access to your place to respond to an injury. When they got there, security let them in downstairs, rode up with 'em on an express elevator, and one of their guys was already in there with this Petrova woman."

"Didn't know that," Nicole's dad said.

"Neither did I," her mother said. "I'm just grateful Teodora knew enough to call 911. But if she had just called the desk, they would have called it in."

"But someone had to let her in," Nicole's dad said, "and if it wasn't you, Ginny, it had to be security."

"Anybody see my problem here?" Wojciechowski said.

"I do," Nicole said. "What was Teodora doing there at that time of the day?"

CHAPTER 64

Shinar

"You'll have to kill me first!" Yadidatum raged at the king.

Nimrod looked first to Ikuppi and then to Terah. "Does she know that can be arranged?"

"Forgive her, Oh Great King," Terah said. "She takes great personal interest in the children she helps birth."

When Ikuppi dragged her away, Terah found himself alone with the king in the echoing court. Nimrod's voice came smooth and low. "You have been a loyal friend for lo these many decades, Terah. We have been through so much together."

"True," Terah said.

"But this, this gift of your firstborn, may be the greatest expression of devotion I have ever received."

Terah bowed as low as he was able. "My lord," he said.

"You know this makes moot your becoming my substitute king, for there will no longer remain a need to appease the gods. You have saved your own life."

"At the expense of my son's?"

Nimrod gazed at him. "You know what my wise men have told me? They informed me your son's birth was imminent, and as always, they were right. But the stars revealed the child's destiny. Were he allowed to live, he would eventually conspire to seize the throne."

"They're sure of this?"

"They know it, Terah! And that would make you the father of a king, having never been one yourself! The lunacy of it!"

Terah wanted to say that his son assuming the throne would mimic the way Nimrod himself had accomplished it. But he had no choice but to carry the subterfuge to its end. He had to appear conflicted, saddened, and yet blindly loyal. Clearly Nimrod had lost any respect he might have had for Terah, believing him so weak that he sacrificed his own son. But then Nimrod had never really respected him, had he? Terah was of a royal line, Nimrod a cursed one. When finally the gods blessed Terah with a son to carry on his lineage, the king demanded the child for his own purposes.

But Terah could compete at deceit.

"Take some time, Terah," the king said. "Prevail upon your wife to understand. I am only acting as the gods lead. They set the stars on their courses in the sky. My oracles have tested these things and are unanimous in their conclusion. You have done the right thing. She will come to see that."

"I can only pray she will."

"I am a benevolent and kind ruler. I would never go against the gods, and they know what's best for you and for Belessunu. I believe they will reward you with another child, perhaps even a son who will not have designs on the throne."

But if he did, you would kill him too. "Perhaps."

"Return to my service when your wounds have healed, faithful servant. And report to me how things go with your wife."

Terah tried to back all the way out of the court but found it awkward with the crutch. "You may turn!" Nimrod called out to him, leaving the throne. Though the king never looked back, Terah thanked him and bowed low before gingerly making his way out.

He repositioned his hood so the guards and other palace personnel would not be alarmed by his face. By now the rumors of why he was there had likely already spread. Some called out congratulations on the birth of his son, but he merely mumbled hurried thank-yous and kept moving.

Terah reached the dungeon in time to find Ikuppi standing behind Yadidatum as she pressed against the bars of her son's cell. She wept as she tried to reassure him. Terah hobbled to her. "You nearly did enough to have me end the both of you!" he rasped.

"Three in one day?" she whimpered. "Would that be enough for you?"

"You can still save yourself."

"And my son?"

The young man look gaunt, scared.

"You know there are no guarantees in here."

"There had better be," she said, "or I will not lie to Mutuum and his wife."

"Keep your voice down, woman."

"If you don't swear my son will be spared, I will do no more of your bidding."

Terah looked around to see who might be in earshot. Leaning on his crutch, he grabbed Yadidatum's garment at the neck and pulled her close. The king he had faithfully served had deceived him in the worst way possible, but Terah's revenge would not be complete unless his own deceit was accomplished in full.

"Listen to me, woman. You will tell the story to Mutuum and his wife exactly as I have recited it to you, or you will never see your own husband or children again. You and this one will be gone before the next rooster crows."

CHAPTER 65

Eleven West

"See why I gotta ask you about your whole day now, Mrs. Berman?" Detective George Wojciechowski said.

Nicole's mother nodded, her brow knit. "Why didn't I think of that? In all the confusion I had it in my mind that this had to have happened in the morning, when Teo was there, because I understood she had found me and called 911. What *was* she doing back there in the afternoon?"

"Did she forget something, Mom? Come back for something?"

"Please don't suggest things, ma'am," Wojciechowski said. "Let me walk her through this."

"Sorry," Nicole said.

"Now, Virginia, you say you were back from your walk —"

"And the bakery."

"Right, in plenty of time to let the housekeeper in."

"Yes. I greeted her as I always do and she responded as she always does."

"What's that mean?"

"Well, I've always been sensitive to the people few seem to notice. I think it comes from Ben's and my travels around the world."

"It's from long before that," Nicole's father said. "You were that way when I met you."

Wojciechowski held up a hand and glanced at Ben. "Let me," he said.

"Of course."

"And you put this Petrova woman in that category why?"

"New, lonely, shy, not comfortable with English. And let's face it, she's on the lower end of the socioeconomic scale, but she makes her living in a rather high-end neighborhood."

Wojciechowski sniffed. "And that makes her, what, lower class?"

"To many, yes. Certainly not to me. I was raised modestly, so I can identify. We were not poor, but we were a one-car family, no exotic vacations, you know."

"I sure do," the detective said. "We didn't do Disney and stuff like that either. Fact, I'm kinda like your housekeeper, on the

325

lower end of the pay scale, makin' my living working largely with seniors a lot better off than me."

"Oh, I imagine you're fairly compensated with such an important position," Nicole's mother said.

"I make more than I ever dreamed, but my salary would be petty cash to you folks."

"Having means was a culture shock to me," she said. "We're very blessed."

"Seems like you got used to it," Wojciechowski said. "And I only told you about me so you'd know I know where you're comin' from about Petrova. So how does that figure in to how you greet her?"

"Well, she's kinda dour, if you know what I mean. Don't know that I've ever seen her smile. So I always try to be cheery with her. I act like her showing up is the highlight of my day — which it sort of is. I can't deny it's nice to have someone clean for me, but it still makes me a little uncomfortable. I mean, I'm perfectly capable. Ben reminds me that since we can afford it and it gives her work, I shouldn't worry about it."

"And you shouldn't tidy up before she gets there," Ben said, smiling.

"So what would you have said to her when she got there yesterday morning?" Wojciechowski said.

Nicole's mother looked up, as if trying to recall. "Something about what a beautiful day it was. Said I'd been out enjoying the sunshine, something like that. She wouldn't look me in the eye. Just nodded, hung up her coat, and changed out of her boots into her work shoes."

"Tell me about her shoes."

Nicole's mom cocked her head, and Nicole could tell she was puzzling out why he wanted to know. "Nothing special. Kind of a scuffed white, sensible, thick soles, sturdy. Looked like they'd be real comfortable, especially in her line of work."

"Tie shoes?"

"Pardon?"

"Laces or Velcro or . . . ?"

"Yes, tie."

"And does she tie them when she puts them on and untie them to take them off, or does she just kick them off and force them on?"

Her mother hesitated. "Such a strange question."

"I got a reason for askin'."

"They're untied when she puts them on, and she ties them."

"Got it."

"Forgive me, Detective, but what does that tell you?"

Wojciechowski ran a hand through his hair. "Good question, and I'll tell you, but first, where does she do this, put her shoes on, I mean? She sit somewhere?"

"No, actually. I've got a little love seat just inside the door and always offer her a seat. But after she hangs her coat, she stands with her back to the wall — right next to that seat — takes her boots off, and puts her shoes on."

"Standing?"

"Yes."

"Ma'am, you've given me the idea that Ms. Petrova's a stocky gal. Thick and sturdy, like her shoes. Am I overstatin' it?"

"No, that's her."

"Kinda surprises me that a woman like that wouldn't sit to change shoes. But lemme ask you, and this is gonna sound weird, but does she lift her foot or does she reach all the way down to put her shoe on and tie it?"

"Can't say I've studied her that closely."

"Think about it."

"I'm getting a little sleepy, sir. Can't understand it, but I am."

"I won't keep you much longer, promise. Close your eyes and remind yourself of her changing into her shoes yesterday morning."

"If I close my eyes I'm afraid I'll doze off."

"No, you won't. We're almost through."

Nicole's mother closed her eyes, then quickly opened them again. "Teo presses her backside against the wall and bends from the waist to the floor."

"She doesn't lift one foot then the other?"

"No."

"Does she put on one shoe and then straighten up and then do the other or —"

"She does them both at the same time. Then she stands up straight."

"You see what I'm goin' for here, Virginia?"

"Not really."

"Look at me. I got a gut, right? It's okay, I can take it. Puttin' on my shoes is one a my least favorite things. We gotta wear these big ol' tie things, and I sit down when I put them on. It's hard for me to bend down there and do even one shoe, so I gotta straighten up and get my breath before I do the other. I wouldn't even dream of tryin' that standing up against the wall. You see how much harder that would be, bending all the way down from the waist?"

"Yes, I suppose."

"What I'm sayin' is, Teodora Petrova seems to be a very flexible woman for her

329

age and size. In fact, for anyone's age and size."

"She's a hard worker, sir. Bending, crouching, reaching. That has to help."

"I'm not concerned about *why* she's so flexible, just that she is. You're kinda petite and active —"

"For my age."

"Exactly, no offense. But you'd be no match for Teodora, would you?"

CHAPTER 66

Shinar

Terah stopped to talk with the dungeon warden in his small chamber on their way out and told Ikuppi to get the midwife into the chariot outside the rear of the palace. He was more concerned about Ikuppi than about Yadidatum when he finally joined them. The man's eyes were full and his lips forced together. "Have someone deliver a chariot to my home," Terah told him. "It need have only one horse, and I will return it when I come back to court in a few weeks."

Without a look or a word, Ikuppi headed to the paddock, spoke to the liveryman, and returned.

"Well?" Terah said.

Ikuppi faced him, silent.

"Did you arrange it?"

Ikuppi nodded and reboarded the chariot. The midwife sat where she had on the way, against the back wall.

"I must sit as well," Terah said, exhausted. Balancing on one leg and supporting himself with one arm would be too much for the trip back. He sat next to Yadidatum and leaned to keep weight off his bitten backside. He lay the crutch across his thighs and it reached the midwife. She glared at him.

"Today fortune has visited you," he said.

"How can you say that? That baby is dead already, isn't he?"

"He may be."

"That is an evil for which you will have to answer to the gods."

"My conscience is clear," Terah said. "This was their plan."

The midwife buried her face in her hands and shook her head. "And you call this fortune?"

"For you, yes! I have the authority to reduce your son's sentence. He will be freed one year from today, whole."

She peered at him. "You swear?"

"I do not swear to you, ma'am. You swear to me. For if there is one breakdown in today's design, losing a hand will be the least of your son's problems. I will have him executed."

She closed her eyes as the chariot began to roll. "I have no choice but to comply," she said. "But I will never forgive you."

"Forgive me? I spared your son!"

"What of Mutuum's son?"

"What you tell him and his wife will become the truth of that tragedy. You would do well to embrace it."

"I cannot do it, sir! Don't make me!"

"Don't be foolish! Ikuppi will vouch for the story, as will my injuries."

Outside the city, Ikuppi yanked the horses to a stop along a desolate stretch and turned to face Terah. "Have you forgotten that Mutuum has already seen you and knows how you were injured?"

"He has not seen my broken nose."

"And you think that will convince him?"

"You and the midwife must convince him. Your job and her son's life hang in the balance — not to mention her own."

"Cover yourself, Terah," Ikuppi said. "A chariot is coming."

It flew past, a king's guard driving two horses. "I told you I needed only one horse," Terah said.

"He will ride one of the horses back to the palace. Did you expect him to walk?"

"You take a sarcastic tone with me?"

"I will take whatever tone I wish. You have forced me beyond my own conscience. You can do no worse to me."

"I could have you imprisoned! Put to death!"

"I would be no worse off. I am already imprisoned by guilt."

"Let's just get on with this," Terah said. "I have told you both, after today I will demand no more than your silence. Breach that and you and your families will pay."

When finally Ikuppi pulled onto the road leading to the servants' quarters, Terah said, "Remember, real tears."

"Ours *will* be real," Ikuppi said. "What about your own?"

"I will weep tears of relief," Terah said.

"You had better pray the gods have mercy on you," the midwife said.

As the settlement came into view, Terah said, "Start lamenting now!"

Yadidatum began wailing, Ikuppi bawled, and Terah shouted, "Oh, woe is me! Woe is me!"

Mutuum and his wife, pale and frail, stood at the entrance to the dwellings. "What has happened?" he shouted. "Where's the baby?"

"What has taken so long?" his wife pleaded. "Where's my child?"

"Oh, woe!" Terah cried. "Woe!"

"The baby has been lost," the midwife said.

"What? What do you mean, lost?"

"Devoured, Mutuum!" Ikuppi said, tears streaming. "The same pack of dogs that attacked the master!"

Mutuum's wife collapsed, and he fell to his knees. "Where? How?"

"Near the house!" Terah said. "We were waiting for Belessunu to awaken when they ambushed us and made the horses rear."

"The child was thrown from my arms," Yadidatum said. "I am so sorry! I blame myself!"

"It's not your fault!" Ikuppi said. "The master leapt out to fight the dogs and was injured even more. There was nothing we could do. One of the horses broke free and kicked at the dogs, but oh, what they had already done to the baby!"

By now a crowd had formed and the tale had spread. It seemed the entire servant village keened as one. Terah struggled to his feet, and Ikuppi helped him out of the chariot. He raised his hand and spoke softly, oozing regret and resolve. "I pray the gods will give you peace, and I pledge generosity from my own storehouse. I will ask Ikuppi to make available to Mutuum and his wife any supplies or foodstuffs they require for the next year. Just know that we all grieve with you and mourn your loss."

Their neighbors encircled the grieving parents and embraced them. Yadidatum trudged from the chariot to her own home. "There is nothing more I can do here, Ikuppi," Terah said. "Take me home."

On the way he said, "After you leave me, take a week's worth of supplies and food to Mutuum and his wife. Then load your chariot and the one delivered to me with as much as you can fit."

"To take to them as well?"

"No, I will show you where to take it. And then nothing more will be required of you."

"I have nothing more to give anyway, Terah."

A cloud of dust ahead became the king's guard riding the extra horse bareback toward the palace. He and Ikuppi merely nodded to each other as he galloped past.

As the chariot rolled slowly toward Terah's place, Ikuppi turned and said, "I wish I had never told you of the king's scheme."

"You would have let him murder my son?"

"Terah! You have not only let him murder a son, you offered him up to the king as a token of worship."

"I did what I had to do."

"And I did what you forced me to," Ikuppi said, "to my eternal torment. You have stolen my soul."

336

CHAPTER 67

Eleven West

Nicole also wanted to know why the new housekeeper had returned to her parents' apartment late the previous afternoon. Obviously that raised questions Teodora would have to answer, but what if she had not been there to discover Nicole's mother on the floor?

Her mother's eyes appeared heavy. "Mom's had enough," Nicole said to Detective Wojciechowski.

"Okay, couple more questions and I'm gone. Virginia, do you remember letting Ms. Petrova in a second time yesterday?"

"I don't."

"What's the last thing you remember between when she was there in the morning and when you came to in the ambulance?"

"Let me think. She was cleaning Ben's den and the guest rooms, and I don't like to hover, so I was watching TV in the living

337

room. I like the true crime shows."

"You remember her leaving?"

Nicole's mother seemed to be struggling. "I don't."

"How about lunch? Remember that?"

"Hmm. I like something light, something I can microwave. Then I usually read after lunch and take a nap before *Wheel of Fortune* and *Jeopardy!* My guilty pleasures. But I must have some sort of amnesia, because I can't remember anything after Teo started on the back rooms."

"Any trouble with her? A falling out? Tension?"

"No," Nicole's mother said. "But she wouldn't have been there all day, would she?"

"That's what I need to know," Wojciechowski said. "CCTV will tell us a lot. But let's say she left and came back. She ever done that before, and why would she?"

Mom just lay shaking her head.

"What do you make of it?" Nicole's dad asked the detective.

"I got a theory, but I'm gonna have to see if it makes sense medically."

"What're you thinking?" Dad said.

"Well, thing is, I don't see a motive, but I'm wonderin' if Ms. Petrova mighta done

338

this in the morning and came back to check on the victim later."

"Teo?" Nicole's mother said. "No! Whatever for?"

"Nobody seems to have a motive, ma'am. You're a tough case 'cause you're one a those saints everybody loves. This woman certainly had the opportunity, and she's big and strong and agile enough . . ."

Nicole's mother turned her head away and took two deep breaths, closing her eyes. "No," she said groggily, "I can't — I can't make that make sense."

"I have to say, I can't either," Nicole said. "If she did do this, when she came back to check, why would she call 911? If she meant to kill Mom, why wouldn't she finish the job?"

Her mother raised a hand. "Don't even suggest such a thing!"

Wojciechowski shrugged. "If I knew, I'd be out of a job. I'll let your mother get some shut-eye, but I got to ask her about what my matron heard her say in the night last night."

"Don't remember much," her mother slurred, "much from . . . from the night."

"Officer Martinez says you told your daughter about a gray metal box with a picture in it."

Her mom lay still, breathing deeply.

"Ma'am?"

"C'mon, Detective," Nicole's dad began, but Wojciechowski stopped him with a look.

"You referred to it as a secret . . ."

"She's asleep," Nicole said.

"Not according to the monitors," Wojciechowski said. "No change in breathin' or pulse."

"You're a doctor now?"

"I'm just trying to clear you and your father."

That roused her mother. "Whatever . . . I said about that . . . nothing to do . . . with this."

"You said your husband didn't know you had seen it."

Nicole's mother just shook her head.

"You need to know, we've taken that box into evidence."

Mom's pulse and respiration increased, but she remained still, eyes closed.

"You've opened the box?" Nicole said.

Wojciechowski tucked away his notepad and picked up his coats. "It's locked, but our guys say they can easily break into it. Which we will do if your father wouldn't rather just open it for us."

"Gladly," her dad said. "Nothing to hide."

"Well, apparently you did."

"Not anymore."

"Want to come with me so we don't have to break into it?"

Her dad rose. "I'll come right back, Nic. I know you wanted to get going —"

"I can wait," she said. She'd hoped to find the box herself, but apparently that was never in the cards. Her parents' apartment was still off-limits, and there was nothing there for her anyway. At least not now.

CHAPTER 68

Ur

Terah could tell from Ikuppi's refusal to even incline his ear to him that pleading was futile. Over the rough half mile from the servant village to his estate, Terah had sat behind Ikuppi on the floor of the chariot and tried to reason with him.

"We have known each other far too long to allow this to come between us, my friend. You cared enough to warn me of the king's intent. You helped me save my child. Food-stuffs and supplies and a little physical labor are all I ask of you now. That and your silence."

Silence he got plenty of, as Ikuppi resolutely facing forward, not even turning his head.

"Just tell me you're still with me, Ikuppi — that you will remain loyal and true. That I can continue to count on you. I got you your job, and there's more I can do for you.

Just help me while I am infirm, and I can ensure the rest of your life will be one of ease. I will even beseech the king to remove you from the front lines, to allow you to only supervise men."

When Terah's compound came into view, he peered over the top of the chariot and struggled to his feet. "Who visits?" he said.

Even now Ikuppi did not answer. Besides the chariot, now with one horse, that had been delivered, a donkey cart sat under the entryway portico, tethered to a post. "A servants' wagon," Terah said. "Whoever is here was not in the servants' village to hear what's happened."

"To hear your lie, you mean," Ikuppi said flatly.

"Oh, now you can hear and speak! The attack on Mutuum's baby is your story too, remember."

"It's a story, but it was never mine."

"Do you not see there was no other way?" Terah said. "It was this or my son! The gods gave me the answer, provided the substitute!"

"So your servants are mere possessions with whom you may do as you wish. Terah, you sentenced that baby to death. You might as well have murdered him yourself."

"We don't know the disposition of the

child. For all we know —"

"Of course we do! The seers consider your firstborn a threat to the throne, and King Nimrod wanted him dead. They believe that was your child! What chance is there that he is still alive?"

"That is not our concern, Ikuppi. What the king does —"

"It is my concern! You are less than a man if you can rid it from your conscience. I cannot."

"See who is within. They must be told what has become of Mutuum's baby."

"Then you tell them," Ikuppi said. "My words have already condemned me. You can ask no more."

He helped Terah down from the chariot and walked him inside. There, two of Belessunu's servant girls tended to Abram. The boy was awake and alert, staring at the girl who held him, tiny hands reaching for her face.

"Your wife is sleeping, master," the other told him. "Oh no, sir! What has happened to you?"

"It is a sad and terrible story, my dear," Terah said. And he told the girls of the attack of the dogs and the death of the baby. Both went ashen.

"You two must get back to your quarters

to mourn with Mutuum and his wife," Terah said. "Meanwhile, we will take Abram to the palace. The king wishes to see him."

"That is an honor, sir," the servant said as she handed the baby to Ikuppi. "But he is too young to travel."

"You would have me refuse the king?"

"Oh, no, sir!"

When the girls had gone, Ikuppi slumped in a chair with the baby in his lap. "Does your lack of shame know no bounds?"

"Ikuppi, think! When the news spreads that I have bestowed my son upon the king, those girls will believe they saw him just before that took place. Otherwise, I would have no choice."

"But to kill them too, of course. Why not? They are merely property. Dispensable. Are you sure you have thought through this entire thing, Terah? When the truth comes out, as it always does, your life will be worthless. How then will you protect your family?"

CHAPTER 69

Vietnam

For six months, Red had kept Ben sane as the lunacy of war and bureaucracy created a living hell for everyone in Southeast Asia. She was twice his age and seemed to be one of few there for the right reasons. She told him her purpose in life was to get wounded soldiers patched up enough to endure the flight home. They called any plane — military or civilian — a Freedom Bird if it went from Vietnam to the States. These long, multistop flights back became the sole goal of most Cherries — new guys — from the moment they landed in the war zone.

Red was attractive but didn't give off any vibe of availability — even to soldiers her own age. "Medical care or friendship is all I offer," she'd say. "There's plenty of young nurses here to fall in love with."

Ben just enjoyed getting to know her and being able to talk through what he could not look away from every day. "Will it always affect me this way?"

"I hope so," Red said. "You don't want to take this in stride, do you?"

"What I want is to quit seeing it even when I shut my eyes."

"Trouble sleeping?"

" 'Course! We must see more than even the guys on the front lines."

"Oh, no question. You can't let it affect your work, but don't expect it to become the norm. Just because you see the docs and us nurses acting like these kids' injuries are nothing we haven't seen before, don't think we wouldn't rather cover our eyes and ears and run away too. But then where would these guys be? As long as they're breathing, we want 'em believing we're gonna get them home."

Ben pressed his lips together as emotion choked him. "I just held a kid's hand while he stared at me, pleading with his eyes. But I was as scared as he was. Everything inside him, from his sternum to his navel, looked obliterated. I told him we had just the surgeon for him. I lied to his face, Red! He didn't need a doc. He needed a miracle. And he didn't get it."

Red pressed a hand over Ben's and whispered, "When I'm home on leave, people

347

tell me my work must be so rewarding. I just say something about the privilege. And it *is* a privilege. But as you're finding out, there's little reward."

"And sure no glamour."

Red nodded. "The gung ho guys sober up quick if they catch duty here."

Venturing into town with Red and her friends took Ben's mind off the carnage briefly. They would head out at the end of their shifts, the nurses always accompanied by men with weapons — or at least boys with weapons. Something about being with Red made Ben feel more like a boy than a man. In his eyes she was a no-nonsense woman of the world. She knew how to have fun but was always in control, and cautious. The first time she'd invited him along, she told him, "In town imagine yourself inside a zoo. Any doe-eyed animal, no matter how big or small or seemingly passive, can be wild after all. And you become prey."

"You're calling the nationals animals?"

"Of course not. I've befriended many of them, and the US is here to protect them. But can you tell a South Vietnamese from a VC? Neither can I. I've treated lots of people who approached a smiling child or a doddering grandma, not expecting to be torn in half."

Ben winced. That was something he hoped to put out of his mind, but if Red intended to remind him he was never really on his own time, she succeeded.

The first several times he went along on a visit to town, the small contingent from the hospital just strolled around, but the others' wariness was not lost on Ben. It seemed they largely ignored the nationals, avoiding their curious glances — he assumed to keep from appearing confrontational. "Occasionally they cause a deliberate distraction," Red said. "Keep a hand on your wallet."

"I'll keep a hand right here," Ben said, cradling his M14.

"That works too," she said.

One evening in town Red led Ben and four of her other coworkers to a restaurant where they were directed to a ridiculously small table. Red assured Ben it would be fine. A waitress passed out menus and stood waiting. Ben felt pressured to quickly scan the menu, but Red said, "Take your time. She's in no hurry."

The six of them decided on a local rice dish they said was common to South Vietnam, but it was exotic to Ben. Red told him it would consist of broken rice with grilled, marinated thick-cut pork and fresh vegetables. She ordered in Vietnamese, and Ben soon discovered why they didn't need more table space. No place settings. They each used chopsticks to eat from a small rice bowl in their hand, to which they added the main dish from a serving bowl on the table. Their beer came with ice, which Red had to assure Ben was safe too.

When their shifts jibed again, Ben and Red and a couple of other nurses headed to town once more. The other three visited a large, multi-booth market under what seemed an acre-long canopy. Ben opted to wait outside. Crowded, noisy, open-air markets reminded him too much of the mayhem at the hospital.

Despite brandishing an M14 and towering over the nationals, Ben felt strangely vulnerable as he sat people watching. Still, his eyes grew heavy and he nearly dozed off in the blistering heat. He forced himself to stay alert. No telling what might happen if someone saw him sleeping, weapon at his side. The last thing he wanted was to send someone, or be sent himself, to the hospital he was trying to avoid.

When Ben noticed commotion at the busy intersection fifteen feet from his bench, he recalled one of Red's warnings. "Keep a hand on your wallet."

This didn't look anything like a manufactured distraction. A beautiful Vietnamese girl with lustrous ebony hair to her waist — she could have been as young as fifteen — had been approached by a young Vietnamese man, maybe in his late teens. He smiled and gestured, but she shook her head.

The girl was tiny and small-boned, with delicate features and nearly translucent skin — except where the sun had bronzed her prominent cheekbones. She attempted to keep walking and the guy stepped in front of her. Ben couldn't read her look. Scared? Puzzled? Or were these just friends bantering? She tried again to move around the boy and he moved again to block her.

Ben rose.

The girl turned around and headed back the way she had come, but the boy overtook her and blocked her again.

"Hey!" Ben shouted. "Leave her alone!"

Both quickly looked his way, and she was clearly terrified. But of him or the guy?

"Not your business!" the boy said.

"It is now," Ben said, approaching.

The boy stepped directly in front of him, glaring. "Nothing to do with you, GI. What're you gonna do?"

"Glad you understand English, son. Let her go."

"Just go back to your bench."

Ben waved her on, and she seemed to thank him with her eyes. She touched his arm as she passed and whispered, "Thank you, sir."

The boy started to follow her, but Ben stepped into his path. "One more step and you'll regret it."

"You gonna shoot me, GI?"

"I don't need a bullet to stop you."

"Then what you gonna do, big man?"

"Take a step and find out."

The teen sneered at Ben, waved him off, and walked the other way, giving him one last look and crossing his fingers at him. What meant good luck in America was this kid's way of giving Ben the finger.

Ben sat back down feeling proud of himself, until he imagined bragging about this to Red and her friends. The tiny Asian had been no real threat, so maybe he ought to change his account to include two adult thugs. That made him smile. And when he did tell the others, he told the truth and they all laughed. "Our hero," Red said. "Don't we all just feel so much safer in his presence now?"

About two weeks later, the little entourage returned to the same restaurant where Ben had been introduced to the iced beer. He sat directly across from Red and stared past her when she said, "Where are you right now, soldier?"

He had to rerack his brain to register what she had asked. "Wait, what? I'm in Nam. What do you mean?"

"Missed you there for a second," she said, a tease in her tone. "Thought you'd left us and were maybe, I don't know, in love?"

"Oh, her?" he said and felt his cheeks flush. "I could swear she was the girl I rescued in front of the market a couple of weeks ago. But she's too young to be working here."

"Anybody working here has to at least be of age," Red said, looking behind her. "That girl's the one? Are you sure?"

"Absolutely," Ben said. "But how old does she look to you?"

"They all look younger than they are. But she's waited on me before. Been here a while. You notice she's in mourning, right?"

"How do you know?"

"Ben, don't stare, but with a face like hers, it's easy to miss she's the only server here in drab colors."

"Hmph, you're right."

"They officially mourn for seven weeks here, but they won't wear bright colors for two years. And that little black patch on her

353

blouse — sometimes those are white — indicates she's lost an immediate family member."

"Wonder who?" Ben said, his eyes still following the young woman.

"Oh, that'd be a good opening line," Red said. "See how far you get with that."

"I'd at least like to greet her."

"Look around, Ben. Take a number and wait your turn."

Soldiers of all ages, ranks, and ethnicities seemed to surreptitiously watch her.

Ben had found her stunning on the street, but when she approached the table, she left him nearly speechless. *"Chào mo. i nguòi,"* she said. He'd been in the country long enough to know that meant "Hello, everyone."

"Hi," Ben managed with a small wave. "Do you remem—"

"It's you!" she said. "I was so hoping to run into you again so I could thank you one more time."

"You speak such good English," Ben blurted, feeling klutzy.

She smiled. "My father taught me from a very young age. It is he who I mourn."

"Sorry for your loss," Red said.

"Thank you. Cancer took him two years ago next week."

"So you're about to burn your mourning clothes."

"Yes!"

"What's that about?" Ben said.

"Let's not get her in trouble for talking while she's working," Red said. "I'll tell you later." She turned back to the waitress. "But may we know your name?"

"Bian Win," she said. "That's how it sounds to you, anyway. *Win* is spelled N-g-u-y-e-n."

"Bian Win," Ben said.

"Yes, but if we are to be friends, you must call me Charm."

"Charm Win. You look too young to be working."

"Oh, I like to look young," she said. "But I am twenty."

Ben could hardly believe it. The beauty he had guessed was a young teen was a year older than he was.

When Charm had taken their orders, the others teased Ben. "She likes you!"

"Nah."

"It's obvious! She lights up when she talks to you."

"Stop. And what's with the clothes-burning thing?"

Red said, "A tradition here is that they wear the same clothes they wore to the funeral for memorial services every seven days for the first forty-nine days. Then they have another memorial on the one hundredth day, the first year anniversary, and the second. Then they burn those clothes and the extended mourning period is over."

"And isn't it true," one of the other nurses said, "that they don't marry while in mourning?"

"That's right. Keep that in mind, Ben."

"Yeah," he said. "Why don't we jump light-years ahead of ourselves. She's probably got guys all over the place."

CHAPTER 70

Ur

Terah sat in the great room tenderly supporting Abram in his lap, the newborn softly clicking his tongue and emitting sighs in his sleep. Terah found himself conflicted, perplexed at how his heart and soul could have callously sentenced one man's son to certain death and an hour later feel overwhelmed with such boundless love for his own son. In the same day he had also threatened the lives of the midwife and her grown son, forced his friend on the king's guard to violate his own conscience and moral code — under a threat to his life and the lives of his family — and was even willing to kill his wife's servant girls if they interfered with his master plan.

But had that idea not come directly to him from the gods themselves? Even the shattered fragments of the idols he had fashioned to represent them seemed to have spoken deeply to his inner being. If that required sacrificing servants or subordinates and even their families, well, the result was all that mattered. If his son was destined to be an "exalted father," whatever Terah had to do to ensure that was the right course.

His problem was separating what he was sure was of the gods and what might have been an intrusion by the one Belessunu believed was the one true God. Which god had led him to a haven where he had been able to avoid death at the fangs of the wild dogs? Which had warned him to worship no other gods? Which had suggested the prophetic name for his son? Terah couldn't shake the feeling that this inscrutable tenderness and love for Abram had salved his conscience to where anything that served it seemed justifiable.

But was it? Or was Ikuppi right, that Terah had abandoned his senses and any vestige of his scruples?

Terah could barely rise and get around with his crutch when not holding the baby, so unless he found a way to safely lay the boy down, he was stuck where he was. He had been foolhardy in sending Ikuppi to do his bidding, leaving him alone with the baby.

Ikuppi returned after a couple of hours, having delivered the food and supplies to

Mutuum and his wife. The king's guard looked miserable, poking his head in the door and saying he had returned to the storehouse and filled his chariot with what Terah had requested. "I'll now fill the other, but I need to know where you want all these goods."

"I'll tell you upon your return, friend, but first may I prevail upon you to take Abram back to Belessunu's side?" Terah grew angry at Ikuppi's hesitation. "I asked only out of courtesy. Just do it."

"Terah, as I have tried to make clear, if you retain any shred of respect for me, you'll refrain from referring to me as your friend. I know well that you consider me your servant, not a colleague, and so I am obligated to merely obey."

"Then do so, Ikuppi! I am tired of your haranguing about this. If you cannot recognize my kindnesses to you —"

"Kindnesses!" the guard said, reaching to take the child. "You merely indebted me for such a time as this."

"Nonsense! Only a friend would have warned me about the king's designs on my son."

"Had I only known what that would generate in your heart!"

"Just be about your business, Ikuppi."

The guard took the baby and appeared to soften. "He does seem a peaceful child. I pray you won't spoil that in him."

Terah just motioned him toward the bedchamber. Belessunu roused as he tiptoed in. "Ikuppi," she said, "where are my servant girls, and Terah?"

"I am here!" Terah called out, hoping to thwart any comments from Ikuppi. "I will join you soon."

Ikuppi emerged, his countenance gloomy, as if he could barely stand to look at Terah. "Just tell me what to do with my cargo," he said. "Let me finish this awful day."

"This is a glorious day!" Terah said. "Abram has been spared and —"

Ikuppi leaned forward and whispered, "You have sentenced your family to a living dungeon. When it reaches Nimrod that the real Amraphel lives and is named Abram, what will you do then, living where you live, doing what you do for the king?"

"That's none of your concern, friend, as your assignment is silence. If the king ever becomes aware, someone is going to die, and it's not going to be me."

"I pledge no further confidence, Terah. I must know the end of your plan."

CHAPTER 71

Detective George Wojciechowski pointed to a chair at a desk in the middle of the common area of the Senior Services and Domestic Violence Unit, where Ben felt conspicuous under the glare of overhead lights. Wojciechowski set the gray metal box before him, scooting into place next to him in a rolling chair.

"We can't do this in private?" Ben said.

"Nobody here knows or cares what we're doin', Doc. What're you afraid of?"

Ben shrugged. "It's just private is all."

Typically Ben retrieved the box every year or two from a spot near the ceiling in the dim lit privacy of his walk-in closet. Reviewing its contents rarely took more than five minutes — just long enough to remind himself of a former life. He couldn't say this was evidence of a self he really knew — just one he remembered from an extended season of anger — and young love. Opening the box in front of anyone else, let alone in a room with plainclothes and uniformed officers nearby and a detective at his elbow, was new to him.

Ben had never fully understood why he kept these talismans from the 1970s. After all, those were his pre-Ginny and, even more importantly, pre-Yeshua years. At times he had tried to puzzle out what made him so livid, so restless, so committed not to just escaping a lifestyle but to also turning his back on everything and everyone he should have loved.

Something drew him to that box every so often, sometimes to appreciate the colossal difference between his old and new man, but always to breathe a heartfelt thanks to Yahweh for the gift of his soulmate. During the early years of his new life, Ben was spurred by the keepsakes to repent of how hurtful he'd been toward his parents. A marine psychologist he had initially distrusted because he was just that — apparently not good enough for private practice — suggested a reason for his regret. Back in the States and slowly recovering from multiple surgeries to render his ravaged hand at least serviceable, the Jarhead Shrink

— as Ben referred to him — said he may harbor repressed guilt over the falling-out with his parents.

"It's not unusual for older teenagers to grow frustrated and long for their freedom and independence," the counselor had said. "Dad and Mom represent the past, traditional values, outdated ideas. The mistake comes when an adolescent rejects them in entirety rather than just picking and choosing his own way and becoming his own person. You turned your back on everything, fled them, fled what they stood for — good and bad — and even fled the country. You admit you weren't even fighting out of any sense of loyalty or patriotism. Ben Berman became the poster boy for the cliché of throwing out the baby with the bathwater."

Ben had to admit that resonated with him, and it didn't entirely surprise him to discover the man wasn't "just a Jarhead Shrink." He was a partner in a huge counseling clinic and served wounded veterans pro bono on his own time. He hadn't even suggested what Ben should do with his angst over the relationship with his parents. He simply cited possible reasons for it and left it to Ben to act upon, or not.

When his mother wrote to ask whether she and his father would be welcome to visit him, Ben immediately responded that he would appreciate that very much. They arrived with tentative smiles — his father literally with hat in hand — and approached hesitantly. Ben spread his arms wide, his left hand wrapped big as a boxing glove. He intended a toothy grin, but tears cascaded as they embraced.

"I need to talk to you," Ben said, voice thick.

"We're here," his father said.

"I missed you. I love you. And I'm sorry."

"It doesn't feel heavy enough to hold a weapon," Wojciechowski said. "What'll we find inside?"

"A few letters," Ben said. "A Purple Heart . . . and the photograph."

"Funny, your wife mentioned only the picture."

"None of the rest of it would have surprised her. Still can't believe she saw it. She doesn't know the combination, so I must have forgotten to spin the dial or put it back. Wonder how long ago this was."

"Glad we didn't hafta bust into it."

"It's irrelevant, you know. I mean, I wish she hadn't seen it, but it's not like some major deal that would make me want to hurt her."

Wojciechowski sat staring at Ben, as if he was done talking about it.

Ben felt every eye in the place on him, but a quick peek told him not one other person in the room showed any interest in him or their boss. He pulled the box closer and held it in place with the stub of his left hand — all four fingers gone down to the large knuckles. Only his thumb remained intact.

Ben rotated the dial to the right to 03, then left to 01, and finally right again to 54. When he slid the release lever, it seemed the click reverberated throughout the room. He was sure that would draw attention, but another glance proved him wrong again. Everyone else appeared lost in their own files or phone calls.

Ben raised the lid to reveal three envelopes containing letters — one from a buddy in his marine unit who had known a nurse friend of his, another from his commander, and the last from a bureaucrat documenting his Purple Heart. The medal itself had slid to the bottom of the shallow box.

His father had been so proud of that. "We prayed for you every day you were overseas," he said. "And you know we're not even sure there's a god!"

"I might be sure now," his mother said. "Honored for you, yes, but so relieved it was not presented posthumously."

His father chuckled. "For so long, when people asked after you, we apologized for where you were. Sorry to tell you that, but no one could understand. But when we learned you were on your way home with a Purple Heart, no more apologizing. What's our son doing these days? Coming home a war hero!"

Ben never felt like a hero, and Nam vets were not exactly welcomed back as such. But he had earned that Purple Heart.

To one side of the box, facedown atop everything else, lay the two-by-three-inch photograph. Wojciechowski handed Ben elongated tweezers with tiny rubber tips. "We may have to fingerprint that."

"Seriously? It'll have only mine and maybe Ginny's. Far as I know, no one else has been in this box."

"Humor me."

Ben gently lifted the picture by one corner with the tweezers and studied the penciled inscription on the back. Wojciechowski leaned close. "You mind?" he said.

Ben shrugged. "Somebody, probably my friend Red, told me to write very gently to keep from leaving an impression on the front."

"Really faint," Wojciechowski said. "What's it say?"

"Charm, 1972."

"That's her name?"

"It's what she asked me to call her," Ben said. "It fit. Her real name was Bian Nguyen." Wojciechowski reached for his notepad. "C'mon, don't write that down. This was more than forty-five years ago. I don't even know if she's still alive."

He turned the photo over to reveal a color image — remarkably unfaded for its age but also brittle.

"Wow," Wojciechowski said, "that's some face. Beautiful, but she doesn't look more'n fourteen, fifteen at most."

"Twenty when I shot this. A year older than me."

Wojciechowski elbowed Ben. "That's what she told ya, eh? Of age?"

Ben looked down. "This was my first love, not some streetwalker. A waitress who wanted to be a teacher."

"Gotcha. Just teasin'. But your wife doesn't know about her?"

Ben shook his head. "Stupid, I know. Ginny told me about previous boyfriends. I told her about a couple of girls from high school and said I'd rather not talk about any after that."

"So she knew there were some?"

"She knew I was a typical soldier. But that wasn't who she was marrying. As long as I didn't bring any diseases into the marriage, she wasn't the type who wanted to hear about recreational stuff."

"But Bian, Charm, was no working girl. So this wasn't just recreation."

"No, she was not. But I just couldn't bring myself to tell Ginny about her. Not sure why."

" 'Course you know why, Doc. You still had a thing for her. Maybe you still do."

"I haven't seen her since January 26 of '73."

"But you remember the exact date. You kept up with her, right? Wrote her? Felt conflicted, maybe guilty?"

Ben nodded. "Conflicted and guilty for sure, but not why you'd think."

"Talk to me, Ben."

"I haven't told Ginny yet, but I have to tell you?"

"You wanna tell me, I can see it all over you. And if it helps clear you, maybe you still don't need to tell your wife."

"Oh, I need to tell her. That's clear. If she kept a picture of a man I didn't recognize, I'd want to know."

"So she finds out you've kept up with this

woman —"

"I didn't mean to imply that. Charm was my first true love. But when I was medevacked home, I treated her shabbily."

"How so?"

"Tucked her picture into my little box and relegated her to my former life. Never wrote, never called."

"She write you?"

Ben shook his head. "Zero contact."

CHAPTER 72

Ur

Terah put a finger to his lips and motioned Ikuppi close, explaining the location of the deep, multi-chambered cave he had discovered. "When you have filled the smaller chariot, I need both of them unloaded there. I only wish I could help. I might be able to in a few days, but this cannot wait, for obvious reasons."

"That is your grand scheme?" Ikuppi said. "You intend to live there the rest of your days?"

"Not I! Belessunu and the boy. The story will go that when she learned of my sacrificing our son to the king, she abandoned me and fled to her homeland."

"And you expect me to transport her and the baby to the cave."

"You know I am unable, at least for now."

"Terah, you saw today the danger of carrying a newborn about. And your wife is certainly in no condition to travel."

"We have no choice! You must be careful, but I cannot risk their being found."

"Getting to the storehouse again, then two runs to your cave with the supplies, will consume the rest of the daylight hours. I won't be able to pick up Belessunu and the baby until much later."

"Taking them after dark is best anyway, Ikuppi, and I will be in your debt."

Ikuppi closed his eyes and backed against the wall by the door. "You have no idea what you owe me. You have made of me a liar, and I am as guilty as you are for the murder of that innocent child."

Terah whispered hoarsely, "We have injured no one!"

"And you believe that exonerates you . . ."

"I will sleep well tonight, my friend, for you have helped spare my family."

"Terah, you have taken leave of your senses."

"I will be sure Belessunu and Abram will be ready by sundown."

"This is lunacy."

"I can forgive your insolence, Ikuppi, as long as I can count on you."

"Until day's end, and then I am finished with you forever."

"And solemnly sworn to secrecy . . ."

371

"Only for the sake of mother and child. I don't care what happens to you."

"I know you don't mean that, Ikuppi, but whatever happens to me had better not be a result of your loose tongue."

"Of that you can be sure. I will remain silent as the dead."

CHAPTER 73

Manhattan

Nicole's father looked ashen when he returned to Eleven West. He would not meet her eyes. "Everything go okay?" she said.

He nodded and busied himself with her mother. He ran a finger across her forehead to keep hair away from her scab, then gently tugged at her bedding.

"She's fine, Dad. You need to talk?"

"Eventually," he said, still looking away. "I know you need to go."

"I can wait," she said.

"No, it's all right. There'll be time. You coming back to spend the night?"

"I can. You need me to?"

He shrugged. "Maybe. I mean, I'll be here. We can talk then."

"We can talk now, Dad, if you need —"

"No, later."

"I'm just going to run home and try to get some work done on the Saudi thing, force myself to open that letter, you know."

Her dad appeared lost in thought.

"Okay?" she said.

"Hmm? Yeah, sure. You go. Have Abigail get you a car."

"It's Saturday, Dad. I'll get a cab."

"She won't mind," he said. "Pretty sure she's in town."

"Dad! She doesn't like doing stuff for me when she's working, let alone when she's off."

"Oh, I'm sure that's not true."

"Last time I asked her to get me a car she said it was cheaper to Uber. Well, I know that."

She could tell she'd lost him again and chastised herself for rehashing her petty problems with his assistant.

"She's just watching out for the bottom line," he said absently.

Always defending her.

"She told me to do whatever I wanted, 'because you always do.'"

"She didn't say that," her dad said.

"What, I made it up?"

"She didn't mean it, not the way it sounds."

Dad could live in his fantasy world. It wasn't that big a deal.

■ ■ ■

"How's Ginny doin'?" Freddie asked when Nicole emerged from the cab at her building. "No bag, so I expect she's still there and you'll be heading back."

Nicole didn't want to get into the attack, so she just updated him on her mother's condition.

"Worse than they expected, huh?" he said. "Too bad. Give her my best. And you're gonna need a ride again when?"

"Couple of hours. I'll call you a few minutes ahead."

On her way up, it hit Nicole. Today was Shabbat! As a Messianic Jew, she did not follow sabbath laws, but the little congregation she and her parents attended did meet on Saturdays. She called to tell them the Bermans would not be there and ask for prayer, but the call went to voice mail. No surprise, the small staff had to be preparing for the service.

As soon as she reached her apartment, Nicole sat, still in her coat, and sliced open the one dreaded piece of mail. She hadn't been this nervous since awaiting the judgment of her thesis leading to her D. Habil. from Universität Berlin five years before.

The doctorate of habilitation was a necessary addition to her PhD from Columbia six years before that, as only with a D. Habil. did she qualify to lead a dig.

Fingers shaking, she found only a single sheet of stationery. Nicole anticipated a denial, pending her fulfillment of a list of requirements. But as she unfolded the page, she could only stare.

دكتور نيكول بيرمان: لقد حان الوقت لمشاهدة ظهرك.

She let the page drop as if it were on fire, dug through her handbag for Detective Wojciechowski's card, and punched in his number.

"Whoa! Slow down there, Dr. Berman," he said. "What's it say?"

"It's just one line in Arabic. 'Dr. Nicole Berman: The time has come to watch your own back.' "

"That's it?"

"Yes, sir, and no signature . . . Detective?"

"Thinking. Gimme a sec."

"Should I be scared? Because I am."

"Listen, don't touch the letter or the envelope again. It's already gonna have your prints on it, and the mailman's."

"Woman's."

"You know her?"

"Sure."

"How's your mail delivered? She bring it right to your door?"

"No, she has a thing she uses to pop open all the boxes in a wall unit in the lobby. She puts everything that fits in there, and bigger stuff she leaves with the front desk."

"Can you see a postmark? Let's make sure this came from overseas."

Nicole squinted. "Looks legit."

"And you know enough about the Middle East to know —"

"C'mon, Detective, I know you know I do."

"So what's it look like?"

"Blue stamped circle with Arabic writing at the top, the date in the middle — a day after the date on the letter. Then at the bottom of the circle, in black, it says, 'Riyadh Post, Saudi Post Corporation.' "

"Okay, hold tight, and remember, don't touch it any more. I'm on my way, and I might bring a techie."

"A techie?"

"A CSI. Don't answer the door to anyone else, and let your downstairs people know we're comin'."

CHAPTER 74

Ur

Terah sat with his crutch in his lap, trying to catch his breath after the conversation with Ikuppi. The king's guard drove the single-horse chariot away, and when Terah could no longer hear it, he gathered his strength and plotted his path to the bedroom. "I am coming to you, Belessunu," he said.

"I would come to you if I were able," she said.

"Save your strength. You'll need it."

"Whatever for, Terah?"

"Give me a moment."

Light-headed, Terah hesitated after rising. He could not afford another fall. On a day when he should have simply laid low to try to recover, he had been up and down and on his knees and outside and back in. Not to mention riding to both his livestock pen a hundred yards one way and the palace more than a mile the other. The stop at the servants' quarters had been nearly as exhausting as his performance at the king's court and in the dungeon.

He pushed aside the drapery in the doorway of the bedchamber and waited again. Belessunu lay on her back with Abram asleep on her chest. She peered over the boy's head. "What have you been doing all day, husband?"

"Oh, to even begin to tell you would take another whole day."

"Well, come and sit, but don't wake the baby."

Sitting on the low mat was the most difficult maneuver of all. It was one thing to make his way about the house, and with help he had been able to climb into the chariot and either stand or sit. But to lower himself nearly to the floor with no support but the crutch, that had already proven something altogether different.

Belessunu pulled her feet to one side to make room for him, but when Terah began to bend, his hands moving down the crutch an inch at a time, his weight shifted and he was unable to catch himself. "Here I come!" he said, keeping a death grip on the wood as his backside headed too quickly to the mat. At the last instant he knew he had to land on his uninjured side or the pain would make him cry out.

Terah fought to keep from slamming down while also shifting to take the brunt of the drop on his good side. He nearly accomplished it, but momentum carried him beyond his balancing point and onto his back he went, swollen feet leaving the floor and following him over. With his sandaled feet in the air, he pushed with the back of his head to try to right himself, but his legs went vertical and the hem of his tunic dropped to his waist, exposing him from his toes to his loincloth.

The crutch had lost purchase with the floor and went tumbling as Terah let out a huge, "Oomph!" and quickly brought his feet back down, trying to cover himself again.

"Oh, no, husband!" Belessunu chortled, covering her laugh with one hand and steadying Abram with the other.

Her chuckling made Terah do the same, and he lay there with his face next to her feet as their laughing shook the mat. The baby coughed and squeaked, which made them giggle all the more. "I must sit up," Terah said. "I can't breathe!"

He planted both palms at his side and rocked, trying to raise himself. But his bad shoulder added nothing to the effort. Beles-sunu pressed a foot under his shoulders, to no effect. Finally Terah was able to roll himself up on his side so he could face her.

"If the boy can sleep through this," she said, "he could become a warrior."

Terah waited until he was able to breathe evenly and rested his head in his hand, his good elbow planted on the mat. "I have no idea how I will ever get up," he said. And they laughed some more.

"Is Ikuppi returning?"

"Yes, but not for some time. If I have to wait, I'll wait, but I was hoping for some food soon."

"Maybe I can get up in a while," she said.

"No, no, as I told you, all in good time. You will need your strength later."

"For what?"

Terah let his head fall back onto the mat and stared at the ceiling. "The king wants to see our son."

"Tonight? Are you mad?"

"Of course not."

"And you must not allow it anyway, Terah."

"Absolutely not. But when I do not comply, he will come looking for the boy."

"We must flee long before that."

"That's what I am saying. But, Belessunu,

I need to tell you what I have done."

"What you have done?"

"He believes he has already seen Abram, though I told him we had named the baby Amraphel."

"I'm confused. You named the boy after the king, and the king believes what? Make me understand, Terah."

CHAPTER 75

Manhattan

Nicole's intercom crackled. "NYPD on their way up, ma'am."

The Saudi letter repelled her as if it had its own malevolent aura. She paced near the door until someone knocked and she saw Wojciechowski through the peephole. A middle-aged Indian with a camera around his neck and carrying an oversized metal briefcase followed the detective in.

"Detective Pranav somethin' or other," Wojciechowski said. "Dr. Nicole Berman, daughter of the vic. Get your explanation outta the way so you can get to work."

The techie delicately laid his case down and presented Nicole his card, which identified him as Detective Third Grade Pranav Chakrabarti, a forensic technician with the NYPD Crime Scene Unit. "We are known as CSUs," he said formally, "not CSIs, as Detective Wojciechowski insists on referring to us. And, as you can see, I learned to pronounce his difficult name, despite his unwillingness to pronounce mine."

Nicole read it perfectly, and he beamed.

"Well, 'scuse me for not havin' a doctorate," Wojciechowski said. "Can we get to this now, Pranav?"

The CSU set up on the table a small tripod for his camera as well as a formation of LCD lights. He quizzed Nicole about how much she had handled the letter and envelope.

"I'm going to photograph them, dust them for prints, and then bag and take them to the lab for more sophisticated testing. Detective Wojciechowski tells me he's trying to see your mail carrier this evening. Fortunately you and your father — and any US postal worker — have your prints in databases to which we have access. We need to determine which post offices this came through to eliminate their personnel and then see if we can lift any other prints."

Chakrabarti went quiet as he worked, and Nicole pulled Wojciechowski aside. "Does this take the focus off my father and me?"

"Sure could be a game changer, assumin' one of you didn't send it yourself."

Nicole puffed. "You just won't be convinced, will you?"

"Lemme ask you this. What if we found your dad's fingerprints on that letter?"

She shook her head. "I can't even invent a response."

"Welcome to my world, Doc. This is the kinda stuff I have to consider every day."

"You're working too hard." Secretly, Nicole was glad he did. The threat had so rattled her she didn't even want to talk about it. "Do you usually work weekends?"

"I wouldn't know what a weekend was," Wojciechowski said. "You think crime takes days off?"

"You love it, is that it?"

That seemed to stop him. "Love it? Well, I sure don't do this for the cash."

"Why then?"

"I'm good at it."

"I can tell," Nicole said. "But that doesn't answer why."

"You really wanna know? Truth is, I'm a justice freak. And much as people want you to believe that all the idealism is drummed out of a cop by the time he's been on the job a coupla years, there's still a lot of us in this for the right reasons."

"What made you that way?"

Wojciechowski chuckled. "Now who won't get off the case? You'd make a good cop."

"You're evading the question, George." In

truth, Nicole was desperate to talk about anything but her own trauma.

"Oh, good one," he said. "I told you when we met that you could call me George, but you don't until you wanna get personal."

"Guilty. So why?"

CHAPTER 76

Ur

Belessunu gingerly repositioned herself so she could put the baby down beside her. She struggled to sit up, her feet spread on the floor, and she held her face in her hands.

"Say something, wife," Terah said. "Please. I did this to save our son."

"I cannot believe you are telling me this. I knew you had abandoned the one true God, but I would not have imagined you were capable of such treachery."

"But I told you, the gods gave me this plan —"

"I do not want to hear that again, Terah! You have not saved this family. You have cursed us."

Her shoulders heaved. "Mutuum and his wife . . . ! How could you do this to them? And Yadidatum! And Ikuppi? To us, Terah! There is so much evil here —"

"Don't cry, Belessunu! Can't you see I

387

had no choice? We can argue about this all night, but I must get you to the cave . . ."

She held up a hand and whispered, "The Lord speaks . . ."

"Oh no."

Belessunu spoke in the flat drone she had used the night before. *"You will be oppressed, and a child shall be preferred over you. Woe to you, wicked one. I shall be hostile with you, for you will reap what you have sown. A woman will rule you."*

Terah became desperate to flee her presence, this presence, but he could not rise.

" 'How dare you crush and grind the faces of servants?' says the Lord your God."

"I reject these admonitions!" Terah wailed, then quieted himself, hoping not to wake the baby.

"Oh, descendant of Noah, why do you not walk with Me in the light of the Lord? You have forsaken the truth for the fables of soothsayers . . ."

"Nimrod's stargazers?" Terah whined.

"Your house may be full of silver and gold, and there may be no end to your treasure, your horses, your chariots. But it is also full of idols. You worship the work of your own hands."

"Pray He spares me, Belessunu, forgives me!"

"You do well to enter into the rock . . ."

"You see, wife? Perhaps it was He who led me to the cave."

". . . and hide in the dust from My terror."

"Oh, Belessunu, I entreat you pray He has mercy on me!"

But she continued, *"The lofty man shall be humbled, and I alone shall be exalted."*

"If I exalt You," Terah groaned, "oh God of my ancestors, will You pardon me?"

"The day of the Lord of hosts shall come upon the proud and lofty . . ."

"But I am not! I humble myself before You . . ."

"You shall be brought low."

Terah grabbed his crutch and struggled to rise, every wound and sore and aching joint pleading for relief. He had to get away from this God. But even as he hobbled out of the bedroom, he could not block out Belessunu's recitation.

"I alone will be exalted, and your idols shall I abolish."

Terah was in the great room now, chastising himself for having not understood that it was this one true God who had already shaken the ground beneath him and warned him. And yet still he was tempted to fall on his face before the remains of his idols.

Belessunu continued, *"In that day you will*

389

cast away your idols of silver and gold, which you made for yourself to worship . . ."

"I will cast them away now!" Terah sobbed. "Oh, I am undone!"

"Terah," Belessunu called in her own voice.

"Spare me, wife!"

"The Lord God wants me to sever myself from you, because, He asks, of what account are you?"

"I am but a man! Sinful and broken! What can I do?"

She spoke for the Lord again: *"You have rebelled against Me, your creator. Alas, sinful man, laden with iniquity, evildoer, corrupt! You will revolt again, for you are sick and your heart is weak. You are unsound from the sole of your foot to your head. Wounds and bruises and sores condemn you. I cannot endure iniquity. When you spread your hands, I will hide from you. Though you pray, I will not hear. Your hands are stained with the blood of the innocent."*

CHAPTER 77

Manhattan

"You're gonna make me tell this, aren't you?" Wojciechowski said. "If you must know, it started with my aunt."

"I'm listening," Nicole said.

"I was eleven, and I had a favorite uncle. Henryk. Went by Hank. I mean, I liked my aunt Lucyna too, but he was the cool one. Lived in Chicago with most of the rest of the family that came over. But he did better than most of the others, so he visited us here at least once a year, usually more. He'd bring me stuff — trinkets, souvenirs, things like that. Told stories, taught me jokes, teased me about bein' a Yanks fan. Said the Cubs could kick our tails. I said, 'Yeah, if they could ever get back to the World Series.' Just a cool guy.

"So this one time he and Aunt Lucy come to visit, and they get mugged right in front of our building. Cab has just pulled outta sight and they're startin' to schlep their bags to the front door. Lowlife comes up, says he's got a knife and wants my uncle's wallet. Uncle Hank starts swearin' at him in Polish, tellin' him he's gonna need more than a knife and all that. The guy pulls the blade and rams it just under Aunt Lucy's sternum and she's good as dead before she hits the ground."

"Oh no!"

"Dad and I run out there. Uncle Hank's bent over Aunt Lucy, screamin'. The bad guy pulls Hank's wallet from his pocket, gives him a bash on the head, and runs off. Dad and I light out after the guy, but I don't notice that Dad stops and goes back 'cause Uncle Hank's on the ground, bleeding. So here I am, no more'n a Little Leaguer, chasin' a violent criminal down the street in broad daylight. He darts into an alley, and I hear my dad scream like I've never heard him ever, calling, 'George! Stop! Get back here!' So I come back. Thing is, I saw the guy, and I coulda picked him out of a lineup. So could my dad.

"Uncle Hank's still in ICU when we bury Aunt Lucy, and all three of us describe the perp to the cops, they get a sketch out to the public, go door to door looking for other witnesses or anybody who might know the guy. And nothin'. Guy literally gets away with murder."

"That's awful!"

"I don't hold it against the cops. They did all they could with what they had. But I've been living with that for forty years. It nearly destroyed our family. Uncle Hank finally went back to Chicago — never came here again. Didn't even want to be reminded of New York, so I never heard from him either. Died when I was in high school. All I wanted was justice. I saw what crime can do. Two people attacked. One dies, one hurt bad, but you can't even count all the victims.

"That's why I do what I do, and I never watch the clock or check the calendar. The wife gets it — well, at least the second one does. I know it's hard on everybody, but justice doesn't wait."

Nicole couldn't speak. She laid a hand on Wojciechowski's arm. "Thank you," she mouthed.

He shrugged. "Fair's fair. Someday you gotta tell me why you do what you do." Nicole wondered if Wojciechowski had ulterior motives for his interest her life's work.

CHAPTER 78

Ur

Terah tried everything in his power to escape the torture in his mind. Was it possible he had been cursed by the god of his forefathers, especially through his own wife? He told himself the child he had sacrificed was a mere servant's baby, but in his soul he feared his namesake's blood *was* on his hands.

Terah forced himself to focus on and worry more about Ikuppi's fatigue than about his own guilt. Surely the king's guard would get over Terah's role in deceiving the king, especially in light of King Nimrod's own deceit. Yet Terah had asked so much of Ikuppi. The man was young and robust, but how much could he endure? When he checked in after each run for supplies and then to unload them at the cave, he looked dreadful.

"Are you all right, my friend?" Terah said.

It was not lost on him that Ikuppi seemed to recoil every time Terah called him friend. But he *was* his friend! What if he had not warned him of the king's intentions? His own son would have been slain by now.

"I just want to finish and be done, done with the task and done with you."

"I understand you feel that way now, Ikuppi, but believe me, we will have better days to come."

"You might," Ikuppi said. "I cannot foresee ever enjoying another day."

"Oh, believe me, when Utu rules the sky again in the morning, everything will seem brighter."

"This is the last supply run to the cave, Terah. When I have unloaded I will return for Belessunu and the baby."

CHAPTER 79

Manhattan

"Before you bag that," Nicole told Detective Chakrabarti, "I need to get a shot of it for my father."

Pranav glanced at Wojciechowski, who nodded.

Wojciechowski's phone chirped. "This's G-Dub," he said. "Good . . . Pick her up and get her to the Central Park station house. Gimme an hour. I'm gonna run the daughter back to Sinai."

He put his phone away. "Found your mail carrier."

"You've got to bring her in to talk to her?"

"People like to help."

"Yeah, but —"

"Life's not fair, Doc. What're ya gonna do?"

"I don't need a ride, by the way," Nicole said. "I'll go back later."

"Not a good idea," Wojciechowski said.

"Unless you know who sent this letter so I can pick him — or her — up right now, I can't let you stay here alone. You'll be safer at Sinai with uniforms outside your door."

"So you think this was more than just intended to scare me?"

"I don't know what to think, but it scares *me*. And it's on me to protect you. You can show your dad the picture of that letter, but you know I gotta follow up with him — see what he makes of it. Meanwhile, you owe me your story." He turned to Chakrabarti. "Pack it up, Pranav. Let's go."

Downstairs, Freddie looked alarmed to see Nicole. "Lemme flag you down a cab." She told him she had a ride with the detectives. "You're not under arrest, are you?" he said.

"No, nothing like that."

"What's going on?"

"Nothing I can talk about right now."

"Be sure to tell Ginny I'm keepin' a good thought for her."

Wojciechowski stopped and spun, peering at the doorman's nameplate. "What's your last name, Frederick?"

"Campbell. I go by Freddie."

"You know Virginia Berman, Freddie Campbell?"

"Me? No, well, yeah, sorta. She visits Miss

Berman now and then. Nice lady."

Wojciechowski seemed to study him. He handed Freddie his card. "You see anything suspicious, call me, hear?"

"I see suspicious stuff all the time. What'm I lookin' for?"

"Anybody askin' about Nicole or her mother, people you don't recognize, that kinda thing."

"You betcha. You suspect foul play or somethin'?"

"Just checkin' things out, Freddie. Appreciate your help."

Wojciechowski told Detective Chakrabarti to drive. "I need to talk to Dr. Berman."

In the car he swung around from the front passenger seat to face her. "I know a lotta your background, but not all."

"You don't have time for my whole story," she said.

"I'm just lookin' for your why. Take me back to high school. I know you were a National Merit Scholar and all that — I hated your type. But you weren't the typical bookworm. You also played, what, basketb—"

"Volleyball. I could've played in college too, but by then I knew what it was going to take to follow my dream."

"Archaeology, right. You know I looked you up — well, had somebody look you up, if I'm bein' honest. But I read all the stuff. You got more degrees than my whole family put together."

"Got the ones I needed."

"And all Ivy League?"

She nodded. "Well, except Berlin."

"And you enjoyed that? All that studying?"

"Not as much as digging, but yes. When you're studying something you love, it can be fun even when it's hard."

"That's what I wanna get to. You love digging. Why? I mean, in the movies it looks like hard labor. Hot, sweaty, dirty, luggin' heavy stuff around. And finding really valuable stuff is rare, right?"

"It's not like Indiana Jones, if that's what you mean."

"Yeah, like that. You're a history buff, okay, but if you're not fightin' Nazis or discovering priceless stuff, what's to love?"

CHAPTER 80

Ur

"Belessunu, you know I would help you prepare for the trip if I could," Terah said.

"That I do know," she said, sadness in her voice. She shuffled between the bedchamber and the great room, carrying small stacks of clothing and personal items, stopping often to steady herself with a hand on the table or having to sit. Pain was written on her face. "You have long been attentive, husband. I do not know what has come over you that you could have —"

"Nothing came over me! Nothing but love for you and our child!"

"Blasphemy!" she hissed. "Do you think I am any abler than you to make this journey tonight? I know we must go, but let me make this plain, Terah. Nothing you can do or say will dissuade me from my devotion to the one true God. He has spoken to me and you know He has spoken to you . . ."

"Please, I don't want to hear —"

"You will hear whatever I have to say from now on. And I am telling you that the worship of any other god, not to mention all these" — she swept a hand over the idol remnants — "will not be tolerated in our new dwelling. Our son will be raised to know and exalt the one true God of our forefathers."

"But —"

"I will countenance no opposition on this, Terah! The Lord has spoken, and so have I. If you command me to abandon my resolve, you will have to bind me and carry me to the cave, else I will stay right here until Nimrod's men find us."

"I want the boy to be healthy and safe," Terah muttered.

"Then you will bring no idol when you visit. And you will not counter anything I teach Abram about God."

Terah nodded miserably. "You understand that I will be your only visitor."

"That will not be easy, but I would not know what to say to any servants anyway. I don't know how you will be able to face them."

"They will feel bad for me, Belessunu! One of their friends' baby was devoured by ravenous dogs, and when the king de-

401

manded their master's son be sacrificed, his wife abandoned him. I will gain much sympathy and respect."

"Your entire life has become a lie, Terah. I don't know how you can face yourself. How will you sleep?"

"I will rest easy, knowing I have done what I had to do to protect you and Abram from the king."

"And now I will do what I have to do to protect your son from you and your murderous, idolatrous ways."

Darkness had fallen when Ikuppi finally returned and set about loading the larger chariot with Belessunu's supplies and making a place for her to sit with the baby.

"Prepare a place for me as well," Terah said. "I have one more ride in me this day."

"I'm glad *you* do," Ikuppi said. "But you have become a burden rather than a help."

"Only temporarily, my friend. Once you deliver me back here tonight, in the coming days we will enjoy comradeship once more."

Ikuppi appeared as weary as Terah had ever seen him when finally he was ready to board his passengers. "Let me start with you, Terah," he said.

Ikuppi tossed Terah's crutch into the chariot, then draped the injured man's arm around his own shoulders and walked him out, propping him against the wheel. He leapt up and squatted to lift as Terah sluggishly climbed in and lowered himself to the floor. No matter how he adjusted himself, he couldn't avoid pressure on his most sensitive injuries. Maybe this was a mistake and he should have said his good-byes inside. But there was more he wanted to tell Belessunu, and it didn't seem right to have another man deliver her and Abram to their new home without his being there.

Ikuppi brought him the sleeping Abram. Terah felt such a blend of emotions he couldn't express himself to his wife when Ikuppi helped her into the chariot. Holding the baby merely confirmed in his mind that, as chaotic as the day had been, the end was all that mattered. He would soon have his family hidden and safe. How he had managed that was between him and his gods.

CHAPTER 81

Vietnam

"Here she comes, Ben," Red said. "He who hesitates . . ."

He whispered, "It's like she's not even real."

"You're hopeless. Find out if she'll see you away from here."

"Not a chance. She wouldn't look twice at me."

"Guess you'll never know," Red said.

"She is fascinating," Ben said. "I'll give her that."

"That's why you can't take your eyes off her? Because she's fascinating?"

Ben waited until Charm's two-year mourning period was over and ventured into town alone for the first time. At the restaurant he asked for a single table in her section and was surprised when she approached with a menu and an iced beer. "My hero," she said.

"Where are your friends?"

"I came to see only you," he said, stunned at her tight-fitting turquoise silk tunic and white trousers. "That is beautiful!"

"Thank you. It's traditional. We call it an *áo dài,* and even men can wear it for special occasions. It would look good on you for New Year's."

He laughed. "That will never happen!"

"I'm glad," she said. "Now, do you trust me?"

"I'll bite."

"You bite?"

"Sorry, it's an idiom. It means I'm listening."

"Father taught me English but not idiom. Or humor. I don't get American humor."

"Anyway, let's say I trust you. Then what?"

"I order for you," she said.

"I definitely trust you for that," he said, handing her the menu.

In a few minutes she delivered steamed long-grain rice smothered in a seafood and vegetable stir-fry. Ben breathed in the aroma. "If it tastes as good as it looks and smells . . ."

"You don't like it, you don't pay."

"And if I do like it, you let me walk you home when you're off work."

"That's my reward for good ordering?"

"It's my reward," Ben said.

"Can I trust you?" she said.

"With what?"

"With me."

"Of course," Ben said. "I don't like the idea of your walking home in the dark. I'm not asking to come in. I'll walk you to your door and disappear. Promise."

"It's a long walk."

"Even better. More time with you."

She smiled. "But I don't even know you."

"I protected you before I even met you."

"From a child!"

"Oh, that hurt," Ben said. "When I tell people about it, I say he was a giant. And ugly. And armed."

Charm laughed. "Okay, you walk me home and protect me from all the giant Vietnamese boys."

CHAPTER 82

Ur

Belessunu took Abram from Terah's arms and hummed to him as Ikuppi feathered the chariot over the rocky route to the cave. They moved little faster than they could have walked, but walking was out of the question.

Terah tried more than once to engage his wife in conversation, but she would not even look his way. He told her she would find the cave cooler, especially at night, and that he would keep stocking her with torches and oil lamps because she could not risk spending much time near the entrance. The cave had to look deserted should anyone happen by.

"This trip will rarely take this long once I am healthy," he said. "I will come every day if I can. I will just have to invent a story for why I continue past the livestock pen. Servants are bound to wonder."

Ikuppi lit a torch and helped Terah inside to a rock ledge where he sat and watched as the king's guard showed her where he'd unloaded all the supplies and food. Belessunu was still plainly ignoring her husband, and when it came time for him to leave, he beckoned her near. She appeared to want nothing less. But Abram was down and still asleep, so she limped to Terah, standing rigid and seeming to eye him suspiciously.

"Farewell, wife, and I will see you tomorrow."

"Examine yourself, Terah. And repent before God."

"I have nothing to repent for," he said. She waved him off and turned away, plodding back to where the baby lay. "I saved our lives!" Terah called after her.

As Ikuppi was pulling Terah up into the chariot once more, he said, "Just look at what we have done."

"What you have done, you mean," Terah said. "You have accomplished much today, and I thank —"

"We have lied to the king. We have murdered a child. We have threatened a midwife and her son. We have lied to grieving parents. We have misled an entire community. And now we have risked two more lives with this ill-timed trip and have left them in the

408

wilderness."

"Protected and out of sight," Terah said.

Ikuppi spat. "We are of all men most wretched."

"Blame it on me, friend. You did only as I asked."

"I should have refused."

"Insubordination is punishable by —"

"How well I know. Already I wish you'd executed me."

"You'll feel differently tomorrow, Ikuppi."

"You are the one who needs to feel differently tomorrow, Terah."

Terah tried to encourage his friend the rest of the way home, but Ikuppi proved as quiet as Belessunu had on the trip to the cave. Terah still talked, cajoled, tried to draw the man out all the way until Ikuppi delivered him to his sleeping mat. "I will need your help in the morning, friend," Terah said. "I will not be able to stand on my own."

"I cannot promise to be here."

"What do you mean? Who else can I trust?"

"I told you, I am done with you."

"But surely not forever."

"That is my wish. Anyway, won't your and your wife's servants arrive in due time?"

"Yes, but —"

Ikuppi laid Terah's crutch on the floor where he could reach it and strode from the room.

"Ikuppi, wait, please!"

But his footsteps continued until the door opened and shut.

"Friend!"

The only response was the clatter of Ikuppi's sword on the side of the chariot as he mounted. Strangely, from the hoofbeats it sounded as if Ikuppi had taken the one-horse chariot rather than the three-horse.

Good man. He is still thinking of his master, even now, leaving me with the larger transport.

CHAPTER 83

Manhattan

Simple and unread as Detective Wojciechowski liked to come off, Nicole found him street-smart and a quick study of people. Either this was his way of indicating to her, without saying it in so many words, that she was no longer a suspect, or he was trying to take her mind off her fear of the threatening letter.

But she had quit worrying about being cleared of anything related to her mother. She believed truth and time walk hand in hand, so both she and her father would be revealed as innocent as they were. And while she was certainly alarmed that someone seemed to specifically target her in the fake letter from the Saudis, she had to admit she had no idea how scared she should be. She was frankly relieved she could still anticipate a genuine response from Riyadh, even if it likely required more work. It was unlikely to constitute a flat rejection of her application.

Her overriding emotions remained anger and frustration that someone had attacked her mother, and she was desperate to know who. Primarily Nicole wanted her mother safe and healthy, but she also wanted justice. Whoever had done this would not get away with it.

In rehearsing her story for Wojciechowski, Nicole was reminded again how she had been shaped by her parents. Sure, her father taking her all over the world and involving her in significant Holy Land archaeological digs planted in her what she believed to her core was her reason for being. But her mother had been every bit as instrumental to Nicole's spiritual life as she had been to her husband's. Her mother had led her father to faith in Christ, and despite not being Jewish herself, had urged him to become a Messianic Jew and always liked to say she had "married into the faith."

Jewish ethnicity is most often connected with a mother's genetics, but Nicole's parents raised her as a Messianic Jew as well. She could not remember knowing anything but that Jesus was the fulfillment of the Messianic prophecies of the Old Testament, which also made her fully expect that He would also fulfill all the prophecies about Him in the New Testament.

To Nicole's surprise, when she expressed that to Wojciechowski, Detective Chakrabarti chimed in from behind the wheel. "So you believe Jesus will return and rule the world for a thousand years at the end of time."

"I do," she said.

"As do I."

"No kiddin'," Wojciechowski said. "Didn't know that, Pranav."

"To my shame," the Indian said. "But the occasion never arose to tell you."

"Yeah, that's not the kinda stuff we usually talk about on the job."

"You might be surprised, George, how many officers are men of faith."

"That would be a surprise," Wojciechowski said. "We can be a pretty earthy bunch. I still remember a lotta the stuff I learned in church as a kid, but I'll never be good enough to be a religious guy."

"Neither will I," Chakrabarti said.

"Nor I," Nicole said, touching Pranav's shoulder and catching his eye in the rear-view mirror.

"What?" Wojciechowski said. "But you both just said —"

"We'll have to talk," Chakrabarti said.

"But I'm most interested in Dr. Berman's story right now. Aren't you?"

"Yeah, Nicole," Wojciechowski said. "But lemme ask you this: You seem like your own woman, makin' your own way and all that, but you give as much credit to your dad as you do your mom for who you turned out to be. That's not the way it's supposed to go these days, is it? Don't women stick together now and kinda downplay always seein' themselves . . . I don't know, only how they relate to men?"

"I get that," Nicole said. "I do resent many of the roles society would like to relegate me to. And, yes, as the daughter of a foundation owner, I have benefited from privileges few others enjoy. But if you don't mind my saying this, Dad didn't get me into Yale or Princeton or Columbia."

"But gettin' to go on all those digs had to look good on your résumé."

"Granted. But they didn't do my schoolwork for me or achieve my grades or degrees. I don't want to brag, but if that doesn't make me an independent woman, I don't know what does. And while I'd love to someday meet the right man, so far I've done this on my own."

"Awright," Wojciechowski said. "Touching stories about all the time you've spent with your mom, how close you are, how you bonded with your dad over digs and all that. But what made the difference for you? What settled it for you?"

"You're looking for my Uncle Henryk and Aunt Lucyna moment?"

"Exactly."

"Nothing quite so dramatic or sad, I'm afraid. For me it was two things: the Dead Sea and the Middle East."

"I love the Dead Sea!" Chakrabarti said. "My parents took me there as a child, before we moved to this country. How I would love to return someday!"

"Huh," Wojciechowski said. "Heard about that place but can't imagine why anyone would wanna go. Hot, dry, full a salt, and somehow below sea level — which I've never been able to figure out."

"Oh, I can just see you there," Chakrabarti chortled. "Can't you, Doctor?"

Nicole laughed. "In his suit!"

"And below sea level is right," Chakrabarti said. "More than fourteen hundred feet! The land around it is the lowest in the world. And the sea is almost ten times as salty as the ocean. Even as a boy, I walked out to where my feet could not reach the bottom and the water was up to my chest, and I was just standing there! It's impossible to sink!"

"You actually went in?" Wojciechowski said.

"I wouldn't have missed it! People come from all over the world to do that. My father laid on his back and read a book."

"But it's called the Dead Sea 'cause all that salt kills everything, right?"

"That's why I find it so fascinating," Nicole said. "The Jordan River is all that feeds it, but every day the sea evaporates millions of tons of water. The minerals left behind are in demand all over the world."

"Okay, I still don't get it," Wojciechowski said. "Sounds like some kinda ecological miracle, but it's stuck in that god-forsaken desert and —"

"That's just it," Nicole said. "My dad told me the first time he took me there that it's not forsaken by God. In fact, he showed me the Bible prophecies that the Dead Sea —"

"Hold on! There's prophecy about this too?"

"You're going to make me show off, Detective, because I've memorized it."

"Why doesn't that surprise me?"

"I'll make this fast. That whole area was once as lush as the Garden of Eden. But you know the story of Sodom and Gomorrah, right?"

"Yeah, fire and brimstone and all that, and some guy's wife turned to stone."

"She turned into a pillar of salt."

"That makes sense," Wojciechowski said.

"Well, we believe God's judgment on Sodom and Gomorrah turned that fertile area into what we find there today. But even after thousands of years, the Dead Sea will rise again."

"So what's the prophecy?"

"Like Pranav said, we believe Jesus will return someday and rule the earth for a thousand years. During that time, the Bible says, water will flow from Jerusalem — in fact from the Temple Mount — and the Dead Sea will be full of fish."

"And you memorized what it says. Let's hear it."

"Okay, this is from Ezekiel in the Old Testament. I can show you the exact reference —"

"How 'bout I just take your word for it?"

"All right, this is what it says: 'This water flows toward the eastern region, goes down into the valley, and enters the sea. When it reaches the sea, its waters are healed. And it shall be that every living thing that moves, wherever the rivers go, will live. There will be a very great multitude of fish, because these waters go there; for they will be healed, and everything will live wherever the river goes.' "

"That's thrilling, isn't it?" Chakrabarti said.

"If you say so," Wojciechowski said. "But I'll say this: if that happens in my lifetime, I'll sign up for whatever Sunday school class you're teachin'."

"If it happens during your lifetime," Chakrabarti said, "that'll mean you became a believer and made it into the millennial kingdom."

"That would surprise more than a few people," Wojciechowski said. "Me included. Okay, interesting place and all that — musta been really somethin' when you first saw it. How old were you?"

"I was eleven," Chakrabarti said.

"I think that's about how old I was when I went too," Nicole said. "But that would have been a lot of years after Pranav was eleven."

"Hey!"

"So you can't spend your whole life studying the Dead Sea, even if that's your thing, so —"

"Actually, some do," Nicole said, "but you're right. That was just one of the catalysts for me. Digs in that whole area woke me up to all kinds of discoveries that just mesmerized me, and I've never lost that wonder."

"Like what?"

"Well, I can't get into the specifics, but here's what happened. From when I was a young teen in the mid-'90s until after I got my PhD, I got to be a volunteer on eight digs in Israel, then was trench supervisor on digs in Syria, Israel, Iraq, and Saudi Arabia. I was then assistant archaeologist in both Iraq and Saudi Arabia, was licensed in four countries, and I've applied to be lead archaeologist for a dig in Mada'in, Saudi Arabia. It's a long shot. I mean, Saudi women have only recently been allowed to drive. So the idea of a woman — an American Christian no less — being approved as a lead is some stretch.

"The last time I dug at Mada'in, I wasn't really assistant archaeologist. I was a little further down the pecking order from the lead, Dr. Mustafa bin-Alawi, and his assistant, Dr. Moshe Greenblatt of Hebrew University in Israel. Dr. bin-Alawi was killed in a plane crash after the dig and before he could begin writing all the follow-up documentation. Greenblatt moved up into his role for that and asked me to take his assistant spot and contribute to the writing.

"So even though I hadn't really been assistant archaeologist, I was credited that way. The Saudis will study my writing and hopefully overlook that technicality and allow me to leapfrog into a lead role next time.

"But here's why I have to get this: My team uncovered — well, I'm being falsely modest — I uncovered a rare find that could be historically pivotal. Without boring you with the details or saying more than I'm allowed to, it's a fragment that — if I can find its other piece — could change the face of the Mideast conflict as we know it."

"You serious?" Wojciechowski said. "I've never understood what's goin' on over there, but it's all you see on the news."

"Let's just say my dream, my goal, is to prove that the centuries-old divide between Muslims and Jews, and ultimately Christians, is based on faulty history."

CHAPTER 84

Ur

Terah lay restless for only a little while after Ikuppi had left. He decided fatigue from such a momentous day overrode any pangs of conscience Belessunu had predicted for him. As he began to drift off, he relished the chance to tell her the next night — when he would check on her and the baby — that he had gone right to sleep. But that wasn't entirely true. Terah's eyes popped open when he realized that two male and two female servants would arrive at dawn as usual, and he wondered whether Mutuum would be among them.

Surely the man couldn't hold against him the misfortune of a chariot accident, or the actions of wild animals. Terah would stick to his story and ask Mutuum what he thought of the gifts Ikuppi had delivered from his storehouse. As long as the midwife Yadidatum upheld her end of the bargain . . . and how could she not with her son's life and freedom — and hand — in the balance? Terah just hoped Ikuppi's penitence would abate with the light of day so he wouldn't feel compelled to waver either.

Satisfied everything was in order, Terah quickly faded from consciousness.

The first hint of the morning sun teased through the wood lattice of his window, and Terah could tell this was going to be one of those cloudless days — twelve hours of relentless heat that sapped energy and strength from even the young and robust. It had been years since he had been either of those, though he was pleased to find he was able to pull himself up to a seated position. He could not stand on his own, however, so he simply waited, affecting a face of mourning. He had to appear overcome by the loss of his only son — sacrificed to the throne.

When the servants knocked, Terah called out, "Come in! I need your help!"

Wedum arrived at the bedchamber door, Belessunu's girls behind him, whispering. "I am at your service, sir," Wedum said. "Is that not Ikuppi's chariot outside?"

"He took a smaller one back last night

and left that one for me. Is Mutuum with you?"

"He waits in the cart."

"I did not expect him today when, as I am, he is grieving."

"It is kind of you to mourn with him, master. But truth be told, he is angry. His wife wants him to thank you for your efforts to save their son, but Mutuum says even seeing you will bring painful images to his mind."

"Tell him I understand and that he need not see me today. In fact, he can take these girls back after they have served me, as Belessunu is not here."

"Not here?" one of the girls said. "Why?"

Terah beckoned Wedum close and whispered, "She has abandoned me."

"What?"

"Have you not heard? The king required of us our son."

"These girls said you told them he wished to see Abram. But what does this mean, he required him of you? To raise as his own? Is he to honor you by making him a prince of the royal household —"

"I fear not, Wedum. I believe he has taken Abram as a sacrifice."

"Oh no! Where has Belessunu gone?"

"She would not tell me. And in my condition I was unable to stop her. She says she will never return because I gave up our son."

"But surely you had no choice!"

"Of course I did not know what the king wanted with him. I assumed just to see him and rejoice with me. But when the king, a god himself, makes a request, what are mortals to do? I pray only that he and the other gods will look upon me with favor for such an offering."

"I am sure they will, master, but what an awful price to pay!"

"I am bereft."

"I am so sorry."

"When you tell Mutuum to take these girls back, see if he is aware of the gifts I had Ikuppi deliver last night."

"Oh, he is aware, master. He and his wife have already begun sharing them."

"Those are not to share! They are for the mourning parents."

"They say it's too much — that you were too kind — and they want others to partake of them too."

"How generous."

Wedum helped Terah up, but he did not immediately assist him to the other room.

"Was there something else, lad?"

"Sir, there is. On our way we passed vultures circling over the wasteland, perhaps

424

four hundred yards to the west."

"That's not unusual, is it? Some animal has left the carcass of a kill for them to pick clean, no?"

"Probably, sir. But we did not want to look."

"Surely this is nothing new to you, Wedum . . . Oh, I see. You fear it could be the remains of Mutuum's child."

"Mutuum refused to look, and the girls thought it bad luck that we just rode on by. They will be reluctant to pass it again on the way back."

"True, master!" one of the girls said. "May we stay here until we're sure the birds have gone?"

"You will prepare first meal for me before leaving. And then Wedum will carry me there in the cart, and we will see if it's anything to be concerned with."

"But we will have taken the cart, sir."

"Mutuum may use the chariot, but tell him to take it nowhere else and return it here tomorrow. Wedum and I will make do with the cart."

CHAPTER 85

Vietnam

Over the next several weeks, Ben invented reasons to get into town to see Charm. He volunteered for supply runs, miscellaneous errands, anything that would get him there, day or night. Some evenings when his shift was over, he would just sit outside the restaurant and chat with her on breaks, waiting to walk her home at the end of the night.

One night Red and her other friends showed up, and she sat with him briefly. "We've missed you," she said, but he saw amusement in her eyes. "Just take things slow, will you? Charm seems like a sweet girl, but don't go falling in love."

"Too late," he said.

"Seriously? You've got it that bad already?"

"I've spent an awful lot of time with her," Ben said. "Even my CO is asking where I've been. I think he knows, but he has a hard

426

time writing me up 'cause I'm such a good worker. Keeps reminding me that even when I'm in town, I'm still sort of on duty. Representing the Corps, on the alert, always armed, all that."

"And if the Cong attacks," Red said, "it's no longer 'sort of' on duty."

"Oh, I know. I used to pray something like that would happen — and I don't even believe in God. I either go home a hero or in a bag. I was okay either way. Now I can't say that."

"Because of her."

"Exactly. Hey, you got your camera with you?"

"No, but one of my friends has hers."

"Do me a favor and get a picture of Charm tonight. She's wearing my favorite outfit."

"I saw. It is beautiful. Of course, she looks good in anything. You two talked about the big stuff yet?"

"Like . . . ?"

"Like you not believing in God? Most Vietnamese are pretty traditional. Lots of gods, actually."

"Nah, we're pretty much on the same page with all that. Her grandparents were proud not to be Buddhist like most every-one else seemed to be, except Catholics —

like the Vietnam president. They belonged to some kind of multi-god group with a funny name."

"*Cao Đài?*" Red said.

"That's it. They were Caodaists, believed in the best of all the major religions, something like that. Charm's parents didn't raise her that way. She's more like me. We say people can believe what they want as long as they don't force us to."

"You're not dreaming about taking her home with you," Red said. "Are you?"

"Can't say it hasn't crossed my mind, but I don't think I could do that to her. She has her heart set on Saigon National."

"The university?"

"Yeah, pedagogical-something or other. Wants to teach young kids. Don't think she has any interest in coming to the States."

"Is she sincere about that, Ben? Not going to the States?"

He shot Red a double take. "Why wouldn't she be?"

"Don't play dumb, Marine. You know a lot of girls here would love nothing more than to escape all this and reach the promised land. And if it means convincing a GI they're madly in love and would follow him anywhere, well . . ."

"Think I could sniff that out pretty quick,"

428

Ben said. "I'm not even sure she feels about me the way I do about her. At least not yet."

"You're telling me you haven't been intimate?"

He shrugged.

"Ben?"

"Not really."

"What does that mean? There's no middle ground there, son."

"I'm not saying I don't want to. We just haven't yet, you know?"

"You've spent the night with her?"

"Twice."

"That's some willpower, Ben."

"Tell me about it. It's just — this is not what that is. There's all kinds of opportunities in town if that's what I'm after."

"You love her."

"I think I do."

"Well, good for you. But if she's not coming your way, and I know you're not staying here, the only option is a couple of broken hearts."

Ben nodded. "You never know. Say we keep in touch, her circumstances change and she wants out — or Nam changes and I want to come back."

"How likely is that?"

"Not very. Just saying."

Red appeared to become emotional and

pressed a finger to her lip.

"What?" Ben said.

She shook her head. "I don't know. You just don't see true love that much anymore. Lord knows, I thought I was in love with my ex. I'm just happy for you, but already sad too, because the odds are so stacked against you."

"Hello!" Charm poked her head out of the restaurant. "Have a short break."

"I'll leave you two," Red said.

"Get the camera," Ben said.

When Red returned, Ben said, "Let me get one of Charm first, then you can shoot the two of us."

She posed, looking shy but radiant. But after he had snapped the picture and tried to advance the film, he found the film was at the end of the roll. Red gave him the picture a few weeks later, and he tucked it into his wallet.

CHAPTER 86

Ur

Once Wedum had helped him rise, Terah was encouraged to find that he was able to walk on his own but still with the aid of the crutch. The ankle remained tender and sore, but he could put a little more weight on it.

Wedum and Mutuum tended to the livestock while Belessunu's servant girls cooked and served Terah his meal. When they returned, Wedum reported that Mutuum had moved to the large chariot Ikuppi had left and was waiting to take the girls back. "He also wanted me to tell you, master, that he will come directly back because we should lead the sheep at least to a shady eating spot before the heat of the day makes them lie down in the sun."

"Do you think that is what has brought vultures?" Terah said. "Some animal succumbing to the heat?"

"It's possible," Wedum said, "but that

would be more likely later in the day. Should we wait until he returns to see what the vultures have flocked to?"

"No, I am ready. And let me walk to the cart. You will have to help me in, but I can make it."

By the time Terah reached the cart, Mutuum had loaded the girls and taken off with the larger chariot. A huge cloud of dust rose on the road behind them. "He is not used to driving three horses, is he?" Terah said.

"He is not, but he is strong and learns fast."

"He'd better be careful with that chariot," Terah said.

"And with those girls," Wedum said.

"Well, yes, of course. I'm feeling better, Wedum, but please do not try to match Mutuum's speed. If there's anything to see, it will still be there when we arrive."

It wasn't long before Terah recognized what the servants had been talking about. Wedum stopped on the road, perpendicular to the activity to the west.

"The birds do not land, Wedum. Very strange."

In the distance two images shimmered in the heat waves rising from the wilderness floor, but Terah couldn't make out the details of either. The vultures seemed to endlessly circle and occasionally one or two swooped, but never far before ascending again. Did that mean their targets were alive, still moving, and they feared them?

"If we approach, the vultures will retreat," Wedum said. "But we must be careful not to become prey of their prey."

"I want to know what is dead or dying," Terah said. "But your donkey would be no match for dogs, especially injured ones, and I don't care to take them on again."

"I will get only close enough to see what the birds are after."

"Slowly," Terah said.

As the donkey tramped over the arid ground, the vultures appeared to become wary and began circling even higher. "They are not retreating, master. They see our beast and us as yet another meal."

"Let's make sure we disappoint them." Terah squinted into the distance. "A horse! Standing! That's why the vultures are shy. He likely whinnies or stamps when they descend."

"What is that he's hitched to?" Wedum said. "A wagon? No! Master, that is a chariot! A king's chariot!"

"Go, Wedum! Who is in the chariot?"

Wedum clicked his tongue and snapped the reins on the donkey's back, but to no effect. He reached back into the bed of the cart where he kept a small branch. He whipped it across the animal's flank, and off they thundered toward the scene.

About thirty feet from the chariot, the donkey skidded to a stop and planted its hooves, locking its knees. Terah cursed the animal and Wedum alternated lashing him with reins and branch, but the donkey would not budge. "Help me down!" Terah said. "Someone lies beyond the chariot!"

Once Wedum had him out and onto the ground with his crutch, Terah said, "Go, man! Who is it?"

Wedum also froze when he got beyond the horse, which was frothy with sweat. Terah hobbled up on his tender ankle. Wedum's voice came high and panicky. "It's Ikuppi, master, in a pool of his own blood!"

"Dead?"

"Covered with flies, and the blood is caked hard."

Terah finally reached Wedum's shoulder. Ikuppi lay facedown, the hilt of his sword nearly buried in the rocky soil, the blade having run him through from abdomen through torso and extending more than a foot out his back. No other hoofprints, footprints, or wheel tracks in sight. The king's guard, whom Terah had recommended for that job years before — and who had warned Terah of Nimrod's plan to slay his firstborn son — had fallen on his own weapon.

Everything Ikuppi lamented over the day before came back to Terah. The man had been trying to tell him of this very plan.

For the first time since he believed the gods had imparted to him this whole scheme, Terah felt a twinge of shame, but not over the loss of a man he had considered a friend. No, he had to confess, he felt relieved. He could have used Ikuppi's help, certainly, but now one of the only two people besides him and Belessunu who knew the truth was unable to reveal it.

That could only work in his favor.

CHAPTER 87

Manhattan

NYPD Crime Scene Unit forensic technician Pranav Chakrabarti swung the unmarked squad car into the Emergency entrance at Mount Sinai. "Let me walk you to the door, Dr. Berman."

"Oh, that's not necessary," Nicole said, touched by his courtliness.

"Yeah, Pranav," Wojciechowski said. "What're ya doin'? This is the twenty-first century and she's a grown woman! Anyway, they're on their way to pick up the housekeeper too. We got to get goin'."

"I'll be right back, George," he said. "Won't be a minute."

"This is kind of you, Detective," Nicole said as he hurried to her side.

"I confess I have an ulterior motive," he said as they walked. "I need you to tell me how I can join one of your digs."

"Oh, Detective, I don't know . . ."

"Please, I know it's for young people and retired people mostly, but it's long been my dream. I have the education and the interest, and I would love —"

"You're way overqualified, and you know it would have to be entirely at your own expense. I mean, volunteers get some food and lodging, but the big-ticket stuff would be all on you."

"Doctor, I have been with the department long enough that I now enjoy a six-figure income and —"

"We dig in the summer so we can accommodate the college kids."

"The summer would work for me!"

"Typically we dig five hours a day for twenty days . . ."

"I get twenty-seven paid days off!"

"And you can take them all at once?"

"If I plan ahead. If it's next summer, I would put in for the time now."

"You know there's no glamour in it. Volunteers get the grunt work, carrying buckets of dirt and rocks, that kind of thing."

"I'm already imagining it."

"Well, don't get your hopes up. You'd have a lot of competition and we can take only so many. Even if you made my list, you would have to be vetted by the host country."

"You have my card. And if I may say, Ms. Berman, as a fellow believer, I know you understand when I say I will be praying it happens."

Nicole couldn't help but picture him as a delightful team member.

But as of now, there was no dig.

The two uniformed officers outside her mother's door had been replaced, so Nicole had to prove who she was yet again. "Okay," one said after checking her ID. "And we're to inform Ms. Jefferson when you arrive."

"You are? What does Kayla want?"

"No idea, ma'am."

They must go to school for this. Do what you're told, but never explain.

She found her mother sleeping, her father sitting with a book in his lap. "You look haggard, Dad. Still jet-lagged?"

"Of course, and thanks."

"I'm just worried about you."

"I know, and I'm worried about your mom."

"She's going to be fine now, isn't she?"

"I hope."

"She's out of the woods," Nicole said. "We just need to worry about whoever did this.

If anyone can get them, it'll be Wojciechowski, don't you think?"

Her dad nodded. "What's the news from
the Saudis?"

"Would you believe I still haven't heard?"

He set his book down. "You opened the
letter, right?"

"You're not going to believe this." She
brought up the photo of it on her phone
and handed it to him.

"You have got to be kidding me," he said,
standing. "Wojciechowski has to see this."

"He just dropped me off, Dad. I called
him right away. They took it into evidence."

"What in the world? 'Watch your *own*
back'? Like they knew about your mother's
back? What are we into here, Nic?' "

A knock came on the door. "Sorry to
interrupt," Kayla said. "If you're in the
middle of something, I can come b—"

"We kind of are," her dad said.

"No problem! You both have my card. Just
call me when it's conv—"

"No," Nicole said. "You're here now. What
is it?"

Kayla looked to Nicole's dad, who
shrugged.

"Well, it's just such a privilege to have all
three principals of The Berman Foundation
in one place, even if our patient is sleeping.

439

The administration wanted me to express their thanks for everything you've done and continue to do for Sinai, and just what you mean to all of us."

"Appreciate that, Ms. Jefferson," her father said. "Do you know if there's any official update on Ginny's condition?"

"I don't," Kayla said, "but I'm more than happy to find out. How about I check with her case manager Monday morning and —"

"Monday morning?!" he exclaimed. "Nobody can tell us now?"

"I'll see what I can find out and get right back to you."

The phone in Nicole's dad's hand buzzed. "Sorry, I need to take this," he said and hurried out.

"Thanks for taking the time," Kayla told Nicole. "I'll let you know as soon as I know anything, but I understand everything is on pace for now."

"You're here after hours again, Kayla. Why's that?"

The young woman smiled, perfect teeth gleaming. "The last line on my job description says, 'Miscellaneous related duties as assigned.' When they call me, I come in."

"Did they call you in tonight?"

"Not specifically, but I am often asked to work after hours when we have VIP patients, and they don't come any more important than her. So, if you need anything . . ."

"I just hate causing you extra, and unnecessary, work."

"Glad to do it. And I'm also grateful for the chance to tell you again that I was serious about joining one of your dig teams some day."

"I know you were, but that's strange."

"Just didn't want you to forget or think I was merely saying it to be polite. And what's strange?"

"You're the second person who's said that in the last few minutes. I can go a month without someone doing that."

"Who was that?"

"You wouldn't know him."

"Well, maybe I'll meet him on the dig."

"Ha! Maybe you will." Having a native Indian and an African American woman on her volunteer team would check off a lot of boxes.

When Kayla was gone, Nicole tiptoed to her mother. Her vitals all read normal on the monitors, and she seemed peaceful. Nicole glanced at her chart at the end of the bed and noticed a nurse had been in to check on her about a half hour before. Nicole decided she could leave her briefly, just to see what was up with her dad.

She found him about a hundred feet down the corridor, studying his phone. He was ashen. "Dad, what is it?" she whispered.

He looked both ways, slipped the phone into his pocket, and said, "Tell me about Mustafa."

"What do you mean tell you about him? You introduced him to me twenty years ago, and getting to be his trench supervisor in '16 was a dream. He was great. He always was."

"You get much time with him?"

"Almost as much as Moshe did, and he was the assistant."

"You mean Greenblatt from Israel?"

"Yeah, I'd been his trench super at Hazor in 2010. The three of us made a good team at Mada'in."

"Mustafa knew what you'd found and why you wanted to go back?"

"Of course, but I figured it would be under Moshe and him again. Who knew? I just wish I could've been there for his funeral."

Ben nodded, his gaze miles away.

"What's going on, Dad?"

He pulled the phone out. "You need to see this."

"Dad! That's my phone!"

"Oh, so it is. Then this was to you, not me."

It was a text in Arabic from a number she didn't recognize — in fact, a number that didn't resemble a phone number, international or not.

هل كنت حقاً تعتقد أن مغادرة مصطفى بن علوي للحديقة كانت عرضية؟

Nicole translated. " 'Did you really think Mustafa bin-Alawi's departure for the garden was accidental?' It has to mean the Islam afterlife, Jannah, right? Doesn't that literally mean 'garden.' "

Her father nodded. "Nicole, do not let this make you withdraw your application from the Saudis."

"Are you kidding? And let whoever this is win? This has to be the same person who told me to watch my back. I'm tempted to answer it."

"And say what?"

"Either 'No, tell me more,' or 'Yes, I knew.' "

"You'd be playing right into their hands."

"But whose hands, Dad?"

"Whoever doesn't want you digging in Saudi Arabia again — enough to attack your mother and threaten you. We've got to get this to Wojciechowski."

"What's he going to do with it?" Nicole said.

"They've got phone techies who can work miracles."

"And you know this how?"

"Crime shows on TV."

CHAPTER 88

Ur

"We must deliver his body to the palace," Wedum said.

"No!" Terah said. "Think, man! Isn't it clear what's happened here?"

"He's killed himself, master. But why?"

"That is not for us to know, but imagine the disgrace, the dishonor, the humiliation of his family. And if the king learns of this, there will be no imperial funeral, only ignominy."

"What can we do?"

"Remove his sword. Place it in his hand as if he used it to protect himself. Then roll him onto his back. Move the chariot far enough away that the vultures will not be scared off by the horse. Once they have begun to devour him, his scent will draw other predators."

"You would have him torn to pieces out here?" Wedum said. "A king's guard?"

"Better than to embarrass his family. Someone will find his bones and the chariot and deduce he was another victim of the dogs. He will be lauded for his years of service to the realm."

"I've known him only a few hours," Wedum said. "But I could tell he was a good man. I don't know if I can —"

"Of course you can! Just roll him up on his side, withdraw the sword, and then leave him on his back."

"Oh, master, don't make me . . ."

"I'd do it myself if I were able. Think of his reputation, his family. Now move!"

Convinced as he was that he had made another prudent decision, even Terah found it hard to watch as Wedum rolled Ikuppi's bloated body on its side to free the hilt from the ground and allow him access to the sword. Wedum gagged as he set his feet and bent to jerk the blade until it wrenched free.

"Now roll him onto his back and place the weapon in his hand."

"Forgive me, master," Wedum groaned, "but I cannot. I already feel I have violated the man."

"Out of the way, coward. A dead man feels nothing, and you know this was his choice."

Terah tottered to the body, put his weight on his left leg, and poked at Ikuppi with his crutch. The man proved heavier than Terah expected. He pushed harder, and though the body rocked, it would not roll over. "Help me, man!" Terah said. "We must be gone before we're seen."

Wedum placed his foot on Ikuppi's hip and pushed him onto his back.

"Now put the sword in his hand."

"Oh, master . . ."

"Just do it!"

Tears rolled down Wedum's cheeks as he obeyed and retreated to Terah's side.

"Now move the chariot and we'll go."

But Wedum found the horse as stubborn as the donkey had been. The whites of its eyes showed terror, and it would not budge. Terah cursed them both. "Help me up in there," he said. "I will hold the reins, and you get out and make the horse move."

When they were in place, Terah leaned precariously on his crutch and Wedum grabbed the horse's bridle. The steed yanked its head back, lifting Wedum off the ground and flinging him aside. "Make him move!" Terah shouted. "Hang on!"

"I need the switch," Wedum said, and he ran back to the donkey cart to retrieve the gnarly branch. He brandished it in front of the horse and raised it as if to strike. The horse reared, nearly hurling Terah from the carriage.

"Give me that and get out of the way, Wedum!"

Terah wrapped the reins around one hand, held his crutch under his arm, and beat the horse's flank with the branch until it nickered and whinnied and finally stomped off in fits and starts. Satisfied he was far enough away from the body to allow the vultures their meal, Terah beckoned to Wedum to help him down.

In the process he nearly tripped over something on the floor of the chariot — the ivory model he had carved of Marduk, the patron deity of Babylonia. It was still intact and as beautiful as the day he had made it. Though it had been a gift to Ikuppi, he certainly had no use for it now. And Terah needed something to begin his new collection.

That night at the cave, Belessunu seemed lethargic and pale in the light of the torches.

"Fortunately, the light cannot be seen from outside," Terah told her. "But you must resurrect that poison you concocted for the wild pigs that ravaged your garden."

"And threatened us," she said weakly. "It was just bat excrement I collected and added to meat I allowed to go rancid. I

448

believe the pigs found it delicious."

"But it left them rotting in the sun."

"Bats live deep in this cave," she said, "so I could collect what I need. But what am I to do with this poisoned meat?"

"We cannot risk wild dogs picking up your or Abram's scent. This place that protects you from the throne also makes you easy prey for dogs."

"Or jackals or hyenas," she said.

"I don't even want to think about it. You deposit the bait around the entrance. Belessunu, are you all right?"

"No, I am not. I'm exhausted and sore and need help here. I know we can't let servants know where I am, but could not Ikuppi bring me — What, Terah?"

"Hmm?"

"At the mere mention of his name you turned white. What is wrong with Ikuppi?"

"Did I say something was wrong with him?"

"Terah, don't insult me. Do you think I don't know you after all these years? What has happened?"

"It's awful, Belessunu. I didn't want to trouble you with this, but Wedum discovered his body in the desert this morning! The wild dogs had overtaken him."

She sat staring. "An armed king's guard

in a royal chariot?"

"Yes! That's why we need the poison, to spread in front of the mouth of the cave for such ravenous and powerful beasts."

"You cannot distract me with warnings about our safety," Belessunu said. "I liked Ikuppi, and I thought you did too."

"Of course I did! He's the one who warned us of Nimrod's plan."

"Then tell me the truth. Is this yet another death for which you are responsible?"

Terah hung his head.

"Oh, Terah, by the time you come to your senses and repent before the one true God, it will be too late! Did you kill Ikuppi because he was a witness to your treachery?"

"No! If you must know, he fell on his own sword, and that's the truth. That he is gone does make it easier for us, however. One less person who could betray us to the king."

"Oh, husband, you are beyond hope. Do you not see why he took his own life? You may as well have murdered him too. At least tell me he will lie in state, duly honored."

"Only his bones remain. We did not want the king to learn of his suicide. This way he will be lauded, yes."

"And what of his family?"

"What of them?"

"They have been left without a husband

450

and father because you pushed him past
what his conscience could bear."

Abram began to fuss. "Allow me to tend
to him," Terah said.

"No! You think I want him comforted by
a murderer?"

"Are you saying I will never again touch
my son?"

"I'm saying not now, Terah. I fear God
must bring you low if you are ever to return
to Him."

CHAPTER 89

Vietnam, 1972

By the end of the summer, peace and rumors of peace changed the nature of Ben and Charm's relationship. Knowing Ben could be shipped home with virtually no notice thrust them together and forced them into morose conversations and even weeping jags that depressed them both. They clung to each other, fearing that any moment might be their last. Ben spent every available night at Charm's apartment, rushing back to his post at dawn.

As the months dragged on, with more news and talk but no peace, they spent more time than ever just walking and talking, telling each other every moment they could remember of their lives. Ben wanted to talk about the future, a future together, but it was just as he had told Red. Charm had dreamt of teaching since she was a young teenager. Escaping to America had never crossed her mind.

"You could teach in the States," he said.

"You forget, I read. Your own magazines say it's unlikely you will be welcomed back. Imagine me. What would I look and sound like to Americans? To them I will represent this war and they will hate me."

"No one who knows you could hate you, Charm."

"But why would they want to get to know me? My English may be good for a Vietnamese, but not for teaching in America. And the US already has good education. It's my people who need teachers."

"I need you."

"I need you, too, Ben, but it would be selfish of me to leave here just for us."

"Just for us?"

"You know what I mean, and you know that I will always love you. You were my first, you know."

He fell silent. Then, "You were my first who ever meant anything."

"You could stay here," she said, looking away.

"But the things I've seen here . . . I hate everything about this place except you."

"And you would have me."

"But what would I do?" he said. "Everything about this place would remind me of stuff I never want to speak of again. Anyway, I have no skills worth anything here."

"You said your parents have means . . ."

"I would never ask them to support me, especially after all I said about them and their priorities."

"We will write," she said.

"Of course. Every day. I can't imagine life without you."

That only made her cry again. "Maybe someday you can visit."

"And find you with a happy Vietnamese husband and a bunch of babies? I don't know."

"Don't tease like that, Ben. You are the one who will find a wife and have a big family. I will be only a memory."

"Don't say that. Don't ever say that."

"We must be realistic," Charm said. "I don't want us to be apart, but we will be, and it won't do us any good to be sad all the time. Let's promise to remember all the fun, all the good times, all the hours together. It will be hard at first, but I won't want to think you're sad."

"I will be heartbroken," he said.

"So will I, but we must promise to overcome it."

"I don't want to get over you," he said.

"I know. It will be for both of us just as if

the other has died. We would grieve, but we wouldn't want the other to worry that we were so sad we could not enjoy life. You know what I mean?"

He nodded, but he wasn't sure he would be able to get on with his life, now that he had found her.

By November, Ben and Charm entered a new phase where they tried spending less time together rather than more. He agreed with her that they needed to prepare for the day they would part forever. It only made sense. It was the rational thing to do. They began by agreeing to see each other only on the odd days of the month. And that's when Ben realized that sense and rationality did not apply to love.

He was miserable without her, and on the odd days they clung to each other even more desperately. But Charm remained the voice of reason. "We're practicing," she said. "And we're finding out how hard it will be. The even days will be everyday when you leave, but time is supposed to heal. I mourned my father for two years. I still miss him, but it is easier. I didn't think it would be, but it is. In December, we should see each other only three times a week — Monday, Wednesday, and Friday."

"Not at all on the weekends?" Ben said. "Is that really what you want?"

"Of course it's not what I want! I want to marry you and live with you the rest of my life. But I can't ask you to stay here, and I don't want to go there."

"Charm, do you feel like if I loved you enough, I would find a way to stay? You can be honest."

She paused. "Sometimes I think that," she said. "But then I know I don't love you any less just because I don't want to go with you."

News from the peace talks in Paris made Ben realize for the first time that the war might really soon be over. He had day-dreamed of getting home, then dreaded it with all that was in him. And now he found himself conflicted. In many ways he missed his parents, even the things he had hated most about them. It struck him that he had never really hated them. He just couldn't abide their thinking, their ways. On the other hand, status conscious as they had been, their foundation had vastly grown and helped a lot of people in a lot of places who had nowhere else to turn.

Ben had always resisted being expected to take it over. That was the rub. The assumption. But at times he considered what he might be able to accomplish with those kinds of resources. Who knew? He might even be able to help Vietnam rebuild and become the kind of a place he would return to and be able to put the slaughter behind him. And that gave Ben an idea. He wondered what his father would think of a fund for Vietnamese who wanted to become teachers. It shouldn't take Charm until she was well into her twenties to even be able to think about pursuing a degree in education. Could The Berman Foundation start a fund, and could Ben somehow see that the first scholarship go to a young woman he knew?

CHAPTER 90

Ur

Terah had healed enough that people didn't blanch when they saw his face. And he had been able to do away with his crutch. He still walked slowly, and he favored his right ankle. But it must not have been broken, because it felt better every day. That toe on his left foot, however, was still sensitive, and he had to be very careful putting on his sandals.

A messenger from the king's court arrived one afternoon to tell him Nimrod-Amraphel requested his presence the next morning.

"Our great king is aware, is he not, that I am not ready to resume my duties just yet?"

"He is, sir. He simply wants a brief audience with you."

Terah made the mistake of telling Belessunu this news that evening, as if it signified some honor.

"Does that put Nimrod back among your

458

many gods, husband? The one who executed an innocent child, thinking it was your own — all the while telling you how pleased he was with you?"

"I should have known you would not understand, Belessunu. I am aware he deceived me, but I remain a valued and trusted confidant."

"Oh, do you? And tell me, Terah, what would the self-proclaimed god and king do with his valued chief officer if he knew your wife and son were here?"

"You know what he would do. My skull would be run through with a sword and I would be buried with all the others who have dishonored the crown. That's why we must hold fast and endure."

"How long can we maintain this ruse, Terah? This is no way for me to live, and certainly no way for Abram to live. Come, let me show you something."

He followed her to the mouth of the cave and peered out to be sure no one was about. She led him to the side of the outcropping where it was clear in the moonlight she had done some digging. "Do you still smell the rancid meat?"

"Of course."

"It's deadly, but it becomes even worse the older it grows. Last night the baby was awakened by the chattering of jackals. I prayed the meat I had laid out would appeal to them, and soon they grew quiet. When I calmed Abram, the animals began crying. They were plainly in agony. This morning I found three lying dead near the entrance. I buried them and added even more meat in the rocks around the perimeter. It gave me confidence, Terah. I fear no animal, but I do fear men. They will not be attracted to rotten meat."

"All the more reason to stay well back in the darkness of the caverns. Men are not able to smell the way dogs and jackals can."

"I have seen or heard no one pass this way," she said. "Day or night."

"Nonetheless, stay vigilant," he said, feeling exposed just being outside.

"I will protect my son with my life," she said, "but I do sometimes bring him out."

"That is reckless, Belessunu."

"I remain watchful. And of course he's too young to comprehend, but he seems absolutely fascinated with the sky. He fixates on the moon and stars, and I have to shade his eyes in the daytime or he would stare directly at the sun."

"Such forays portend only danger," Terah said. "If you persist in this, I do not want to hear of it."

"You'll hear more than that. I want you to know what I'm teaching the boy."

"Teaching him? He doesn't understand one word."

"He will. I tell him of the one true God, the Creator. I tell him God put the moon and the stars in the sky and gave the sun to warm us during the day. I tell him these orbs are not gods but creations of the Lord God Almighty. By the time he walks on his own, he will see the folly of pagan gods and worshipping anything or anyone but the Creator. He will understand the senselessness of idols made of wood and stone and ivory and gold and silver. He will know the one true God."

Terah hung his head and led Belessunu back into the cave where he sat on a rock ledge just inside the mouth where the moonlight still reached him. "Would you sit with me, wife?"

"I prefer to stand," she said.

"Must you despise me so?"

"Oh, Terah! I don't despise you. I will defy your ungodliness, and I hate how you have sinned against the God of our forefathers. But that is because I love you. I care for you. I long to see you return to your belief in the Lord Himself. I tremble at the thought that you have strayed so far from

461

Him that He might never take you back, even if you see the depth of your wickedness. I want you to know my resolve and hear my opposition to your depraved schemes. But I do not want you to think I despise you. Do you not see the altar I built?" She gestured toward what he had assumed was her oven.

"I thought Ikuppi built that for you."

"This is not where I cook, husband. It is where I offer sacrifices and pray for you."

Terah found himself speechless. *For me, when she thinks as she does about what I have done?* He buried his head in his hands. "Belessunu, is it possible we might one day return to the delight we once knew in each other?"

"That I leave entirely to you, Terah. I cherished the man I married in my youth. And I miss him. Should he return, so would I."

"I am here," he said.

"No, you are not. You will return to me only when you have repented before the Lord your God and He has forgiven you. He might require you recompense those whose lives you have destroyed by your selfish decisions."

"But I spared our son's —"

"At the cost of so many others! The

462

injuries you have inflicted reach far beyond the lives of Mutuum's baby and Ikuppi. Think of their families, think of the midwife, think of your lack of faith in God to protect the son He promised would himself become an exalted father. God does not lie. How could Abram become a father if the king were to kill him?"

"Belessunu, let me hold him. I know you think me evil, but he is my son. My arms ache to cradle him."

"Perhaps in time," she said, deep sadness in her voice.

CHAPTER 91

Manhattan

"Hang tight," Wojciechowski said. "I'll send a car."

"I hate leaving Ginny by herself," Nicole's dad told the detective.

"I'd like you both here. Can someone else stay with her? We shouldn't be more than an hour."

"Well, at least one of us will be there," Ben said.

"I'll be fine," Nicole's mother said. "I'm ready for a little dinner anyway, so staff will be around."

While they were waiting for the ride to the Central Park station house, Kayla showed up to report she had talked with Dr. Thorn to get an update on her mother's condition. Nicole talked with her in the hall. "Bet he wasn't happy to be called at home."

"He wasn't. Especially this late. But he did say he was concerned about something he referred to as 'sundowning.' "

"What's that?"

"I took some notes. Best I understand it, Sundown Syndrome refers to changes in behavior late in the afternoon or evening with Alzheimer's or premature dementia."

"Which he determined my mother doesn't have."

"He said that, but he also said to watch for things like agitation, delusions, paranoia, or disorientation. He said he's trying to get at why her mental acuity seems to come and go."

"But as far as how long she has to stay here . . ."

"He's guessing up to another week."

Nicole told Kayla she and her father had to be gone for about an hour. "Any chance you'll still be here when we get back?"

"If you need me to be."

"Well, we're just a little skittish about leaving Mom alone."

"The officers will be here."

"I know, but we prefer someone who's here to look after her specifically. They're just keeping people out — which is great, but . . ."

"Pleased to sit with her," Kayla said.

"You're a lifesaver."

■ ■ ■ ■

At the precinct station house, Wojciechowski sat hunched over Nicole's phone. "Can't believe you both know Arabic. I wouldn't have even known what language this was if it hadn't been for the letter you got, let alone what it says. Gotta be the same guy though, right? That what you're thinkin'?"

"Seems like it," she said. "But what do we know? You're the expert."

"Not when it comes to this foreign stuff. I don't know what to make of it. But you're sure whoever it is is referring to this Mustafa guy?"

"That's all it can mean, in my opinion," her dad said. "Question is, does this person really know whether the plane crash was an accident, or is he just taking advantage of the situation to make Nic wonder."

"Somebody in Chock-a-block's department can determine whether this text came from overseas. Maybe Pranav himself."

"Chock-a-block?" Nicole said.

"I'm tryin' to get a handle on his last name 'cause he gets mine right and makes me feel bad."

"You'd better stick with his first name."

"Anyway, he already decided the stamp

466

and postmark and envelope and paper are Middle Eastern on the one you got at home. Print results ought to be up soon. We already released your mail carrier. Told us what she knew, which wasn't much. Noticed it because it was foreign but says you get a lotta that kinda stuff."

"Foreign mail, sure, but nothing like that."

"Here's Chaka Kahn now," Wojciechowski said as Pranav swept in and handed him two manila folders.

"Thank you so much for trying, Detective Woe Jeh House Key," the Indian said. "You see how easy it is to master a difficult name if you just invest a little time?"

"You're a better man than me, Pranav," Wojciechowski said. "Whaddya got?"

"All the detectable prints on the envelope trace back to Ms. Berman, the mail carrier, and postal workers in other cities whose prints are in our system. So, just as we suspected. The originator wiped his or hers off. As for the letter, the only prints are Ms. Berman's and they're consistent with un-folding it, not folding it or stuffing it in an envelope. And as I told you, Detective, all the elements appear to be genuinely Middle Eastern, and sent from there. The second file is the translation of the other document you gave me and our best assumptions."

467

Wojciechowski gave him Nicole's phone. "How long would it take to determine if this message was sent from over there too?"

"A software package on my phone can do that in no time." He forwarded the file to his own phone, punched a few buttons, and said, "Saudi Arabia."

"You're sure?" Wojciechowski said. "Couldn't have been faked?"

"Someone tried to hide it with a random number, but one hundred percent it's from there."

"Think you deserve the rest of the night off, Pranav."

"Oh, come on, Detective. Repeat after me, Chak-rah-bar-tee."

"I'll work on it."

CHAPTER 92

Shinar

In spite of himself, Terah carried Belessunu's encouragement with him to the palace the next morning. How indeed could his son become an exalted father unless he escaped execution by the throne?

King Nimrod-Amraphel greeted Terah with a huge smile. "This is the way life should be — my chief officer in the court!"

"An honor to see you, my lord," Terah said, bowing.

"And it's good to see you getting around much better!"

"Thank you, oh Great King. I expect to return to my duties in just a few days."

"Excellent! Your selfless devotion and worship have endeared you to me and to the realm as never before. I know it could not have been easy."

"It has been difficult. In fact, Belessunu has not forgiven me."

"I pray she will come to see that my stargazers are never wrong, and I will also beseech the gods to favor her with yet another child, this time either a daughter or a son without designs on the thro —"

"Begging your pardon, Excellency, but my wife has left me."

The king scowled. "That is an outrage! How dare she? Where has she gone?"

"I do not know, sir. I suspect back to the land of her people."

"Abandoning a marriage contract with a member of the royal staff is an act of treason punishable by —"

"I pray mercy for her, sir. She is heartbroken and not thinking."

"You believe she will come to her senses and return."

"I pray so."

"In the meantime, as I promised, you have access to my entire concubinage. Enjoy as many as you need for as long as you wish."

"Thank you, my lord, but just now I am in mourning."

"For?"

Does the king mock me or is he stupid? "For the loss of my son, sir, and the absence of my wife."

"Well, yes, but I have just awarded you the remedy!"

Terah bowed again. "Deep gratitude, sir."

"Unfortunately, I have more sobering news for you, my friend."

"My king?"

"The body of one of the guards you hired for me some years ago has been found in the wilderness, though it took some time to determine it was he. Ikuppi appears to have been devoured by wild beasts and his carcass picked clean by vultures."

"How tragic! I had heard he was missing, but I had hoped for a more pleasant outcome."

"Because you knew him, I have decided that you should take charge of his memorial. Spare no expense and laud him with every honor due such a faithful servant of the throne. I have every confidence in your ability to bring esteem to the crown through this celebration. And when it has been accomplished, and you are back to your usual post, I have a most interesting challenge for you."

"A challenge?"

"The most extensive and ambitious project in all the decades you have been with me. When your time finally comes and the gods welcome you into the heavenlies, this will be what you are remembered for."

"Humbled, Your Highness. And curious."
"All in good time, Terah."

CHAPTER 93

Vietnam, 1973

Friday, January 26, Ben appropriated a Jeep late in the afternoon and raced into town. He found Charm leaving her apartment for work, leapt out, and ran to her. She froze and her eyes grew wide. They were seeing each other only on Mondays and Thursdays by now, and he had just spent the previous night with her.

"I'm not to see you until Monday," she said, a cry in her voice. "Tell me you are not leaving!"

"Just got word," he said, breathless, and pulling her into a fierce embrace right there on the street. "They're going to sign the peace accord in Paris tomorrow and announce an immediate ceasefire."

"They've been saying that for years," she said, her lips at his ear. "It's always going to be tomorrow."

"This looks legit. I have to be back at the

hospital in twenty minutes. We're on high alert."

"For a ceasefire?"

"We're likely going to be the only ones observing that," Ben said, "because we've had it here and want out. And our guys think the VC is mobilizing right now to get in their last licks before it goes into effect."

"Last licks?" she said.

"Another idiom, sorry. The North won't likely honor a ceasefire anyway, but they know it's coming tomorrow. This is their last chance to attack without facing war crime charges. I gotta get going right now."

"Will I ever see you again? . . . Ben?"

He clung to her, trembling. She forced him back and searched his face. "Promise me I'll see you before go."

"If I can, of course!"

"Promise me, Ben."

"You know I will if there's any way . . ."

"Promise!"

"I promise," he said and kissed her hard and long, as if imprinting herself onto him for the rest of his life.

Ben sprinted to the Jeep and sped off with a wave. Before his last left toward the hospital, he heard gunfire and spun in his seat to see outnumbered South Vietnamese troops engaging the VC. He hadn't ever seen Cong troops in the city — at least that he was aware of. He U-turned too fast, tipped up onto two wheels, and nearly threw himself from the vehicle. The Jeep bounced down, and he floored the accelerator back toward Charm. She stood frozen at a corner.

"Was that gunfire?" she cried.

"Get back home, now! Go! Lock yourself in and stay low! Go!"

"Be careful!" she yelled, and he was relieved to see her running back toward her apartment. He would never make it to the hospital on time, but all he cared about now was getting there in one piece.

Ben stayed clear of the regular route and bounced through ruts and high grasses to go wide around where he had seen VC. He grabbed his M14 from the back and laid it across his lap, clicking off the safety. Would his last day in this god-forsaken country be the one that saw him fire his weapon other than on the target range?

Ahead maybe a half mile he saw where he could reconnect with the road to the hospital, but already coming his way were US trucks he knew would be packed with navy and marine personnel, barreling toward town. Ben made a beeline toward them, planning to fly up onto the road just as they passed and head straight to his post.

He was within a hundred yards of the road when a dozen or so VC burst from the tree line to his left, firing at the trucks. Too late to avoid them, he kept the accelerator to the floor and bounded wildly through the grass. Ben propped his weapon in the crook of his left arm and opened fire. They'd not even seen the Jeep coming and several dropped in the grass. He had dreaded this moment, forced to kill enemy troops, and had worried what it would do to him. But in the moment he had no choice. He was protecting his mates and hopefully thwarting an incursion into the town where his beloved had barricaded herself. And anyway, his barrage was sure to cost him his life. He couldn't hold off all of them, and he'd driven right into their line of fire.

Ben knew his only hope was to keep firing and keep heading directly for the road. The hospital loomed less than half a mile away, so he only hoped if he was hit, he could keep the Jeep going straight until he wound up there. Once he thought going home whole or in a bag would make little difference. Now all he wanted was to survive.

Bullets clanged off the Jeep chassis, and he quickly abandoned the plan to aim straight for the hospital complex. He zigzagged, still with the road in sight. As he soared up onto the shoulder, the second truck passed and comrades waved at him and pumped fists as they took aim at the VC. Ben saw no other traffic and so burst onto the pavement, but before he could steady the Jeep, a rear tire blew and now he was all over the road, skidding, sliding, and about to roll. He fought the wheel with both hands, and just when he thought he had steadied the vehicle, his rifle slid off his lap, and two VC popped up from the ditch. He would pass within inches of them, unarmed.

Both had weapons raised. Ben grabbed his from the floor, raised it, and fired, hitting the first man in the Adam's apple and seeing him drop. The other opened fire as Ben instinctively threw up his hand, dropped his rifle again, and yanked the wheel to the right. The explosions from the VC's weapon deafened him, and he had driven through the hail of bullets. The Jeep tumbled and rolled, throwing Ben and his weapon clear. He wound up on his back on the other side of the road, unable to move.

The VC approached to finish him off, but he saw the man fall under a fusillade of gunfire. Ben knew he'd been hit himself though, because something had splashed all over his face and blood covered his camos from his shirt to his boots. He reached to feel his face but had no feeling in his hand. Held before his eyes it was twice its normal size — fingers splayed like those on an old-time baseball mitt, and his palm look like raw hamburger. Light-headed and losing blood, Ben could make out corpsmen running toward him. The men in the first truck had obliterated what was left of the Cong he'd driven through, and those in the second had taken out the one who shot him.

Fading fast, Ben believed beyond doubt he was dying. Comforted that he was not alone, he imagined four faces hovering over him and realized they were the only people in the world he cared about. Charm, Mom, Dad, and Red.

Ben realized he was still alive when he heard American voices saying Communist troops had attacked four hundred villages in a South Vietnam land grab. "They take town?" he mush-mouthed, trying to force open his eyes.

"Well, look who's decided to join us for breakfast," Red said.

"You sound gorgeous," Ben said.

"You haven't looked at me yet, Marine. Nobody looks good this time of the morning."

"Time is it?"

"A tick after oh four hundred, buddy."

"I been out since sixteen hundred hours?"

"You deserved the rest, hero. You may be the reason this town is still out of the hands of the North."

"Charm safe?"

A pause. "Haven't heard otherwise."

The bright lights forced Ben to open his eyes only in stages. Red leaned over him to block the worst of it. "You do look gorgeous," he said.

"Great," she said. "Gorgeous to a busted-up corpsman young enough to be my son."

"How busted up, Red?" He held up his left hand, wrapped in gauze and the size of a volleyball. "Looked pretty bad when it happened."

"Everything else will heal, Ben. Bumps, bruises, contusions, sprains. But you know we don't give you any bull here. There's not much left of that hand."

"Am I gonna lose it?"

"You've already lost most of it. Sorry. In layman's terms they saved your thumb and your big knuckles. In therapy you'll be hearing the medical term for what's left. You've still got your metacarpal bones up to the heads. Where your hand meets your fingers, that's the MCP joint. The metacarpophalangeal."

"So, no fingers."

"Have to scratch your rear with your right hand. You are right-handed, correct?"

"Well, if I wasn't I am now."

"You were. I'd have noticed if you weren't."

"When can I get back to town?"

"You're not going back, Ben."

"Got to. Promised."

"Sorry. They're trying to get you on a Freedom Bird before noon. Doc doesn't like moving you this fast, but you can rehab close to home, and there's no telling what's gonna happen here."

Tears rolled from the sides of Ben's eyes.

"You shouldn't feel any pain yet," Red said. "You okay?"

"Not that kinda pain," he said.

Ben was suffering both kinds of pain when he was loaded onto an evac plane at eleven hundred hours. A morphine drip could barely keep up with the throbbing hand, and he knew better than to make any decisions in that state. And yet he did anyway. He made a difficult one he wasn't entirely sure of, except that he was determined not to change his mind. He was glad he couldn't make it back to town, because he didn't

480

want Charm to see him this way. She'd only worry. He was never going to see her again, he knew that. And writing to her? Maybe it was selfish, but that would be too painful.

Charm would have to become what she had once predicted she would be to him. A cherished memory from a land he never wanted to visit again.

At a layover in Frankfurt, Ben caught wind of rumors about a direct hit on the hospital they left that morning. "Massive casualties," someone said.

"Staff?" Ben asked an officer.

" 'Fraid so."

"Can you check on a name?"

"I can try."

And it hit Ben that he never knew Red's real name. She'd become one of his dearest friends, a parent in the wilderness, and he'd never asked her name.

"Rank? Serial number? Anything?"

He shook his head.

"That's gonna make it awful hard, corpsman."

"A nurse named Red, that's all I know. Early forties maybe."

"I'll do my best. No promises."

More than a day later they landed in Washington, DC, where patients would be

481

treated until they were stable enough to be assigned to facilities closer to their homes. The process of disembarking proved laborious, with several still on stretchers. The officer Ben had asked to check on Red approached and handed him a folded sheet of paper. "I'm sorry, corpsman," he said.

Ben had to shake it open with his good hand.

CASUALTY REPORT
US Navy Nurse Lieutenant Lucinda Bishop, DOB May 15, 1930
DOD 1620 HRS, January 26, 1973, Vietnam (exact location classified).

CHAPTER 94

Shinar

Only a slight limp remained from Terah's night of terror with the dogs. Without it he'd have had a bounce in his step from the praise Nimrod lavished on him for the success of the Ikuppi memorial pageant. It had begun with a parade led by Ikuppi's wife and three children followed by his remains in a coffin — most unusual for a commoner. Terah had had the bones wrapped in a reed mat, and just before burial the box would be opened and a bowl of water placed near the mouth of his skull. Terah had considered placing the Marduk idol in with him, but that seemed such a waste.

Royal singers, instrumentalists, and dancers accompanied the procession — which was populated by hundreds of citizens assigned by edict to join and mourn aloud. The parade paused briefly at the palace, where the king himself appeared under an elevated portico and delivered a tribute Terah had written. It brought the assembled to tears, or at least they pretended it had.

Belessunu urged Terah to allow the truth to pierce his heart during the festive march to the cemetery and not forget that it had been he who had pushed Ikuppi to take his own life. "But I cannot let on that this was how he died," Terah said.

"True," she said. "But you know."

Throughout the day, despite that Ikuppi's widow thanked Terah over and over for so honoring her late husband, Belessunu's admonitions affected him. In fact, all the decisions he had made since hearing of the king's intentions for Terah's son stabbed at him in moments of reverie. So much so that Terah tried to busy himself every hour of the day so his mind and conscience would be occupied and he could evade the truth.

And finally King Nimrod-Amraphel summoned Terah for a private audience, at which he was to learn of the project he was to superintend — the one the king promised would become his eternal legacy. This meeting was not at court but in an antechamber where Nimrod normally met with his top military leaders or his stargazers. Today it was just the king and Terah.

He had bowls of figs, quinces, and pomegranates delivered and urged Terah to try these along with olives "for a delightful contrast of tastes." The king imbibed wine while Terah enjoyed a rich, dark beer. He was careful not to have so much that it clouded his judgment, because Terah rather savored the nectar of prestige.

It seemed Nimrod was at the peak of his power and glory and influence, and he revelled in it. It wasn't typical of him to dress in his royal finery for private meetings, but today he was resplendent from his heavily bejeweled crown to his thick, colorful, flowing robes to even his embroidered shoes. Terah thought the royal scepter appeared out of place too, but there it stood, propped against the king's chair — itself nearly as ornate as his great throne.

Nimrod had stationed outside the door an obsequious adjutant even older than Terah. Shamash was known around the palace as a fawning sycophant who groveled for any chance to serve the king. And Nimrod seemed to love barking his name. "Shamash! Wine!" "Shamash! Bread!" Today it was, "Shamash! The tablets from the engineers!"

Shamash would toddle in, humming as if he could barely control his ecstasy at serving. He bowed and scraped and always retreated by backing out. Age had cost him some of his agility, however, and often he backed into the doorframe, which sent him reeling into the door — which he grabbed to keep from slamming into the wall. He would bow some more, begging a thousand pardons, and ever so quietly close the door, waiting for his next summons.

Nimrod stood and carefully arranged the thin cuneiform plates on the table before Terah. Elaborate sketches had been pressed into the now hardened clay, depicting various stages of a colossal building project. The king crossed his arms and appeared to wait for Terah to fully comprehend each rendering. Finally, as if he could no longer contain himself, he said, "You see?"

"It's beautiful, my lord."

"Isn't it?"

"I confess I can barely picture it finished," Terah said.

"Allow me to give it some perspective. You see this last image, showing all these elements — underground foundation, base, cornerstone, first level — all as one finished piece?"

"I do."

"Do you think it is life-size as it is depicted?" His eyes grew with obvious expectation.

"I rather think not, Excellency. If these are from the engineers, this must be as big as the palace itself."

"Do you know how tall the palace is, Terah?"

"I am no engineer, but I would guess thirty cubits, somewhere around fifty feet."

"Excellent eye, my friend! Let me tell you how much larger Nimrod's Babylonian Tower will be . . ."

"Larger than the palace, already the largest structure in the realm?"

"Much!"

"I do love the name."

"Appropriate, don't you think? Already the entire kingdom is known as the Land of Nimrod, and I cannot deny I have grown it as if I created every city with my own hands."

"Of course it's appropriate. This is your empire."

"It is!" the king exulted. "And every foe, every pretender to the throne I have smashed!"

The door swung open, and the old man bowed low. "At your service, my lord!"

"I said 'smashed,' not 'Shamash,' fool!"

And back out he went, begging forgiveness and careening through the doorway.

The king broke all protocol by grabbing

487

his scepter, using it as a walking stick, and marching all the way around the table to stand next to Terah. Terah began to rise, but Nimrod said, "No, sit, sit!" And with a grand gesture he indicated the last clay drawing. "That, my loyal, steadfast servant, shall rise more than eight thousand feet!"

Terah could not speak. He mouthed, "More than a mile and a half?"

"I am the only deity on earth bound by a physical body, Terah. This will allow me to ascend to my fellow gods."

Terah shook his head. "Astounding," he said. "And your idea?"

"Of course! What mortal could conceive of this?"

"Not I!"

"No, but you are going to see to its construction."

"My King! I am deeply honored by your trust and confidence, but I am neither engineer nor builder."

"I have all of those I need, friend! What I need are laborers from throughout the entire realm, ships and camels with which to transport them here, places for them to stay, food for them to eat, materials with which to create my tower. And I need someone to arbitrate when the inevitable disagreements arise between all the experts.

That will be you, the one I trust above all others in the kingdom. You need not know any of the details. You are charged with seeing it gets done. Everyone will answer to you, and you will answer to me. And may the gods favor you."

Bursting with pride and purpose, Terah was also overwhelmed and apparently couldn't hide his greatest fear. "What troubles you?" the king said. "I thought you would be overjoyed."

"Oh, I am, Highness! I just worry that I have enough years left to accomplish this massive task."

"Those who know these things say it can be completed in fewer than fifty years. I will grant you at least that many more years of life."

"You will?"

"I can and I do," Nimrod said, placing a hand atop Terah's head and sending a chill down his spine. "Consider it done! May you engage this greatest of all tasks with the passion of a newlywed."

"Just one more question then."

"I'm sure there will be more than that, Terah, and I grant you this assignment so that I am required to do nothing but watch it rise. What is your question?"

"You may have just answered it, sir. I was

wondering where you would like this constructed. But if you hope to observe our progress daily —"

"And without leaving the palace."

"— that gives me direction."

"Follow me, Terah," the king said and led him to the other side of the palace to the portico from which he had addressed Ikuppi's funeral procession. "I want to be able to see it from here, and no doubt you'll want it as close to the river as possible, but not so close that the ground is too moist to support it."

"Brilliant idea, my King. No surprise."

CHAPTER 95

NYPD Central Park Precinct Station
Manhattan

"Is Teodora here?" Nicole asked Wojciechowski. "I'd like to get a look at her."

"Was s'posed to be, but no. I was gonna interview her in here." He opened the door to a sparse room with four chairs, two on either side of a wooden table. "You'd a been able to see and hear it all on monitors out there. Let's sit. We gotta talk."

"So this is what it's like to be a suspect," Nicole said. "Sitting across from you in an interrogation room."

"I guess," Wojciechowski said. "I like bein' on this side a the table." He tapped two file folders on the table and set them aside. "Time to give you guys a look at where we are. I know the clearin' phase was tough. It always is. I never cleared two PhDs at once, ya know. I get a few MDs through here because of the senior angle, and a lotta times they *are* guilty. I was pretty sure you two were innocent from the beginning, but I had —"

"Could've fooled me," Nicole's dad said.

"— I had to follow through, Doc, you know that. I been wrong before. It's been awhile, but it happens. Anyhoo, my gut tells me the letter and the text today would have been enough to clear you anyway."

"But there's more?" Nicole said.

"A lot more, ma'am. We got a confession from the housekeeper, Petrova."

"Really!" Nicole said. "You suspected her, but I never saw that coming. I doubt Mama did either."

"She actually confessed?" her father said. "Or did you confuse an old woman for whom English is a second lang—"

Wojciechowski stopped him with a raised hand and pulled a photocopy from one of the files. "Don't know how many languages you guys know. How 'bout Bulgarian?"

"That's more Nic's bailiwick."

She shook her head. "I know a smattering of Slavic languages, but Bulgarian is tricky. It's one of the Southern Slav tongues and —"

"You lost me already, Doc. Just lemme say we were pretty sure we had her dead to

492

rights. The closed-circuit TV feed showed her goin' and comin' Friday morning, just like your mother said. Then it shows her coming back, same afternoon. Everybody else on the video is recognized by the front desk people and security. They come, they go, no one uses the back entrance or exit.

"We try to track her down, wanna find out what she was doin' there that time a day, what happened, all that. Found out she stays in a tiny room with a bath upstairs in a house not far from where she goes to church." He turned over a page in the folder. "Bulgarian Orthodox Church on West Fiftieth. We call the landlord, who says he and his wife don't really know her. She's quiet, no phone, minds her business, pays her rent in cash on time every time. Our guys ask if they came over to ask her a few questions would she be there. Landlord says sure, she's upstairs now. They head over.

"Turns out somebody screwed up and forgot to tell the landlord not to tell her we were comin'. When our guys get there, he says his wife thought it would be only courteous to let her know so she'd be dressed and everything. Next thing they know, she's on her way out, wearin' that big, white parka and carrying her Bible and a purse. Tells 'em she's going to church for a few minutes but she'll be right back.

"Squad car heads to the church, finds some kinda assistant parish priest who says a woman fitting Petrova's description — heavy coat and all — had been there nearly half an hour, sitting in a pew and writing on a pad of paper. He'd asked her if she needed any prayer or counsel and she just shook her head. Said she had exited through the rear of the building between five and ten minutes before.

"They ask him what's out back and he says just alleys. They take a look back there, follow the alley south between buildings to Forty-ninth and see a commotion to the west, just short of Eleventh Ave. Bus sittin' cockeyed in the street, sirens in the distance, people huddled over a body at the curb about twenty feet beyond the bus."

Nicole flinched. "You're not saying . . ."

"Bible wound up in the intersection of Forty-ninth and Eleventh, purse hit a building on the northeast corner. Petrova dead. If the impact didn't kill her, her head slammin' the pavement did. Witnesses back up the driver's story that she was standin' on the sidewalk on the north side of Forty-ninth and he was headed to the bus stop just past Eleventh. Says next thing he knows she takes two giant steps right in front of him. Didn't even have time to hit the brake."

Nicole covered her mouth. Her dad whispered, "Awful. So she'd written her confession, is that what you're saying?"

"One of our guys found it in her purse. Our people translated the original and came to some conclusions, but before I show you that, see if you can make out anything from what she wrote."

He spun the sheet to face them and Nicole leaned close. "I don't get the flow," she said, "but I see words I recognize. 'Guilty . . .' 'Sorry . . .' 'Ashamed . . .' 'Scared . . .' 'Father . . .' There's a name. 'Dimitar.' 'Feel bad for Mrs. Berman.' 'Forgive me . . .' Something about a Middle Eastern man . . . 'Persian? Arab? Syrian?' 'Threatened family.' And then something about Jesus. Looks like 'receive me.' Then 'I believe Jesus. My name means gift of God.' What's it all about, Detective?"

"We'd run her name through Interpol like we do with any foreign suspects. When she heard we were coming, she might've wondered if we knew. Turns out her father, long dead, was Dimitar Petrov. Don't know how he got mixed up in it, but he was busted years ago for a Syrian arms deal. That's more than nine hundred miles from Bulgaria, so it was probably all about money."

495

Wojciechowski pulled another document from a folder. "Here's what our guys make of this. Bottom line, obviously somebody doesn't want you diggin' in Saudi Arabia."

"I'm getting the picture," Nicole said. "But it's not the Saudis, is it?"

"Looks like a rogue agent, this Persian she talks about. She doesn't know where he's from, but probably because of the connection with her late dad, he threatened her family if she didn't do this for him. She wouldn't have had any idea why. Ben, we're thinking he may have even gotten to your former housekeeper, paid her off to get herself fired, and made Petrova look like the perfect replacement."

"Which she appeared to be," her dad said.

"After studyin' the CCTV, the time line, your mother's memory, all that, our people think Petrova did this before she left in the morning. Then, maybe 'cause a her religion, she regretted it and went back to see if Virginia had survived."

"All this just to keep me from leading a dig in Saudi Arabia? Why? Threaten me? Attack my mother?"

"Whoever this is," Wojciechowski said, "what are they so afraid of? What do they think you're gonna find?"

"The question is how do they know what

I'm looking for. Lots of people dig over there. Only Mustafa and Moshe knew."

"Somebody told somebody," Wojciechowski said. "But Saudi Arabia's way outta my jurisdiction. Anyway, you two aren't people of interest anymore, and we can turn the rest over to Interpol."

"And we just fend for ourselves?" Nicole's dad said. "Whoever this is is still out there."

"Oh, if he comes here, we'll get 'em," Wojciechowski said. "I'm just sayin' you want Interpol on this if he's trying to pull the strings from over there."

"I'm not withdrawing my app," Nicole said.

Her dad snorted. "They're trying to scare the wrong family."

Wojciechowski returned her dad's box to him and said, "Whatever you do, be smart. We'll get this guy, but stay alert."

"Don't worry."

"And it looks like you don't have to tell your wife about the box or the picture unless you want to."

"Yes, you do, Dad."

"I know I do. It's long overdue."

CHAPTER 96

Ur

"A tower to reach the gods," Belessunu repeated back to Terah. "And so your deceiver, the one who believes he's assassinated your own firstborn male child, puts you in charge of a project designed for his own aggrandizement, and all is forgiven."

"I wouldn't say I have forgiven him, wife. But I cannot help but feel honored and trusted."

"Oh, he trusts you, all right. He trusts you to fulfill his every desire. As he has obligated your next fifty years, would you care to know my plans for the next ten? I plan to so immerse our son in the work of the Lord God that when he is able I can get him to the land of his ancestors. I pray Shem remains alive long enough to tell Abram all he remembers of the great ark and all the wonders of God. I cannot imagine telling him what his father is doing for the self-proclaimed deity king who murders perceived enemies on a whim."

"The boy has a right to be proud of his father."

"His father has a responsibility to make him proud."

"You will not take him from here. I forbid it."

"You have lost your authority over me or the boy," Belessunu said. "Would you like to know what the Lord God Almighty says?"

"No! Spare me that!"

"I will not. He says, *'The earth shall suffer for its sin, for they have twisted My instructions, violated My laws, broken My eternal covenant. I will consume the earth with a curse so its people must pay a price.'* "

"I am leaving," Terah said.

"Listen as you go!" she said. *"I will punish the gods in the heavens and the proud ruler on earth. The glory of the moon will fade and the brightness the sun will wane, My armies of heaven shall rule."*

"Please, Belessunu, stop!"

"You will call on your idols for wisdom and be found wanting."

CHAPTER 97

Eleven West
Monday

"You sure you want me here for this, Dad?" Nicole said. "Seems it's between you and Mom."

"I want you here," her mother said. "Whatever this is, you ought to hear it too."

Her dad nodded. "I'm just sorry I never told you, Ginny. You told me about your previous relationships —"

"Which didn't amount to much. So this was a relationship?"

"It was."

"In Vietnam?"

"Yes."

"Did you love her?"

"I thought I did. Well, yes, I did. And hard as it is even for me to believe, while it was deep and meaningful and special, especially at that time in my life, I can tell you honestly, even at its best it was nothing like what we have. I can't deny we were in love, but I don't want you to ever think it holds a candle to —"

"I've never doubted your love, Ben. It just gave me pause to find that picture and wonder. And to learn she was someone so special to you, and I have never heard of or about her."

"That's all on me. I regret it and I'm sorry. Sorry for not telling you. Sorry for hiding the box. Sorry for leaving it out where you could stumble onto it."

"Did you sleep with her, Ben?"

"May I tell you the story from the beginning?"

Ginny nodded, and he told her everything, leaving nothing out. It was the first time Nicole had heard how he had been wounded.

"I never saw her, talked to her, heard from her, or wrote to her ever again. I didn't want to see another death notice like Red's, so I was relieved when my father told me that the proxy scholarship from the foundation had been used by Bian Nguyen at Saigon National Pedagogical University. All I know is that she graduated. I don't know where or when or if she ever used her teaching degree or even whether she's dead or alive."

Nicole's mother's eyes were full. She

reached for him and he took her hand. "She sounds like a wonderful woman. And so did Red. It sounds like Red helped you grow up too. Forgive me for doing the math in my head, but while Charm is our age, do you realize Red would have been nearly ninety by now? Those women helped make you the man you became, Ben, and I'm grateful for both of them."

"But I was lost without you," he said.

"Who knows how receptive you'd have been if you'd never met Charm? I'm curious enough to maybe look her up myself some day. She opened your mind, developed your heart."

"It shouldn't surprise me you'd be so good about this," he said. "Forgive me?"

"Of course. But there had better be no more secrets."

"Promise."

That afternoon in the corridor at the hospital, Nicole called the doorman at her building and asked if he'd do her a favor.

"Anything," Freddie said. "You know that."

"When you get a minute, just see if I've had any packages arrive, anything too big for my mail slot."

"I'll check right now. Hang on . . ." She

heard him entering, checking with the front desk. "Just one," he said. "Thick, padded envelope from Saudi Arabia."

"Freddie, could you have that messengered to me here at Sinai? Just tell them Eleven West and put it on my bill."

"You betcha, Doc. And how's Mom?"

"Better. Much better."

"And did the cops find there was foul play?"

"I'll you the whole story in a few days."

ACKNOWLEDGMENTS

Byron Williamson, Jeana Ledbetter, and Leeanna Nelson at Worthy.

Dr. Craig Evans, consultant extraordinaire.

Walt Larimore, MD, friend and medical consultant.

James Scott Bell, friend and legal consultant.

Natalie Hanemann, deadeye editor.

Lynn and Debbie Kaupp, indispensable assistants.

Alex Field, agent nonpareil.

Dianna Jenkins, my heart.

ABOUT THE AUTHOR

Jerry B. Jenkins's books have sold more than 70 million copies. Twenty-one of his titles have reached the *New York Times, USA Today, Publishers Weekly,* and *Wall Street Journal* bestseller lists. The phenomenally best-selling Left Behind series inspired a movie starring Nicolas Cage. Jenkins has been featured on the cover of *Newsweek* and his writing has appeared in *Time, Guideposts, Parade,* and dozens of other periodicals. He and his wife, Dianna, have three grown children and eight grandchildren and live in Colorado.

The employees of Thorndike Press hope you have enjoyed this Large Print book. All our Thorndike, Wheeler, and Kennebec Large Print titles are designed for easy reading, and all our books are made to last. Other Thorndike Press Large Print books are available at your library, through selected bookstores, or directly from us.

For information about titles, please call:
   (800) 223-1244

or visit our website at:
   gale.com/thorndike

To share your comments, please write:
   Publisher
   Thorndike Press
   10 Water St., Suite 310
   Waterville, ME 04901